AS EVIL AS . . . CHILD'S PLAY

Annalie uncapped the toothpaste tube and squeezed a precise, green-speckled caterpillar wave across the bristle. She ran the water hot, warmed the toothbrush. 'Got some respect comin', Lord knows, least from my own son.' Thrust the brush against the upper gum and agitated her hand angrily up and down, side to side. 'Can't help . . . what I do . . . got to make a living . . .'

The froth turning crimson now around her lips, Annalie slowed, watched the mirror, feeling more than peppermint cold, a scratching, at first no more than an abrasive, purging discomfort; but then the pain – delayed like a paper cut – rising to consciousness. Annalie stopped, raised a disbelieving hand to the mouth of the woman in the mirror.

Quickly grabbed the tube, breathing faster, pressed the paste between her fingertips, felt the ground glass mixture slice into her skin . . .

The Prodigy

M. JAY LIVINGSTONE

SPHERE BOOKS LIMITED
30/32 Gray's Inn Road, London WC1X 8JL

First published in Great Britain by Sphere Books Ltd 1981

TRADE
MARK

Set in Lasercomp Times

Printed and bound in Great Britain by
©ollins, Glasgow

Acknowledgments

The author wishes to thank the following people for their help: Gerald Levitin, Traffic Commissioner, City of San Francisco legal advisor; Dr Richard L. Schoenbrun, Tiburon, Belvedere Isle, California medical advisor; and David Perlman, Science Correspondent, San Francisco Chronicle.

The author also wishes to acknowledge his indebtedness to the following works and organisations: *Alice in Wonderland,* by Lewis Carroll; *The Tempest* by William Shakespeare; *Bridge of San Luis Rey,* by Thornton Wilder; Berkeley Young People's Liberation House as reported in 'Some Liberated Children' by Susan Berman in the *San Francisco Chronicle,* September 29, 1974; and United Press International.

TO my wife,
for my children

THE PRODIGY

The child's sob in the silence curses
deeper
Than the strong man in his wrath.

The Cry of the Children — Stanza 13
– Elizabeth Barrett Browning

Every year in the United States, 200,000 youngsters under he age of 18 are arrested and detained at least a few days in ail for offenses which no adult could be punished for. Although not all those held in jail pending a hearing wind ıp with long term sentences – four months to two years or nore – a lot do, perhaps as many as 40,000 a year.

Washington Post, Monday, January 5, 1976

"I got my Rit-lin; you got your Dex. Slip us a pill; we won't e wrecks." These new words to an old jingle illustrate how lrugs enter the classroom. New juvenile junkies aren't ushed by shady characters but by schools, physicians, harmaceutical companies and parents. Almost half the ıation's kids are now deliberately drugged because "their ehavior bothers adults."

The Myth of the Hyperactive Child: And Other Means of Child Control by Peter Schrag and Diane Divoky – Pantheon

Teachers, traditionally more progressive in their thinking, ıow are militantly demanding law and order in the schools even at the price of children's rights. "This is a war," says 'im Walsh, Security Director of George Washington High School in New York City, "and we need to keep every veapon in our defense arsenal."

Washington Post, Monday, January 5, 1976

ONE

I: *Friday, 5 August, 1977*

The following news story appeared on page two of the Cleveland Herald:

A DRIVE AGAINST
CHILDREN IN PORN

Cleveland – A New York-based group launched a campaign yesterday against use of children in pornographic films and magazines, and its president urged members of Congress to see for themselves why a crackdown is needed.

Against a backdrop of slick magazines featuring children in nude poses and indulging in a variety of sex acts, Dr. Judianne Densen-Gerber said at a news conference in Cleveland that there is a $1 billion annual traffic in such material, and it is sold all across the country.

She said there is evidence that parents and guardians 'sell' their children for such purposes, and that children as young as three are involved.

Densen-Gerber is president of the Odyssey Institute of New York, which deals with the abuse of children and which conducted antipornography demonstrations outside adult-material stores yesterday in New York, Philadelphia, Cleveland, Detroit, Chicago and Flint, Michigan.

Densen-Gerber said she hopes to win passage of laws requiring licensing of materials involving children, and harsh penalties for sexual abuse.

She also wants specific prohibitions, under child

abuse and neglect statutes, against the use or selling of a child for sexual purposes.

At the news conference featuring excerpts from two films of young children engaged in sexual activity, she said the campaign already has resulted in removal of such material from pornography shops in Washington and New York.

Although most of the publications and films come from California, she said there is evidence of porno operations in Cleveland, Cincinnati and Flint, Michigan. Boys and girls between the ages of three and seventeen are featured. One film at the news conference was called 'Suzy and Her Little Brother,' with a ten-year-old girl showing her eight-year-old brother the aspects of lovemaking, including oral-genital contact, manual contact and actual intercourse.

There was a hint of local scandal at the end of the news conference when a retired lawyer, Ozzie Witherbee, urged that an immediate investigation be initiated in Erieview Heights, a wealthy Cleveland suburb. He intimated that a prominent attorney, a school board official and a juvenile court probation officer were involved in a ring producing homosexual films featuring subteen boys.

Accompanying Witherbee was Aaron Farrow, a twelve-year-old student at Erieview Heights High School who told those in attendance of the induction of another student, Martin Kyle, aged eleven. According to Farrow, the Kyle boy was placed in the Cohasset County Juvenile Detention Home when he tried to expose the ring. He was later killed, allegedly by three other detention home inmates. A hearing is scheduled for October 3.

Densen-Gerber said she would look into the matter.

II: Saturday Afternoon, 6 August

A children's liberation club known as 'The Home of David' met in the basement recreation room of a private residence at 2780 Bellevue Boulevard in Erieview Heights.

The purpose of the hastily called meeting, in the worlds of Aaron Farrow, the group's leader, was to 'decide what steps should be taken to prevent further "inductions", and what actions must be initiated to deal with adult offenders, either immune or above the conventional procedures of law.'

The tone of the meeting was composed yet determined. The five members, all but two in their subteens, were quickly brought to order by the Farrow boy, a prodigy pianist who, last May, performed Rachmaninoff's Third Piano Concerto with the Cleveland Orchestra.

Following the reading and acceptance of the minutes from the prior meeting, Aaron Farrow made his introductory remarks:

'As you know, Marty Kyle was one of the charter members of our club. He helped draft our constitution. He was one of us. He became involved . . . with certain adults in an effort to help other kids who were being exploited. He felt he could do this directly, by talking to the kids, telling them about us, and by appealing to the reason and decency of the adults involved. He didn't fail. He simply wasn't allowed to finish what he set out to do. He didn't succeed. As we now know, his method was wrong. He met force with words. It didn't work. So! What can I say. We learned from Marty.

'I called the meeting today to review the actions we discussed two months ago at Marty's house, and which were to be taken only as a . . . last resort. I don't like it, but there it is. In light of what has happened, are there any objections?'

'No!' the other children shouted in unison.

'Then we'll proceed. Amy, were you able to get a manual from Southwestern Furnace Corporation?'

Amy Witt, a frail yet energetic thirteen-year-old, stood up. 'Yes, but I haven't read it. Sorry, Aaron, you know how it is.'

'I know, Amy. I also know how it can't be from now on. Does it contain the correct model number?'

'Oh, sure, but Aaron, I . . . '

'Problem?'

'Only that I'll need some help. I'm lousy with electrical diagrams, you know that.'

Aaron turned to his younger brother, Robbie, aged ten. 'Robbie?'

'No hassle. The wiring's a snap.'

'How much time before you finish the automobile prototype?'

'I'm doing a fire engine. It's more fun. I figure another three, four weeks. Any rush?'

'None right now,' Aaron answered. 'Just want to be ready.'

'Don't sweat it,' Robbie sighed.

Aaron turned to Chris Kasko, the largest member of the group and who at fourteen was also the oldest. 'Have you contacted the pet store, Chris?'

'Right. They think I'm nuts.'

The others laughed. Aaron didn't. 'So?'

'It'll take them three weeks to get the cricket cage. Something less to get the . . . tenants,' he smiled. 'Time enough, I figure.'

'How about the baling wire?'

'Don't need it. A coat hanger'll do just fine.'

'For picking your navel!' Aaron snapped. 'Let's get it right.'

'Okay, okay . . . ' Chris stared out the window, still uneasy at being ordered around by a boy two years his junior.

Aaron paused and put his hand on Chris's shoulder. 'Hey.

Come on, Chris,' he said softly, 'you know what I'm saying. It's just . . . Marty.'

Chris looked up at him. 'Sure, I know. It's scary stuff, that's all.'

'Want out?'

'No way, man, just . . . just hoping there might be another way. You know?'

'Marty hoped so too, and look where it got him.'

'I know, I know. Whatever.'

Aaron looked at Peter Robinson, the only black boy in the group. 'Pete, your home scene's pretty together now, right? I mean your mom's off your back and all?'

'She's never around to be a problem,' he shrugged. 'Things could be worse. Long as I stay forgetful and shut my door at night, I'm okay.' He glanced around the room self-consciously.

'No guilt!' Aaron said firmly. 'Remember? We didn't start it.'

Peter nodded. 'You got it.'

'Okay. I'll need your help here in the recreation room with the wall chambers, mounts and housings. We'll have to work afternoons when my mother's off spinning her wheels at civic functions.'

'No problem.'

'I'll leave it to you to rent the drill. And we have to figure what we're going to use for insulation, otherwise . . . '

'Dry ice,' Camilla Saddleford interrupted. 'At least it works in principle.'

'That's brilliant strategy, Cammie,' Aaron smiled proudly,

Cammie smiled, her nose an accordion of freckled wrinkles. 'That's what you say; I stink at chess.'

'How much time will the dry ice buy us?'

'A two-inch thickness ought to be good for twelve to fifteen hours.'

'All right!' *Aaron beamed. 'Have you been able to locate some curare?'*

Cammie frowned. 'That's a toughie. It's illegal, you know.'

'That doesn't stop them.'

'I know, Aaron, it's just that when you're older, you can get anything you want.'

'Not any more!' Aaron snapped. 'At least not at our expense.'

'Hey, Aaron,' Peter threw up his hand, 'What about this guy, Packer? When's he get here, and what do we do about him?'

Aaron leaned against the brick fireplace, his back to the group. 'Some three weeks. I'm not sure about him.' He turned around. 'Let's wait and see. He might be all right.'

'Fat chance!' Peter snorted.

'We'll see,' Aaron insisted. 'Let's not make the mistake of dealing in absolutes.'

'Oh, shit, Aaron!' Chris got up and shambled to the door, turned around. 'I'm with Peter. What is this, anyway? Your best friend gets killed – and you know the other guys in the home had nothing to do with it – and you start gettin' soft on this guy Matthew Packer? A guy you've never seen? I don't believe it.'

'Not soft – fair. Let's see where he's at.'

Chris, at the door, took a deep breath. 'Meeting over?'

Aaron looked at the others. They nodded. 'Hang on a minute. Let me just say this before you split, okay?' They nodded again. His voice was quiet. 'We exist because we must, okay? We'll do what we're going to do because we must, okay? Otherwise we'd end up like Marty. It'd take the law three years or better to get justice for Marty. And even that's a risk: a good lawyer could get the thing flushed down the tubes. You know the fix. You know the loopholes. But that still doesn't mean we go out and react blindly. Ozzie Witherbee warned us about that. He said, 'Don't get caught up. Don't lose reason.' He glanced at Chris. 'That's why we wait to find out what Matthew Packer's all about.'

Chris nodded, smiled. 'A gentle warning, Aaron? You

know, the old thing about an ounce of prevention is worth a pound of. . . '

'Such as?' Aaron watched him closely.

'Just a threat, a little scare – no big thing, no hurt, I promise.'

'Like what?'

'The gas station bit.'

'And I'll bet you've already got the particulars.'

'Seventy-Six VW bug. Beige,' Chris rattled off, 'Oxitron station at the corner of Colby and Van Dillon. Half a block from his apartment.'

'Jesus, Chris,' Aaron shook his head, always a little wary of Chris's proclivity for research. 'And you'll do it, I suppose.'

'Can't. My parents know him. Have to be . . . '

'East Chester?'

'Right.'

'Keep it harmless.'

'Of course.' But the look wasn't a guarantee.

'Meeting adjourned,' Aaron said.

The others got up and left the room. Chris waited at the door until they had disappeared upstairs.

'Thought you couldn't wait to get out of here.'

'Had a question.'

'Shoot.'

Chris shut the door and faced Aaron. 'You go over to that garage you were tellin' me about, where they were making that film? The one with Marty?'

Aaron saw the drift. 'That's right . . . '

'You go inside?'

'No. Not right away.'

'What happened?'

'there was a brolen window pane in back. I thought I'd be able to look inside without being seen.'

'You mean you got caught?'

'Right.'

'Jesus, Aaron, what happened?'

'Things.'

'Like what?'

'Like forcing me to watch.'

'Marty in there?'

Aaron nodded. 'Tied up. On a table. Face down. Some old guy, sweating, crouching over him.'

'Recognise him?'

'No . . . not him.'

'The others?'

'I saw them.'

'Well?'

'I recognised some of them.'

'Who were they?' Chris's breathing came faster.

Aaron shook his head. 'Not now, Chris.'

'Why not how?'

'There's no point. Later you'll know it all.'

'That's no answer!' Chris shouted.

'It'll have to do.'

'Jesus, Aaron, can't you at least tell me why?'

'Ever wonder why I'm here and not with Marty?'

'I don't give a shit why you're here and not with Marty! What're you, God or somethin', deciding when's the right time for everything?'

'Come on, Chris, take it easy. We've got a long way to go.'

'I can't take it easy, I've got to know. Now!'

'Know what?'

'Was my father in there?'

'No, Chris. Not your father.'

1

There are times you start off doing something you don't want to do and end up being glad you did. This wasn't one of them. This was one of those times I started off doing something I wanted to do and ended up being sorry.

People still come up to me and ask, 'Hey, you're Matt Packer, right? The guy who taught that Farrow kid how to make film?' Then, with a knowing look, 'I mean *that* film?'

'I was around,' I answer.

'Oh, come on, what do you mean, "around"?'

'I mean, he made his own film. I was around teaching him how. The rudiments. I sure as hell didn't tell him what to shoot. Don't lay that one on me.'

There are still times I wonder why I helped create such a monster. Yet in truth, it was the monster that created me. Nothing I could have done would have altered the Aaron Farrow master plan. Like Doctor Edward Teller, I had been unaware of the final consequences. And, like most of us, the final horrors would leave me with twenty-twenty hindsight.

It was almost a year ago that I got the offer to teach at Erieview Heights High School in Cleveland. I was producing a comedy show at the time for one of the networks in L.A. And had been on and off for eleven years. Several shows, on and off the air: eleven years of carbon copy days. The offer to teach film-making was appealing. Even at one-fourth the salary, I'd be quadrupling my sense of accomplishment. I was prime for change. But sure as hell, not for Aaron Farrow.

My classroom at Erieview High was located at the foot of the school auditorium, just to the left of the stage. It was used for rehearsals, speech classes and meetings of the school's fledgling film group.

When I entered the classroom that first morning on opening day, 12 September, my attention had first been caught by a red-leafed coleus sitting on a radiator at the foot of a window. It had leaves better than six inches in width. This in itself might not have been that noteworthy, say to a botanist experimenting with a super-growth plant food. But when I touched one of the leaves, the entire plant wilted and gave off a foul odour. As I backed away, the leaves continued to wither, and in the morning sun I could perceive heat waves rising from the shrivelled and colourless remains.

As I wandered around the room, not knowing whether I should admit my blunder – or to whom – I was disturbed, even mystified by the sophistication and obvious value of the film equipment I found. The group was decidedly not as amateur as I'd been led to believe. This puzzled me as I'd been briefed that I alone would be responsible for requisitioning any necessary supplies. I was astonished to open a camera case and find a 16-millimeter Arriflex, which retails for $5000, not including lenses and motor. My intention had been to order a used and inexpensive Super-8.

In one corner of the case was a script, the title stencilled across a red cover: *The Bridge of Erieview Lake*. I opened it to the first page.

'It's a rough draft.'

'Oh?' I turned around, startled, as if I'd been caught snooping in someone's diary. I looked again at the title page for the name of the author. Aaron Farrow. I should have guessed.

'Am I to assume I'm meeting the author?'

'I wrote it,' he corrected.

'Same thing, isn't it?'

'No,' he answered simply. 'To become an author, one must first learn how to write.'

I returned the script to the case. 'A pleasure to meet you, Aaron,' I said flatly.

'And you'd be Mister Packer?' He sat down in a chair near the front of the room.

'That's right.'

'Producer of *Three to Make Freddy* and *Sunday's Fun Day*.'

'You seem to know quite a bit about me.' I crossed to the desk at the front of the room.

'On the contrary, Mister Packer. I know you have a twelve-year-old daughter named Margie. Other than that, I know nothing at all about you.' He flipped through some pages in his notebook, then looked up at me, unsmiling: 'Unless, of course, you'd prefer to be known solely as the creator-producer of those two . . . shows. *That* would indicate a great deal about you.'

I sat down and pretended to organise my notes and books on top of the desk. 'I take it you don't care for the shows,' I said evenly, feigning disinterest.

'They're intended as children's shows?'

I looked up, perplexed. 'Of course, they're chil . . . '

'I personally don't care for them.'

'That's what I was picking up. Anything in particular?'

'Of course. They're insulting. However, I understand adults find them entertaining.'

'A few,' I lied.

'More then a few, Mister Packer, if the last Telepulse audience rating is any indication.' He absently thumbed an index tab in his notebook. 'Shows ostensibly produced for children, but viewed by adults who are amused at seeing children reflected according to adult definition.'

'It's not quite that simple.' I'd heard of precociousness, but this was absurd.

'It's close enough, Mister Packer. Who's more qualified to judge than the purported target audience?'

'All right then, *Mister* Farrow, just what would you suggest?'

'Using advisors and writers the same age as the audience you seek to attract.'

'Totally impractical.'

'Really?'

'Of course.'

'Because it mades such perfectly good sense?'

I leaned forward. 'No, not at all. because it's a perfect illustration of youthful idealism: purist, unbending. You are totally unaware of the politics in . . . '

'Fortunately,' he interrupted, 'we now have you here to remedy that situation. We *do* have the capacity to learn. But I'm being redundant. You're already well aware of that, I'm sure.'

'Listen, Aaron, I'm here to teach film-making. Not film politics.'

'From your own experience, Mister Packer, I'm sure you realise they are one and the same. As with anything else. Matter of fact, our film will deal with politics . . . in the extreme.'

Five other students burst noisily into the room cutting off my attempt at a reply. They were followed by boisterous groups of twos and threes. I was frankly grateful for the interruption. I'd begun to feel cornered. Obviously, I'd romanticised my new assignment, expecting, I suppose, to walk into a hushed room of avid film groupies. After all, I'd made a sizable concession by having my name removed from network television credits and added to the roster of local teachers. My thanks was a mini-Einstein named Aaron Farrow. It was going to be a rotten opening day.

III: Noon On Saturday, 13 August

Annalie Robinson awoke with a start, propped herself up on one elbow. She glanced at the empty space next to her, smiled, shook her head. He'd been an asshole. No wonder Peter had stormed out the evening before when – what was his name? – had played grab-ass around the dinner table, breaking a lamp and scaring the cat out of eight lives. And made her laugh so hard the tears poured down her cheeks.

That's why the suddenness of awakening: nothing had happened. Annalie looked out the window. A drizzly, grey day, inside and out. It reflected her mood and the colour of her last five years. Shook her head and wondered aloud about Peter, 'Not like you, boy, not when you gets all steamed up and stompy like that.'

Swung her legs off the side of the bed, looked into her slippers, held up her robe. 'I remember the last time, Peter Robinson,' she scolded, 'right after you come home from joining that uppity lib club for kids up there in Erieview . . . '

Turned the robe upside down and shook. 'Put a dead hamster, half a dead hamster in my pocket, half-eaten by Cat, the back half, still warm, my God! 'nough to scare pee out of flies. What you got now for Mama?'

She slapped her slippers together to verify their emptiness, tugged them on, stumbled toward the bathroom to clean the night before out of her mouth.

She switched on the light, lifted the toilet seat, peered into the bowl. Safe. Opened the shower. Empty. Inventoried the medicine cabinet. All in order. Except for a small note taped to the middle shelf. Annalie smiled, chuckled. 'Why, Petey, you're gettin's much lip as your daddy had.'

'Laughter at the expense of
others carries the highest
price. Smile carefully, Mama.'

Annalie uncapped the toothpaste tube and squeezed a precise, green-speckled caterpillar wave across the bristle. 'That boy gonna get more than laughter out of me, he keeps up with dead rats and smart-ass talk around here.'

She ran the water hot, warmed the toothbrush. 'Got some respect comin', Lord knows, least from my own son.' Thrust the brush against the upper gum and agitated her hand angrily up and down, side to side. 'Can't help . . . what I do . . . got to make a livin' . . . shit.'

The froth turning crimson now around her lips, Annalie

slowed, watched the mirror. Feeling more than peppermint cold, a scratching, at first no more than an abrasive, purging discomfort; but then the pain – delayed like a paper cut – rising to consciousness. Annalie stopped, raised a disbelieving hand to the mouth of the woman in the mirror.

Quickly grabbed the tube, breathing faster, pressed the paste between her fingertips, felt the ground glass mixture slice into her skin.

At 12.20 p.m., half a block away from Annalie Robinson's apartment, a clerk, in the local grocery store tossed a tarp over the sidewalk display shelves. The rain fell harder, and automobiles sent grimy waves splattering at his feet. Cleaving through the frying bacon sound of tyres on wet streets came a woman's scream. Distinct. The clerk stopped, shook his head, stepped back inside the store. He'd heard it before. It was a lousy neighbourhood.

2

As the last of the students took their seats, I collected the yellow homeroom cards scattered on my desk and began to check them off against my master list. I glanced around the room from time to time on the pretext of pairing up a name with a face. Would there be more than one perverse genius, or was Aaron Farrow a solo act?

At the centre of the usual student maelstrom was an island of calm: five students were gathered close around Aaron Farrow, talking quietly, their copies of *The Bridge of Erieview Lake* open in front of them. Surrounded by chaos they reflected not only concentration, but something more. Something I saw rarely in adults, never in children. Something that arouses my apprehension, because I've seen it cause as much ugliness as beauty. Determination.

My uneasiness grew. They were *too* composed, too committed.

I had the feeling Aaron Farrow was as much leader as

member. Perhaps, a guide. He talked easily to the other five. They listened, asked questions, commented. There was no sign of condescension, of proselytising, in his answers, only a sincere effort to communicate clearly. He was a slight boy, but there was strength in his directness. Though not handsome, or even good-looking by most standards, he had a beauty; he drew the others to him invisibly, inexorably. His fine blond hair fell evenly, spun off a cowlick in the middle of his head. His eyes were the main source of his magnetism. Black. Not brown – black. All pupil against a blue-white cornea. Bright and penetrating, as if a pair of klieg lights at a film premiere had reversed their polarity and were sweepimg white sky with black beams.

He talked with his hands. Or rather, he conducted his words. So supple were his gestures, I doubted he had wrists. Graceful yet not effeminate. There was music there somewhere.

I decided to meet the moment head on; moved around my desk to the front of the class and shifted a one-armed chair to a position where I could face them. The uproar quietened to gentle murmurings.

'Hi. I'm Matthew Packer. Matt for short. I'm to be your homeroom counsellor for the semester, but since my only experience in advising kids has been with my twelve-year-old daughter, I'm a novice. Despite this rather obvious shortcoming, the administration has seen fit to cast me in the role of counsellor . . . for better or worse. It may be like asking Freud to teach automotive engineering, we'll see.

'Any questions? About anything?'

Those around Aaron Farrow rurned to him. Except for one girl, who stared at the charred remains of the coleus on the radiator. Aaron's hand shot up. My stomach lurched.

'Yes, Aaron?'

He stood up and folded his hands behind him. 'Mister Packer, since you're brand new to teaching, may I ask why it is you wish to teach?'

'Oh, Jee-sus,' the lone toughie moaned, slumping diagonally across his chair. 'Another Farrow spectacular.'

'Aaron, that's not very nice,' one of the Attentives whispered. Aaron ignored them. He stood calmly, awaiting my reply.

'Well, Aaron,' I answered, 'since you're new to film-making, might I ask why it is that *you* wish to make film?'

He tilted his head, gave the slightest indication of a smile. It was as if he'd expected far less and was moderately satisfied with my response.

'You shall see in good time, Mister Packer – all in good time. But tell us,' he paused, watching me carefully, 'will you teach what you know, or what you believe?'

'What I know.'

'Thank you.'

'I'll discuss what I believe, Aaron, providing there's interest in it.'

'That would depend on the value of what you believe, would it not?' He sat down and immediately returned his attention to his peer group. He hadn't expected a response – the question had been deliberately rhetorical. I'd been warned about the Farrow boy's brilliance, but not his acerbity.

'I believe there is value in what anyone believes, if for no other reason than to reaffirm or strengthen one's own positions.'

He smiled. 'for those of us who still find that necessary.'

I had a sudden urge to smash the little bastard. On the other hand, I respected his intelligence, though abstractly, as one would marvel at the micro-transistorised circuitry of a solid-state amplifier. I felt mildly threatened, but perhaps this was no more than my own unfamiliarity with an extraordinary situation.

I spent the rest of the ten-minute homeroom period calling out names and committing the faces to memory. The last girl raised her hand just as the bell over my head clanged. I sat back in my chair, relieved, and remained motionless through the stampeding exodus. One of Aaron's group closed the door behind her. Someone else immediately reopened it. The loner. He shuffled over to me, hands shoved deep in his pockets. Whan he reached the desk, he looked around the room, nodding and blinked a couple of times as he worked his gum from cheek to cheek.

'Yes, Roderick? It is Roderick, isn't it?'

'Rod,' he corrected, 'Rod Angstrom.'

'What can I do for you, Rod?'

'You read the script?'

'Aaron's?'

'Um-hmm.'

'Not yet, no.'

'Think you'd better.' The nodding continued.

'Good?'

'Dunno. Never finished it.'

'How come?'

'Got kicked out of their club. They took my copy away.'

I regarded him sceptically. Aaron was half his size and probably two-thirds his age.

'I know what you're thinkin',' he continued. 'How'd they get it from me?'

'Well, Rod, the thought had crossed my mind . . .'

'Easy. Seven to one. I once saw a guy they'd worked over. Used to be in on it myself.'

'Rod, look, I'm not . . .'

'One big bruise, if you overlooked the cuts. Not pretty. Believe me, Mister Packer, I handed it back nice and easy.'

'Working a guy over is a little tough to swallow Rod, considering your size and . . .'

'Look, Mister Packer, I'm not kiddin'. And I'm not

talkin' neither. I know better. Just . . . read the script. That is, providin' you can get your hands on a copy.'

'What's so important about the script?'

He smiled and leaned on the desk in front of me. 'Hey, I said, "I'm not talkin" . . .'

'Come off it, Rod, cut the melodrama and say what's on your . . .'

'You've got a featured part, Mister Packer. And it isn't what you'd call . . . the hero's role. That is, unless you're some kinda sickie.' He turned his back and walked to the door. 'See ya,' he tossed off as it was closing behind him.

I sat back and closed my eyes, thought about leaving Cleveland before setting up bag and baggage in the middle of some bizarre punk rock scenerio. Thought about disturbed kids, like Rod. About ambivalence, arch-enemy of mine. That's where Aaron Farrow didn't fit. That's where Aaron was different from Rod. And me. He knew exactly what he was doing. No doubts. To see this in a child is remarkable. To see it in Aaron was downright frightening.

I was feeling uneasy as hell about Rod's warning, yet intrigued to find myself in the middle of a script in which I was already a feature player. Without having read for the part. Twenty minutes at the school and it was time to find out what was going on.

I'd stay. But where to begin.

Get to know them. Rod and Aaron. The others. How many? Where to start? Student files containing personal histories. In the administration office. The script. I was sure *The Bridge of Erieview Lake* would put me in touch with at least six students, to say nothing of having the opportunity of seeing myself as others saw me . . . before they'd even seen me. The files would give me a thumbnail and a pulse. But nothing to trace the labyrinthine twists of a prodigy's mind.

IV: Monday Morning, 22 August

At precisely 8 a.m., Robbie Farrow, Peter Robinson and Amy Witt huddled in the entryway of Chasen's Hardware and Electrical Supplies at Erieview Square, waiting for Mr Osgood to open for the day's business.

It was a crisp, windy day, paper scraps hurtling by at ankle level and pedestrians, heads drawn, turtle-style, down into upturned collars. Robbie held a master list as Peter and Amy crosschecked items from their own crumpled slips.

'Mortar?' Robbie asked.

'Two, ninety-pound sacks,' Peter answered.

'That be enough?'

'Should be. Epoxy?'

'Got it.' Robbie checked off the items.

'Cinder blocks?'

'Right.'

'You taking care of all the electrical?'

'Is water wet?' Robbie smiled.

'Where we gonna get the drill with a masonry bit?'

'Landis Rents. Over on Apling Boulevard.'

*Peter shook his head. 'Je-*sus! *How the fuck we gonna drill in your basement without your mom knowin'?'*

Robbie smiled. 'She knows. She likes me and Aaron building things. Always told us, "Satan finds some mischief still for idle hands to do." '

'If she only knew,' Amy said quietly.

'How we gonna pay for all this, Robbie?'

'Charging it to my parents' account.'

'Oh, wow!' Peter covered his eyes in mock disbelief, 'I can't stand *it. Can you dig the irony?'*

'Of course,' Amy said quietly.

'Aaron calls it poetic justice,' Robbie said.

The door opened to the clatter of brass bells attached to the jamb. 'Well, well, Robbie, what brings you out so early?'

'Hi, Mister Osgood. Just got some stuff to pick up.' Robbie handed him the list.

'Looks like another project.'

'Guess you could call it that.'

Osgood paused halfway to the counter, whispering, '. . . mortar, cinder blocks, lead sheeting, copper tubing,' stopped and turned to Robbie. 'Good grief! What're you guys building, a fallout shelter?'

Robbie shrugged. 'Guess you could call it that, Mister Osgood, but actually it's a fort for our backyard.'

Amy looked at Peter and smiled.

Peter shook his head. 'Oh, wow,' he whispered.

Osgood chuckled. 'Got too much here to take with you. Can your dad pick up the order?'

'Nope. Need it delivered, if that's okay.'

'Later in the week?'

'Can it be tomorrow at four?' Robbie asked.

Osgood smiled. 'What've you got, a deadline?

'Guess you might say so. Actually, it's a summer project for school.'

'Waited 'til the last minute, eh?'

Robbie nodded. 'You know how it is.'

Osgood watched the children leave, muttered a few unintelligibles about over-indulgent parents as he tallied the order. Almost $00. He'd better give Mrs Farrow a call. Then again, he'd better not. She might cancel.

On the way to the rapid transit stop, nothing was said. As the bus came into view, Peter murmured, 'There's no way, man, no way we're gonna keep this quiet. This is nuts, Robbie, you know that?'

'Trust Aaron,' Robbie said. 'He knows what he's doing.'

'What makes you so damn sure?'

Amy turned to Peter before boarding. 'Because we're right,' she said quietly.

3

I got up and crossed the room to the camera case in the far corner. The script wasn't on top where I'd left it. I opened the case. Not inside. I hadn't seen Aaron take it. One of the other students?

By the time I got to the administration office the corridors were quiet. I'd been there once before when Bill Kasko, an expatriate writer from Hollywood, had set up the job interview for me with Gabriel Saddleford, the principal. The name sounded embossed. But at his insistence, everyone called him Gabe – his effort at being a member of the team, a chum. To me he would be Mister Saddleford to the end. I'd pictured him as a venerable Mr Chips in black robes and baggy trousers collecting like melted wax on his shoes. The original resembled a portly David Niven.

The interview had made me nervous. I was convinced that without Bill's recommendation I never would have been offered the job. He'd related the behind-closed-doors conversation later that same evening. I'd been waiting in the outer office, flipping through *National Geographic*, watching the shadows of pacing feet beneath the door.

'A little on the flamboyant side would be my assessment, Bill,' Saddleford had said.

'Just nervous, Gabe,' Bill had countered. 'Behind the glibness, he's a very sensitive guy. Really. After a few weeks he'll fit right in. I'm sure it's just a matter of time.'

'Weary of "Hollywood Babylon" . . . is that it?'

'Weary of being something he isn't, that's all,' Bill had answered.

'Erieview parents wouldn't warm up to a guy who's into kinky scenes, Bill.'

'Neither would I.'

'Very well, then. We'll give it a try.'

'Thanks, Gabe.'

'A trial semester. That's all. Then we'll review the situation.'

'Fine.'

'Better fill him in on Aaron Farrow. *Without* details, if you don't mind. Simply a few well-chosen words of caution.'

'He's handled evough adult prima donnas, I doubt if enfant terribles will phase him.'

'Care to reveal the source of your confidence? Or is it just that with the passage of time the incredible has become commonplace to you?'

'Not at all. I simply feel the less attention paid, the better.'

'Bullshit! I couldn't disagree more. A healthy respect for the little bastard is not only advisable, it's precautionary. We still don't know whether we're dealing with a "bad seed" or a saint. Do I make myself clear?'

'All right, Gabe. I'll mention it in passing. I just don't want to blow things out of proportion.'

'I assure you, Bill, you couldn't. No matter what you'd say.' Then Saddleford had smiled and backed off. 'Perhaps you're right. Don't want to draw too much attention to the matter. No, I certainly don't. Ah, well, it should prove a provocative confrontation.'

'As provocative as the one with Sylvia, I'd be willing to bet.'

'You already know *that* outcome,' Saddleford had said.

'Do I?'

'Of course. The inevitability of the spider and the fly – played out in a most . . . enticing parlour.'

When Bill had rejoined me in the waiting room, his smile

had telegraphed the good news. We'd retired to a local bar.

'Sylvia who?' I'd asked, after two drinks.

'Farrow. Aaron's mother. An . . . unusual woman.'

'And?' I'd pressed.

'I think it's best you find out for yourself. Without any . . . promptings.'

'Come off it, Bill, you've got my curiosity up.'

'Your problem,' he'd snapped.

His abruptness had startled me. 'Okay, *okay*. I sure as hell didn't bring it up.'

'And you sure as nightfall aren't letting it drop, are you?'

I had. Quickly. The subject had never come up again. For good reason.

Then, as now, only the lonely sound of a secretary's typing attested to life in the building. I'd met her during the initial interview, Agatha Wickware, an efficient, asexual spinster with the inevitable gilt chain attaching her glasses to her neck like a miniature pulley system to hoist them on to her nose. Nubby ears spilled out of her clasping earrings, partially hidden behind tight, orange curls. She was of the Thirties, yet energetic and naturally delightful. I liked her instinctively.

'Mister Packer, how nice.' She sat back. 'How was the flight in?'

'A bore, Miss Wickware. I had to sit there and watch *A Little Night Music* for the third time.'

'Had to?'

'If a film's tunning, I'm compelled to watch. It's similar to television addiction. Saddleford in?'

She nodded. 'And available.'

Saddlefork swung around from his window as I closed the door. 'Well, Packer, I see you survived the first ten minutes. Come to resign?'

'Not yet, no. However, I'm feeling I'd better reserve the right to change my mind.'

'Not into dedication, hmm? How'd it go?'

'Not bad. Didn't win them, didn't lose them. Some fencing.'

'Oh? Anyone in particular?'

'Aaron Farrow. Name ring a bell?'

Saddleford smiled. 'Oh, my,' he sighed. 'Yes, I was anticipating something of that nature, but certainly not so soon.'

'I'm beginning to understand why.'

'Some of it perhaps. But, not all I assure you. Sit down, sit down.' He motioned at me as if waving goodbye with a handkerchief. I did. In one of those exhaling, red-leather chairs in which the chill seeps through your clothing.

'Let me explain the boy as best I can. Once every fifteen, twenty years or so an Aaron Farrow passes through a school like this; *once*, through a city the size of Cleveland. In generations past they've simply been described as geniuses or prodigies. They're pure platinum to some teachers, *beteš noires* to others because you know you've got a Mozart or a Machiavelli in your hands, and just possibly the sculptor is going to make the difference. Today the situation's considerably more . . . complex, more sensitive than it's been in the past. Aaron happens to come along at a very bad time.' He sat down behind his desk and elaborately cleaned and relit his pipe.

'Why's that?'

'Because rarely before,' he puffed, 'have we we lived in an atmosphere of such permissiveness and rebellion. Oh, I'm not talking about the usual revolutionary movements that crop up from century to century. Today, if you've got a chip on your shoulder and a substantial ego, you can give birth to just about any movement you wish. We've had women's lib, gay lib, ecology freaks, zero-population growthers, pro-abortionists, anti-abortionists, you name it. Causes are all the fashion.'

'What's that got to do with Aaron?'

'Permit me to digress, Packer, to give you some insight into the boy. Aaron is *twelve* years old – four to five years younger than his classmates. With an IQ of one-ninety-one, he couldn't have been held back. He's incredibly precocious.'

I winced. 'You don't have to tell me.'

'Aaron's brilliance was almost immediately obvious. Recognising when he was only two years old that their child was exceptional – and undoubtedly intoxicated by the stir he'd created among local educators and psychologists – his parents initiated a programme of private tutors. By the time he was five, he'd made his first tour of Europe, during which he'd composed two sonatas for string quartet. He entered the Eastman School of Music in Rochester when he was seven. At eight he became interested in telepathy, and was put through a series of tests at the Stanford Research Institute in Palo Alto, where he purportedly scored higher than Uri Geller.

'At the virtual insistence of child psychiatrists who feared he would become totally disoriented from reality and our society, Aaron was enrolled in public school. Tenth grade. Ten years old. Possibly it was too little, too late: he kept to himself. Spoke to no one. Last spring, at the age of eleven, he performed Rachmaninoff's *Third Piano Concerto* with the Cleveland Orchestra. The reviews were raves. All he lacked was the physical power to properly deliver the fortissimo passages. And now he's twelve . . .'

'I can't believe he's twelve!'

'*Nobody* believes he's twelve, Packer. But there we are, don't you see? There was also a time when the world was flat and films were silent.'

'And what now, for Aaron? Music?'

'Unfortunately, no. About nine, ten months ago, feeling he had achieved all he could in the music world, Aaron turned his brilliance, his determination, his . . .' Saddleford stopped abruptly, frowned, absently tapped his pipe on the edge of his ashtray. He wore clear polish on his perfectly manicured nails. His voice, too, had been emery-boarded to produce well-rounded words, belying, I was sure, some ragged emotions lurking below.

'Yes?'

'Well . . . I was going to say "obsession". Yet that isn't entirely accurate either. In any case, he turned all his energies to an entirely different and unrelated field, and came up with a very personal cause.' Saddleford reached over for his pouch and began to fill his pipe again.

I slouched in my chair. His sense of dramatic pause was flawless. And irritating. 'Which was?'

'Children's liberation.'

'Oh, Christ. I was afraid of that.' I was trying hard to avoid the implications.

'There it is,' he shrugged.

'Children's lib,' I repeated.

'Right,' Saddleford nodded, puffing on his pipe.

I sat back, my mind trying to fit together a puzzle with pieces missing. Was it coincidence? 'My daughter was a member of a lib club, too, back in L.A. I wonder . . .'

'The home of David?'

'That's it. Same one. "Home of David." Jesus! I suppose she'll affiliate here . . . if she hasn't already.'

'Wouldn't be at all surprised,' Saddleford shrugged. 'So, then. You already know all about it. Not to worry.'

'I'm not so sure. You see, I *don't* know that much about it. We never discussed it really – I mean, in other than the most casual terms. Of course, there were the usual accusations of my sounding like a father and acting like a parent and being an adult *adult*, God forbid. I don't like to pry. She deserves her space.'

'Very wise, I quite agree.'

'Maybe not.'

The bushy eyebrows came together like iron filings over a magnet. 'I'm not sure I'm understanding you.'

'How much do you *really* know about this lib bit?'

'Enough.'

'But not a hell of a lot.'

'*Enough* . . . to assume they aren't out to make trouble.'

'So far,' I said.

'Oh, Packer, don't be an alarmist. You know how kids are – secret meetings, codes . . . surreptitious nonsense. Nobody *ever* knows for sure what they're up to. And though they may be precocious, they're still kids. I suspect it's all quite harmless.'

I sat forward. 'Mister Saddleford, can you tell me this: What do they want liberation *from*?'

'Adults.'

'Of course. Very well, then. I have an idea. Let's give it to them and be done with it.'

I didn't want to pursue the subject further without first talking to Margie, without confirming or refuting the flood of suspicions I was experiencing.

'Packer,' he took a deep breath and said patronisingly, 'if you sincerely want to communicate with Aaron Farrow and his group – no matter how ludicuous this whole lib affair may seem on the surface – might I suggest you approach the subject with a little less levity.' He let out a large puff ball of smoke. 'Show a little tolerance, man. It's the only way you can hope to get through to them, I assure you.'

'Mister Saddleford,' I sat back and tried to approximate his seriousness, 'I would *very* much like to. However, you must admit, strictly from one adult pig to another, that the whole notion *is* preposterous. I mean, when *I* was in high school I was hung up on kishtail convertibles, necking in the balcony of the neighbourhood movie theatre on Saturday afternoon, and boobs – any boobs would do. Now it's this children's lib crap. It isn't exactly hiding *God's Little Acre* under your mattress, but it's the same principle,'

I ended with a quick smile and shrug. 'It *is* an adolescent fad, don't you agree?'

Saddleford nodded pompously. 'Perhaps. I understand your position. However, I'd urge you not to discuss Aaron's film with him as a "faddist" endeavour. It's serious stuff.'

'*The Bridge of Erieview Lake*?'

'I believe that's the title.'

'I've been told I have a role. Have you read it?'

'No. No one has. Other than a few trusted members of his own circle.'

'How many in the group?'

'Locally, six or seven.'

You mean Cleveland locally?'

'I mean Erieview Heights locally. Citywide I believe the figure is close to forty, perhaps fifty. I don't know what the figures are for New York and Los Angeles.'

I was feeling uneasy again about how little I knew. Margie hadn't revealed much at all. Had it been deliberate? 'It would appear the movement already has a fairly substantial foundation.'

'Yes. And growing steadily, though cautiously. Or so I'm told.'

For several moments Saddleford sat quietly and puffed his pipe, eyeing me as if to weigh my reactions. It was all supposed to seem perfectly harmless. But something didn't feel harmless. Especially Margie's keeping it all to herself. It wasn't like her. Or maybe it was, and I'd misread the signals.

'Hey, pigeon,' I'd said to Margie, one night at dinner before leaving Los Angeles. 'How's the idea of moving to Cleveland strike you?'

'Fine,' she had answered simply, through a mouthful of strawberry shortcake. Too simply.

'Wouldn't mind?'

'Nope.'

I'd been startled by her equanimity. 'You mean changing schools wouldn't bug you?'

'Not at all, why?

'You wouldn't have the beach outside your front door, or your children's lib group.'

'Oh, Daddy, come off it – you make it sound like Columbus's first voyage or something,' she had said with mock impatience. Too exaggerated. Too flip.

'I know, I know. I just thought the possibility of moving might come as a surprise.'

'Especially since we've been discussing it for the last year.' A twinkle and a wry grin.

'We have?'

'Of course.'

'When?'

'*Con*stantly, silly. All your talk about getting out of the smog and heat and,' she had mimicked me, shaking her head, lowering her voice, 'that lousy job with all the bellyachers and pair . . . para . . . what do you call them?'

'Parasites.'

'See?' A magnanimous tilt of the head.

'Guess so. Memory like a sieve.'

'No, just tuned out.' She had put her elbows on the table and rested her chin on folded hands. Her attitude had been calculatedly conspiratorial. 'So tell me how *you* feel about it?'

'About what?'

'Moving to Cleveland.'

'From good to great, depending on the day. I'd be teaching film-making at a high school. Place called Erieview Heights. A suburb.'

'Sounds like an adventure.'

'Want to join me on it?'

She had come around the table, hugged me and said, in

her most adult manner, 'By all means. I think you've made a very wise decision, Daddy.'

'Thank you.'

'I'm really looking forward to it.'

'You're . . . sure about all this?'

'Absolutely.'

She'd left the room with a stack of dishes. I'd started to pursue the matter further, then decided to pass. No particular reason – the unread evening paper on the couch, a certain not caring. Though something about the whole exchange had been subtly off-kilter, I'd shrugged it off as just another unimportant item I was sure had originated in the usual place: the fertile hideway of Margie's adolescence, where I'd also discovered closed-door phone calls, carbons of poems and quotations sent to people I'd never heard of in the Los Angeles area, and news clippings of fires involving fatalities, which had given me pause, but not alarm. The stealthy stuff of Captain Marvel code rings in my day. Or so I'd assumed at the time.

The tapping of Saddleford's pipe brought me back to reality. 'Are they marching?' I asked Saddleford.

'No,' he said.

'Do they protest?'

'Not publicly that I'm aware of.'

'Then, what do they do?'

'Meet. Talk. Ask your daughter. It all seems pretty cerebral,' he shrugged.

'Disturbing is more like it.'

'Possibly, if you're inclined to regard such matters in that light.'

'How can you avoid it?' I asked. 'No buttons, no demonstrations, no picnics. They haven't even tried to throw you out of office.'

'Yet,' he puffed.

'The only thing we know they've done is to deliberately *avoid* attention.'

'Possibly. Then again, your apprehension may be nothing more than your keen sense of melodrama.'

'Well, if you'll pardon my theatricality, children's lib is a long way from stick-ball.'

'When were you in tenth grade, Packer?'

'Fifty-one, Fifty-two, somewhere in there.'

'It's a long way from "somewhere in there".'

'Evidently.' I made a move to get up. 'May I look through the files for my homeroom students?'

'Of course.' Saddleford crossed to a filing cabinet and riffled through the folders. 'Let me offer you some professional advice.' He didn't look up. The offer sounded more like a demand.

'All right.'

'Give the Farrow boy plenty of free rein. Don't inhibit him, no matter how trying the situation may become.'

'Isn't that a little . . . over-indulgent?'

He pulled out a stuffed manila file. 'No . . . it would be exceedingly wise.'

'You know, Mister Saddleford, I can't seem to shake my feeling that there are things being left unsaid here. Am I being an alarm . . .'

'Because they're unknown!' he snapped defensively. 'Look, Packer, an apple is best when it reaches its peak of ripeness which, ironically,' he waved the file at me, 'happens to be the very same moment whan it begins to rot.'

'Now that's a little recondite for me. I'm sorry, I've always been lousy at riddles.'

'The Yin and the Yang, Packer! The eternal tug of war between good and evil.' He slapped the file into my hand. 'I do hope you're better at prudence than you are at riddles. Yes?'

'Thank you.' I crossed to the door and smiled good-naturedly, trying to make light of his dark seriousness. 'Guess I'm sorry my daughter married out of her religion, that's all.'

Saddleford sat down and tapped the dead ash from his pipe. 'Mine did too, Packer. Mine did, too.'

Possibly a look passed between us. Nothing of great import. Could have been my imagination. Or possibly no more than a mutual wariness of an unknown, an interest in something we knew very little about and were both hesitant to pursue.

As I walked back down the corridor, I realised I was a long way from situation comedies.

V: The Last Day Of August 1977

Fred Witt came home tired and grouchy, a headache pressing forward from behind his left ear towards the back of his eyes, a throbbing complaint born in long hours of drinking the night before – a night of slamming doors to shut out the shrillness of his wife, Elizabeth, still mourning a baby born dead, three years before, and to avoid the eloquent silence of his daughter, Amy, hidden behind other doors of her own construction.

Always the same Elizabeth theme – a new child, beautiful and smiling, alive, her immortality. Always the mute daughter, Amy, his by a prior marriage, silent, withdrawn, a constant reminder of the failure of his second union.

If he left, there'd be nothing for him. In staying, he could at least feel the energy of bitterness.

The night before, Fred Witt had easily – by habit, by default – felt nothing, nothing, as he watched Elizabeth in their bedroom, as motionless and familiar in her corner as the sad-eyed Pekinese in his basket beneath her chair.

Nothing, as he slapped Amy, twice, three times – to hear a sound, any sound, to prove there was life in this house, that he was not as he'd come to fear living in a graveyard of his own construction.

He sat on the edge of his bed. Elizabeth was with her social worker sister, Constance, a pathetic spinster in Akronm discudding, he was sure, the imagined marvels of present and future, if the baby had only lived. Amy was closeted in her room, he assumed, or perhaps at a meeting of her lib club. Little difference.

Time to fog away the sounds, to silence the foul-mouthed young inmates at the detention home, to ease the unrelenting guilt for promising the boys they could go home sooner if they'd just . . . cooperate. One film? That so bad? One, brief afternoon in return for a life of freedom? He could fix it: a small price to pay.

Fred Witt pressed his hands to his head as he kicked the bedroom door closed behind him, took a deep breath of relief as he crossed the room and reached into his bedside table for the plastic bottle of Eye-Ease drops. Removed the cap. Lay back on his bed. Held his right eye wide with the thumb and index finger of his left hand. One quick pinch. Two colourless drops.

Amy glanced up from her biology text as she heard the stumbling and thrashing from down the hall, the thump of a chair knocked over, the breaking of glass, a strangled cry from a place she knew by heart. It was only a glance, however. She had an exam the next morning. And the vial of concentrated eye solution Cammie Saddleford had given her was tucked safely in the bottom of her book bag. The note she'd typed at school was pinned to the visor of her father's car.

He would read it in a day or two. Perhaps three, Cammie had said. With his left eye.

If a man destroy the eye of
another man, they shall destroy
his *eye.*

– *Hammurabi, King of Babylon*

4

As I scanned the student files back in my classroom, I began to sense the futility of searching for clues I had hoped would be wedged between grades and birthdates, sports and church activities. I closed the last folder and damned my lousy memory. Obviously I'd missed something along the way, samewhere: something of Margie, of Malibu, the lib group. Maybe even of my ex-wife. Had I been manipulated? And if so, why Cleveland? I reviewed the prior year in hopes of locating a thread.

There had been eleven years of computerised existence with my wife prior to the divorce: cocktails at 5.15, supper at 6.15, sex on Tuesdays and Saturdays at 11.45 but not before brushing my teeth. She'd been programmed by an antebellum Texas family where you dressed for dinner and undressed in the dark.

I was granted custody of Margie, not because I requested it, which I had, but because her mother wanted it that way: it would give her second husband time to adjust without the added difficulty of a stepchild. Margie had just turned ten at the time. Had she interpreted her mother's decision as rejection?

We rented an old, mildewy beach house with yellow shutters in Malibu. She enjoyed the clean air and being able to see the horizon at the ocean's end. I watched happily as her hair grow long and freely on her golden shoulders.

We'd become easy with each other, yer the unanswered questions lingered. We played Scrabble and Monopoly, whenever I could find the time. My therapist had recommended more time, but I always fell short. He'd prescribed candour to offset the lies that had riddled the marriage. But there was too little, too late. Margie'd looked elsewhere and found a local chapter of a children's liberation club.

I had encouraged her to be spontaneous. I wanted her to see that all doors were open, that all clothes could fit. I had been determined that Margie would have the freedom to settle on her own identity when and where she chose, and by the end of our first two years together, she was running a gamut of possibilities. She was well on her way to becoming her own person. And so, last thing I expected was the bond that developed between Margie and Aaron. At times I was sure it must have been psychic.

On the way to our apartment after our arrival at Cleveland Municipal Airport, Margie and I had been driven up streets they called boulevards with names like Bellemont, Van Dillon and Kensington. The houses were monuments, great Georgian and Tudor beasts with leaded-pane eyes and pouting semicircular driveways. I felt distinctly uncomfortable, as if we were transients being regarded with disdain by these homes, as they sat back comfortably on their deep pile lawns, languidly smoking their chimneys. Old money. The palaces of Mather, Singer and Ponderbrook. Basements with billiard rooms and attics with ballrooms. Margie had sat silently, as impressed and fascinated as I was. Had there been more to her silence?

Our furnished apartment was near Colby Road overlooking the rapid transit, midway between Erieview Square and Canterbury Center. It was in a brick building with freshly painted white shutters and walkways winding through manicured privet. The mailboxes were brass, The front door was solid oak. We were to be substantially housed.

The morning following our arrival, Margie and I had sat down to grapefruit halves, toast and Instant Breakfast.

she'd inherited my aversion to heavy morning meals. At an earlier age, I might have suspected father-emulation, even with regard to food, but she'd become so thoroughly invloved with her children's lib group that thoughts, statements and actions tinged with parental influence were cauterised.

Even that first morning, I'd sensed something. There was a buoyancy, a strength I hadn't seen before. She'd been watching me. and I could tell by her cheshire smile that she'd drawn some uncomplimentary conclusions. 'Yes?'

'Oh, nothing. I was just thinking.'

'Thinking what?'

'Nothing in particular,' she had answered, pilfering the time to fabricate an evasive answer.

'Mar-gie!' I had warned. I hated the game.

'*Crinkles* around the eyes!' she blurted, jabbing at her grapefruit. 'I hope I never have to grow old.' She looked at me hard. Her intensity had surprised me. 'I mean, is it awful growing old? Really awful? I mean, don't you feel it? Doesn't . . . doesn't your body ache or something?'

'Listen . . . *kid*,' I had leaned forward, 'it might interest you to know I wouldn't go through my teens and twenties again for anything in the world.'

'That's because you're older now.'

'Well, of *course* I'm older.'

'You're not understanding.'

'Perspectives change as you get older.'

'Oh, Daddy, that's a parental cliché and you know it.'

'I'm sure it is.'

'Well then?'

'Sometimes it applies.'

'Not often.'

'Well, thanks for a "sometimes".'

'Don't you understand,' she asked with blue-eyed intensity, 'that fresh ideas, fresh thinking and new concepts come from new people?'

'"*New people*!" What's that, the libber's battle cry?'

'Sometimes it applies,' she said smugly.

'Margie, love, they're only new to you because *you* are.' I had tried for gentleness. 'When you're my age, you begin to realise they aren't new at all but shared with many others along the way before we were born.'

'How depressing! that's just another example of middleaged rigidity.'

'Oh, quit parroting your lib garbage!'

'It isn't lib garbage any more than yours is parent garbage!'

'Okay, okay, then look at life this way: as a timeless collaboration of all people that transcends centuries as well as age groups.'

'Jeez, I hope I die before I start to rationalise like that.' She stabbed with her spoon to emphasise 'die' and 'that'.

'Listen, little miss know-it-all, just because you lucked out with a one-sixty-eight IQ and skipped a couple of grades doesn't mean you've attained satori.'

She looked at me coldly. 'You're beginning to sound like a father, you know that?'

Her whole dialogue had become more pointed than in Malibu, as if, like a Catholic visiting the Vatican, she was now closer to the energy source of her beliefs.

'Why, isn't that remarkable?'

'Why, isn't that predictable?' she had mimicked.

'Perhaps it's simply ear of the listener.'

'Whatever . . . it doesn't mean you have to *be* like one. This *is* nineteen-seventy-seven, you know.'

'What's that supposed to mean, that my views are out of the Dark Ages?'

'Not . . . quite.'

As she went her way to the kitchen, I had noticed she was suddenly turning into an attractive young lady. There was only the beginning of a bosom, but her waist, fanny and hips had certainly put their act together. She still had too many teeth for her small face, but her mother's side of the family had always been a collection of wide grins and blue eyes. Margie had also inherited the eyes, the luminescent blue, of sky after a spring shower. It was a birthday when she smiled and a memorial service when she was brooding. 'Well, what then? Vintage World War One?'

'Oh, come off it, Daddy! Let's just call it a classic example of avoiding the issue. And *that* happens to be timeless.'

I had crossed to the front door and picked up my briefcase. 'Ready to go?'

'Still avoiding the issue?'

'Stop crowding me! Let's get a move on!'

'First day jitters?'

'In a hurry,' I corrected.

'We have half an hour.'

'I want to be early.'

'Revealing nervousness . . . '

'Revealing diligence! Now, dammit, get off my back!'

She brushed by me at the door. 'Okay, okay, anything you say. Next thing I know you'll tie me up and tape my mouth shut.'

'And why, pray tell, would I want to go and do thing like that?'

'So you won't have to hear the truth.'

As we approached the school, we passed impeccable brick and clapboard homes all neatly lined up like laying chickens, and looking as pampered as the morning students hatching out their front doors. It was a set for idle thoughts. Surely, nothing grotesque about deliberate trees. Nothing suspicious about lawns trimmed under a jeweller's eyepiece. Nothing sordid about a white steeple crowning the school like a monument to purity. Why be apprehensive about children in clusters, landscaped along the sidewalks, against the railings and on the grass? Why feel uneasy when Judy Garland, Mickey Rooney and Donald O'Connor might pop up from behind a hedge?

We had entered the large, double-entry door at the front of the school. Waxed linoleum, stale T-shirts and awakening radiators. Shouting kids, slamming lockers, a clanging bell demanding the school come to order. Chaos.

Margie left for the administration office to be assigned her homeroom number. I had sadly watched her dissolve into a crush of students twice her size. Plucky kid – no longer a kid, walking tall. Where had she learned her fearlessness? Was it possible I'd done something right? Possible. But evidently not enough to right years of wrongs. That was to fall within Aaron's jurisdiction.

Like it or not, Margie was my only link to the libbers' plans. As I returned the files to Saddleford's office, I resolved to have it out with her at dinner that evening.

VI: Labour Day, 1977

The first day in the transformation of the basement recreation room at 2780 Bellevue Boulevard, the last day of summmer for school-bound children; the beginning of Aaron's plan which, not coincidentally, would also complete the blueprint stage for the foundation of the Home of David; a day of high anticipation, of concept becoming reality.

Peter had already begun work with the electric drill. Fitted with a masonry bit, the drill cut through the mortar cementing an English Cross pattern of bricks with the ease of a hot knife slicing butter. At his feet, in front of the fireplace, were brick and pointing trowels, a bolster, a hammer, a jointer. A stack of bricks formed to his left. White dust filled the room, settling on all surfaces. Furniture lost its colour as if sealed in Egyptian tombs, and the faces of the children paled.

Cammie Saddleford approached Aaron carrying two one-gallon containers. 'These should be kept in a safe place, Aaron. Cool and dry, if possible.'

'The wine cellar. It's never used.'

'Won't your parents ask?'

Aaron shook his head. 'Don't be silly. They only ask when I'm sick.'

Robbie crouched in front of the only door to the room, a corroded lock mechaninsm at his feet, and a shiny brass assemblage already being fitted into the cavity left by the old. He paused, looked up, shouted: 'Aaron, you want a dead-bolt mechanism wired in here or what? Might be more efficient, less chance of a fuck-up.'

'That's fine,' Aaron smiled. 'You're operating under the assumption they'll deduce five steps ahead of the lock situation. It'll never happen.'

In a far corner, Chris Kasko sat surrounded by various shapes and thicknesses of glass. He held one after the other up to the light emanating from the windows. Aaron approached, sat down next to him.

'How's it goin'?'

'Fantastic!' Chris shook his head, 'Look at these! It's like walking through a museum of photo-optics.'

'They'll work?'

'Perfectly. Look at this.' Chris held up a circular disc, roughly four inches in diameter and a quarter-inch thick. 'Tempered glass, like Pyrex . . . or those petri dishes we use in biology. Heat-resistant. No distortion.' He picked another of identical dimensions, held one in front of the other. 'Like storm windows. Mount them three inches apart for a constant temperature within the chamber. Though the aperture's only four inches, they'll preserve the function of wide-angle lenses. Plus – get this! – plus the existing light in the room will be plane-polarised.'

'Will they allow the . . .'

Chris nodded. 'Jesus, Aaron, you'll see the whole room, the whole goddamned room in a constant light. Something happens at the foot of the wall below the chamber . . . you'll see *it!'*

Aaron stared at the discs, then turned to Chris. 'Everyone *will see it.'*

5

The remainder of that first day passed quickly. The schedule was light. My last class was at 3.25 p.m., after school let out. An elective. Fundamental film-making. Six students. Seven, if Margie made it. The libbers.

Unfortunately, I was late. In desperate need of a breath-catching cup of coffee, I'd indulged in a regathering of forces. After lunch I'd checked out my mail slot in the administration office. Along with three offerings from the academic bureaucracy was a brief note from Rod Angstrom, asking for a private meeting the following morning: 'It's urgent, Mister Packer. I know what they're up to.'

When I entered the room, the seven were collected in front of my desk. Margie had received her permission. I smiled, she smiled. The feeling persisted that I'd been set up by my own daughter.

Most classes of seven or eight fan out and sprawl. Not so, this group. It was like a choir. Their decorum had finishing-school polish. They weren't talking among themselves. They didn't look at each other. Including Margie, the newcomer. As if sensing presences was all they needed. The wordless stares were for me, unblinking, expectant, unafraid. Only my daughter gave off minimal warmth, and this was blunted by her self-consciousness.

I started to sit at my desk, but thought better of it. Enter. Join. Make them feel I was one of them rather than some six-foot-one adult chauvinist. I pulled a chair around to face them, glanced down at the seven class cards neatly stacked on Aaron's notebook.

He stood up and handed them to me the moment I saw them. 'Did you touch the plant, Mister Packer?'

'Plant . . . ?' Again that uneasy feeling.

'The coleus,' he smiled, nodding towards the window.

'Yes . . . yes I did. I'm very sorry. I had no idea it would . . .'

'Entirely understandable, Mister Packer. It would have been dead by nightfall in any case,' he continued to smile.

'You . . . find it amusing?'

'Only in that it offers a harmless illustration of how man destroys what he doesn' t understand.'

'I think that's a little far-fetched, Aaron. How would I have . . .'

'My aplogies,' he sat down. 'I'm being premature.'

I watched him in hopes of further explanation. His hands were folded in his lap. The subject was at an end.

'Shall we proceed then?' Silence. 'Very well.' I looked at the top card. 'Let's see here . . . top of the stack is Amy Witt.' I glanced up. A tentative hand raised. 'All right. Next is Aaron, whom I know. Robert Farrow?'

'Robbie,' he corrected.

'Robbie it is. What have we here, a little adolescent nepotism?'

'My younger brother,' Aaron said coldly, 'and would be my brother even if we didn't share the name. He's only ten, but has special permission to attend. I'll be responsible. He's not to be graded.'

'Can if he wants to be,' I offered.

'Doesn't want to be,' Robbie shook his head.

'None of us want to be,' Aaron added, 'but it would appear necessary.'

'Why's that?'

'Which?' he took a deep breath, expressing his tenuous

patience. 'Why none of us want to be, or why it's necessary?'

'Both.'

'Grading is a socially acceptable form of discrimination practised by the adult community to legitimise brain-washing and calculated to dissemble its real motives.'

'Which are?' It was a question I wasn't sure I wanted to ask.

'To establish a competitive environment for the young, thereby maintaining the health of the adult corporate state.'

('I *can't* believe he's twelve!' I'd said.)

'To pit child against child, thereby weakening by division and precluding the strength of a youthful collective.'

('*Nobody* believes he's twelve,' Saddleford had agreed.)

'Grading is guilty of all that?' I asked.

'Please don't play games, Mister Packer. It is a ridiculously transparent and antiquated system, and to deny that is to cast doubt on your own ability to to reason.'

'Guess I never gave it that much thought.' My ears began to burn.

'I hope that won't become a problem.'

'Possibly yours, Aaron!' I snapped, tiring of his condescension, 'especially if you don't do better about getting around your age discrimination. Unless I'm mistaken, you're hopefully here to learn, and I'm here to teach.'

'Oh, spare me, Mister Packer. Spare us your clichés. We're always in school, because we're always learning. We're always teacher *and* student. You have nothing to learn from us?'

'A great deal, it would seem,' I nodded.

'And if you're not learning, you're not living, in which case you shouldn't be allowed near a school. Correct me if I'm wrong, but I seem to recall a statement of yours that our comments would be welcome at any time. "So please don't be shy"? A mere six hours ago, I believe. Now why don't you proceed with the added absurdity of roll call so we can learn something today without getting bogged down with petty emotionalism.'

I sat quite still and gritted my teeth. ('. . . no matter how trying the situation may become,' Saddleford had said.) I'd been laced before, but never by a twelve-year-old. To be honest, I didn't know how to handle it. In my job I'd stood nose-to-nose with the best. This time I decided to listen. It was a new cast and a different location.

'I think I understand your position.'

'Do you, Mister Packer, do you really?'

'Not all of it, no. Not yet. But enough so that I'll make a deal with you and say, "screw the grades."'

The other students looked at each other with something resembling disbelief. Margie stared at me, pride mixed with surprise. I'd made a dent. Margie turned to Aaron. He didn't smile, didn't loook at the others, simply continued to stare at me with a glowering intensity.

'What are you doing, Mister Packer?' His tone was wary. 'What game show are you producing now, the "I want to communicate" hour? Or, possibly a brisk turn at "Close the Gap?" Or is it the "Win Them by Pretending to Join Them" ruse?'

'No game, Aaron. No pretence. Want to defend your stand against communication?'

'In order to defend something, Mister Packer, one must first establish the possibility that there is something to defend, and since there can never be anything but the most primitive communication between us, defence is pointless.'

'Even primitive man believed in give and take, Aaron, come on!'

'How can that possibly apply here?'

'I drop the grading, you get off your soapbox. Fair?'

He looked startled. 'You're joking.'

'No. You're bullheaded.'

'You can't drop the grading system around here.'

'Because you say I can't?'

'Because they won't let you.'

'Who won't let me?'

'The school administration.'

'*My* problem.'

'You mean we all get an "incomplete"?'

'If *you* mean I get some co-operation. Shall we screw the roll call as well?'

Two of the others tried to stifle giggles. Aaron shook his head, the first glimmer of a smile playing at one corner of his mouth. 'What're you, crazy or somethin'? They won't let you get away with that crap around here.' A kid's voice, a kid's words. I was reaching. By not being bulldozed.

'That is also my problem,' I said, tearing up the yellow cards, then handing the big halves to the others. 'Here . . . we all do it. It's good therapy. Up the system! Aaron?' I handed him his card. 'One other contingency . . .'

The glimmer left, the card went slack in his right hand. The guard stepped in front of his voice like a mute in the bell of a trumpet. 'And what would that be, Mister Packer?'

I indicated the others. '*You* introduce me to your friends. Without files, charts, letters and figures, I should at least know them by your definition. Don't you agree?'

He listened. He nodded once. 'On one condition.'

'Which is?'

'I introduce them *my* way.'

'Absolutely.'

I was not prepared for what happened.

Aaron looked at the others and smiled, a broad, open, fresh smile. He looked from one to the other, each returning the smile with as much warmth as the one given. Including Margie. Which surprised me. Perhaps it was a ritual practised in all chapters.

He moved from student to student, touching an arm, a shoulder, ruffling some hair. He spoke to each. Softly.

'Hey,' he said. 'All *right*,' he said. 'Okay,' he whispered. One girl stuck out her tongue. 'Right on!' he laughed. Suddenly I was in a room with kids – honest-to-God, scuffed-up, tattered-Levi's kids. It was good to see.

Aaron paused behind Amy. He put his hands lightly on her shoulders. She looked up at him, then back down, reached up and poked him in the ribs with her thumbs. As he began to speak, she looked at me and held her smile.

'This is Amy Witt, Mister Packer. Her father's a juvenile court probation officer at the Cohasset County Detention Home – supposedly. He's – into other things. Her mother drinks heavily. When her father comes home, they drink together, and Amy stays in her room with the door shut. When she was six, she'd go with her mother to the corner bar every Friday night, where they'd have to pick up her father and drive him home so he wouldn't spend the week's paycheck in one night – so there'd be enough money left to cover the grocery bill. His buddies would bounce her on their laps and pinch her buttocks.' He lifted her hands lightly, inadvertently. I could see the watermark tracings of scars circling her wrists. 'Amy didn't think she was pretty. Not because of the welts on her cheeks or the stripes she got on her legs every time her father whipped her with a coat hanger. Just plain because she didn't think she was pretty – for whatever reason. A form of blindness. Since birth.'

Aaron's voice had changed. It was soft and soothing. The words were different. They came from a different and simpler place. 'We had a talk one day last year after school. Out on the lawn. I told her she *was* pretty. Especially in the shade of the trees, because then the bruises didn't show, they just got mixed up with leaf shadows. After that she always wanted to sit under a tree with me in the afternoon when school let out. Now we sit in the sun, too. Because now she knows she's pretty anyway – no matter what her parents think about her or do to her.'

He moved on to Robbie, his brother, and put his hands

on his shoulders. 'Robbie likes "Robbie", not "Robert".' Our mother likes "Robert", because that's where her head's at. Not too serious yet, as long as her attitude doesn't get beyond the name stage.

'Robbie's a mechanical nut. He can do things with machines and electricity James Bond wished he'd dreamed of. Got that model fire engine you built?'

Robbie looked apprehensive. 'You sure?'

'He's okay,' Aaron assured him.

Robbie removed a small replica of an antique fire engine from his lunch pail, along with what I assumed to be a pocket computer. He put the model on the floor and started tapping the buttons. It sped across the floor, stopped within inches of the wall, reversed, and began braiding between the legs of the desk chairs. A small light started spinning, and a siren cut the stillness of the room, the sound of whistling between teeth.

I was sincerely amazed, yet didn't want to appear awed. 'Pretty impressive,' I said.

Aaron moved to the boy next to Robbie. 'This is Chris Kasko. He thinks he's tough.' He flipped Chris's hair across his forehead. 'He thinks his hair's tough. Girls think he's foxy. He's into optics and astronomy. Chris's father teaches here, as you know. His mom is a pharmacist in a local drugstore where she rips off her weekly supply of uppers. Comes on like Phyllis Diller at the breakfast table. We call her 'Saccharin Kasko' because she artificially sweetens anything from mental cruelty to death.'

The kids laughed. Chris looked around, breaking up. 'It's true, she's a total gross-out.'

'She hates spiders and snails,' Aaron continued, 'which she claims are bad for her weak heart. But, what can be bad for something that's malevolent in the first place? They don't like Chris. Told him so. Told him he must be an example of a recessive gene – or maybe he really isn't theirs, maybe they got the babies mixed up in the hospital. He eats in his room. Prefers it that way. He does his thing, they do theirs.'

'Especially at breakfast,' Chris mumbled.

I'd never known Bill and Peggy well enough to discuss parenting in depth, but cruelty was unlikely. Or I'd been unaware.

'Chris used to steal a lot of the time,' Aaron continued. 'He was like a yo-yo in and out of Juvenile Hall. Used to beat up on me a lot, too, because I'm smaller and younger, and everyone pointed at me and said I was brighter and pointed at him and called him "DumbDumb" and "Slugger." I told him to lay off. I told him to quit getting pissed off at me, because I really wasn't what he was pissed off at. We talked a little after that. We talked mostly about forming a club, about what to do about it all – about mums on pills and fathers who drink and kids who get whipped with coat hangers.' He continued to speak as he moved to the next student. 'We're not completely sure yet, but we've got a beginning, we've got some plans. We want to make a film that shows it like it is. It's beginning to fall into place.' He looked blankly at me, his voice flat. 'We're beginning to know.'

'I'd like to hear more about it.'

He moved on. 'This is Peter Robinson. You look at him through adult eyes, and your first thought is "black".' We looked at him and thought how awful it must be to be a black kid in Erieview High. He was one of three who got bussed in here to fulfil some adult committee's definition of integration. He said where he comes from down in the Century Park district, they call it "Erieview White's High School." That's for openers.

'One day the rest of us wore shoe polish and applied white pancake to Peter. Saddleford sent us home for misbehaviour. Didn't think it was amusing. Course not. Neither did we. That wasn't the point. Each day for the next week, we wore shoe polish, and Pete stayed black. But each day, we deliberately left one of us white and picked on him, Pete being in the majority for the first time in his life. Each of us had our turn at being alone.

'Then an odd thing happened. The other students began to pick on us too – called us names and hung around after school so they could hit us and throw things at us, pretending like it was kidding but really meaning it. We almost found out what it's like to be black. We also found out it didn't matter to us, okay. And it doesn't matter to Peter now, here at school, anyway. We have the same stuff going on underneath. About ourselves. About others. Between us. At this age. The shit comes later. Now we don't think in black and white any more, and hadn't until our parents laid that number on us. Now we think in younger and older. Now we share a minority group. It's just a different kind of persecution. Now we're all just a little bit black. And Peter's mother acts just as white as ours.

'One night when he was eight his baby sister started crying in her crib, the way all babies do when they get hungry in the middle of the night. Only that night was different. As he was about to turn over, Peter saw his father come into the room and walk slowly to the crib. He had a pillow in his hand. He lifted it and then slowly pressed it down over his baby sister's face. He held it there. And Peter kept very still. He squeezed his eyes shut and held his breath so he wouldn't make a sound. So he wouldn't be killed too. When he couldn't hold his breath any longer, he opened his eyes and saw his father's face in the light from the crack in the door, smiling, standing tall and still in the silence. His father's . . . gone now. His mother cleans homes for Erieview whites during the day. At night and over weekends, she hustles around the downtown hotels.' Peter looked down. Aaron paused.

'Once you discover colour, language and place don't mean anything but interesting things to be learned and enjoyed, you also discover the only real difference is age. You have to be sixteen, eighteen and twenty-one to do certain things, to be a certain way. That's like saying you have to be an adult to think, Mister Packer, because it's only the adults who make the laws and set up the rules. Isn't it?' He shook his head. 'Well, spare me that scene, man. First you want us to emulate you,' he jabbed his finger at me, 'and then you pass laws to make damn sure we do.' His eyes narrowed, his voice tightened. 'We have some new laws. Only this time they're written by us. And they apply to you.'

Margie looked up at him, eyes knitted, a slight warning frown, an almost imperceptible shake of her head. Aaron appeared bewildered, as if returning from a trance. Margie's expression disturbed me. It was her first day, yet the look had indicated familiarity.

The whole situation was becoming difficult for me. I had had to restrain myself from interrupting Aaron on several occasions. ('Give the Farrow boy plenty of free rein,' the man had insisted.) Christ, I had a raving tyrant on my hands! I told myself: This *is* the opening of negotiations. And tomorrow, the world?

There was something far more upsetting in Aaron's words and the reception they enjoyed among his peers than the cause. It was partly a matter of attitude. It was partly a co-operative consciousness. I'm no evolutionist, but there was something there, uncomfortable and threatening.

Though Aaron had the facility with words, he was expressing an ailment common to all – an injured part of them which they felt in the same place and with equal distress. They communicated according to the signals and responses of one nervous system; a cluster of synapses.

Disquieting. Because I recoil from the emotional binges of fanatical groups. Because I distrust absolute answers, and the false omnipotence they promise; their narcotic ability to drive sane people into collective madness. This was exactly what Aaron was talking about. This was precisely what they were rebelling against. Yet they were too young to understand that they were employing the identical means to reach what they considered their unique end. I hoped some day they would be able to look back with a perspective that would allow them to smile at themselves. It was a faint hope, however, nothing more. Something I felt, churning, something I saw, disfigured, was coldly insisting on just the opposite.

VII: Saturday, 10 September

Aaron stood inside the fireplace of the basement recreation room, staring out through the hole cut by Peter the preceding Monday. By inserting his head into the square opening he could see the entire room. His mother would be in the overstuffed chair, his father on the bench to the right of the door. The Saddlefords would occupy the couch, the Kaskos on the pool table bench. Packer? He would wait and see.

Amy was busy sewing a small, plastic zipper into the back of the couch. She'd already completed her work on the armchair. Aaron had watched fascinated, a proud grin easing up into his cheeks; he marvelled at the exactitude of her incision in the upholstery, the meticulous removal of a precise amount of stuffing, the cautious insertion of the magnesium reservoir, and finally, the flap of proper thickness and length to hide the zipper which closed the chamber. She was a seamstress-surgeon.

Aaron walked to the windows, checked the backs of the drapes. Magnesium strips were strategically stitched into the fabric at the rear of the folds, so as not to be visible from in front. Cammie's idea. Amy's perfect execution.

It was coming together. Three more weeks and the room would be ready.

'Nice work, Amy.'

'Hope it works.'

'Your father say anything?'

'Not a word. It's been very quiet.'

'Perhaps we've been able to help him see things in a different light.'

'I doubt it.'

'That's the trouble with all of this. So do I.'

Aaron went to a foot locker in the corner, flipped the combination lock briskly three times, lifted the lid. He reached inside and pulled out several cans of exposed film.

'Sixteen-hundred feet.' He shifted them from hand to hand, as if gauging the weight of the images. 'Love to see this stuff.' He stacked them again, returned them to the locker. 'Wonder if we can trust Packer to develop it.'

'Won't we have to?' Amy asked.

'I suppose.'

What if he . . . says something?'

Aaron shrugged. 'He has weaknesses.'

Amy stopped sewing. Her fingers ached. 'How about the throw rugs?'

'They can wait until next week. Let's go up to Connor's. I'm starving.'

Amy got up smiling. 'I think I could handle a chili-dog.' She picked up her down jacket. 'I'll sure be glad when this is all over.'

Aaron shook his head as they left the room. 'It's just the beginning, Amy.'

6

Aaron introduced the others with less rhetoric. 'This is Camilla Saddleford, Mister Packer, a fantastic chemist. She could make ginger ale from castor oil. If you can't stomach squash, she could make it taste like french fries, with twice the nutrition and half the calories. Unfortunately, she hasn't come up with anything from a test tube to make a human being out of her father, our pontifical principal, Sir Gabe.

'It was her coleus you wiped out. In finding a powerful growth accelerator, she inadvertently succeeded in establishing an extreme cellular sensitivity. Similar, in a way, to haemophilia in humans. The slightest temperature change causes cell disintegration and immediate putrefaction. Don't worry, she'll get it right before she's finished.'

'How about Marty Kyle?' Chris broke in. 'Tell 'em about Marty.'

Aaron hesitated, glanced at the others. Their watchful silence indicated agreement with Chris. 'Marty was . . . killed,' Aaron began, staring out the window. 'In a detention home. They tell us other kids in the home did it. If so, they were put up to it.'

'Do you know that for sure, Aaron?' I asked.

'Course,' he turned to face me. 'The three involved were released the next day. It was a set up.'

'That doesn't necessarily mean . . . '

'There *is* no other explanation, Mister Packer.'

'Tell him the rest.' Chris insisted.

'A group of our community's . . . finer citizens were shooting skin flicks with kids. Marty tried to stop it. That's all.'

'That's *not* all,' Chris blurted. 'Tell him about . . . '

'I said, "that's all!"' Aaron's look pressed Chris into his seat and ended the introduction. He moved slowly, thoughtfully to a position behind Margie's chair.

'Margie you know – or think you know,' he smiled enigmatically. 'She's a whiz at history and law and can spot our mistakes before we make them.' He sat down.

'We hope,' Margie smiled.

I nodded and thanked Aaron. I wanted to appear neither awed nor hostile. 'And how does all of this apply to film-making?' I asked evenly.

Aaron looked disappointed, then resentful. He had closed the door again on his easy openness.

'First, know what you want to say. Right, Mister Packer? Then make your statement. We know what we want to say about adult tyranny. Showing it will be saying it without words. We also know what we want to do about it, but we need the help of others. The film will demonstrate our need, and we hope it will enlist the necessary aid.'

'Okay, let's get started. I suggest we begin by learning how to use that sixteen-Arri over in the corner.'

'We know how. We've already shot over sixteen hundred feet.'

'Has it been developed?'

'No.'

Amy shook his arm. 'Ask him the other thing, Aaron, about all our stuff.'

'Can we enlarge super-eight to sixteen?'

'Sure. You'll have some quality loss.'

'How so?'

'Graininess. A washed-out look. Loss of detail and crisp lines. Closer to the look of newsreel footage.'

'Great! that'll be perfect for those scenes. I *want* them grainy.' His smile was self-satisfied.

'What scenes are those?'

'In due time, Mister Packer.'

'Aaron . . . ' I sat up in my chair and leaned forward. 'Do you want my professional counselling or not?'

'That's why you're here.'

'Then tell me something. You have the camera . . . '

'We have five cameras. Four super-eights belong to us.'

'All right, five. It would appear you know how to use them. You know what you want to say. You have a script. What is it you want me to teach you? Why do you need me at all?'

'Staging, lighting, sync-sound, scoring and editing,' came the unhesitant reply. 'The stuff we've shot is all documentary style. Cinema verité. Nothing slick. That would detract from our truth.'

'All right.'

'Also processing and printing. Can we do that right here at the school?'

'No way. Unless you know where there's a hundred thousand in alumni funds lying around.'

His face fell, as naturally as a kid who'd just been told he can't go to Disneyland. 'Oh, Jesus, no!'

'What'll we do, Aaron?' Peter whispered.

'Hey, slow down, that's no big problem,' I said. 'There's a lab downtown. I've already checked it out.'

'Yeah, sure, but can we *trust* them?' Aaron asked.

'To what? Develop the footage?'

'No, not to *look* at it.'

'They've got to, Aaron.' I was baffled. 'How else are they going to colour-correct your print if they don't look at it? How else will the negative cutter be able to do his job?'

'They gotta do that too?'

'Absolutely. But what's the big deal? They could care less about what you guys are shooting.'

'Hey, maybe he's right, Aaron,' Chris said. 'To them we're just a bunch of kids shooting home movies.'

'No way a bunch of kids would have shot what we've already shot,' Aaron said slowly, as if projecting the scenes through his mind. 'Then again,' he mused, 'why would they have to know a bunch of kids shot it in the first place?'

'Whoa!' Chris looked at Aaron. 'Right!'

'Hey, come on you guys,' I said. 'What've you shot, the inside of the Pentagon? I promise you, they've seen everything there is to see on film, including some of the raunchiest, hardcore films in the business. They're happy as long as they get paid.'

'Okay,' Aaron said, picking up a tote bag next to his chair. 'Okay, let's try it. Will you take it in?' He handed me the bag. 'Say it's stuff you've shot?'

'I'll take it in . . . '

'Call it stuff you've shot, okay?' he insisted.

'I guess so.' I was curious as hell. 'All right, if *I* see it? I mean, if I supposedly shot it, I ought to know what I shot, right? In case somebody asks?'

He paused. 'Some of it.'

'Not all of it?'

'Not until it's finished.'

'Why?'

'Mister Packer, consider: Films made for kids today are made by adults as adults see us. Our film will be for kids, but it will be made by kids . . . and it will be of adults as *we* see *them*. It won't be pretty.'

'So? Sounds fascinating.'

'Your value judgements and suggestions would be biased and would serve no practical purpose. Do you understand? I'm sorry. I don't mean it as a put-down . . . exactly.'

The qualified apology indicated a certain progress. 'I see. Purity?'

'Something like that.'

'What if I promise not to say anything?'

'Mister Packer,' Aaron smiled knowingly, 'that would be virtually impossible. You'd have no recourse.'

'Will other adults be allowed to view the finished product?'

'*Only* if accompanied by a child. After all, every motion picture rated R or X is off limits to us,' he laughed lightly. 'Just because they show someone balling or using the word "fuck".' Now I ask you, Mister Packer,' he tilted his head impishly, 'do you really think the finest little boys and girls of today don't know most all there is to know about balling and when to use the word "fuck" to its best advantage?'

'Point well made.'

'And at what time in your own life did you use four-letter words with consistency, vigour and a conspicuous absence of guilt, Mister Packer?'

'Touché, Mister Farrow.'

'Not at all, Mister Packer,' he bowed his head in mock acceptance of his victory. 'Not at all.'

'But, Mister Farrow,' I asked teasingly, 'if I'm to play a featured role in your picture, shouldn't I at least be allowed to read the script?'

The change in atmosphere was audible: a collective caught breath.

'Rod Angstrom . . . ' Aaron said in a slow whisper. His eyes snapped through me and the wall beyond. The smiles of the other children disappeared in unison. Their heads jerked towards Aaron.

'Pardon me,' I said.

'He didn't know,' Chris said reassuringly.

'He knew,' Aaron said.

'Who knew what?' I was lost.

'What'll we do, Aaron?' Amy asked.

Aaron's eyes refocused on me. 'Rod Angstrom. He's turned Uncle Tom.'

'I'm not understanding . . . '

'Of course not!' Aaron snapped. 'How could you? There's no way you can understand something you know nothing about.' He turned to Amy. His composure returned, his voice softened. He'd made a decision. 'It's all right, Amy.' He looked at the others. 'It'll be all right.'

'You sure?' Peter asked.

'Yes. Very sure.'

The other children shifted back into their original positions. What I had sensed as some kind of energy presence dispersed. Aaron looked back at me. 'I see the moviola arrived.'

'A . . . around two this afternoon.'

'Will you teach us how to use it?'

'Sure.' I felt telieved. 'Let's get it on.'

What followed was pleasure. They devoured every instruction with an enthusiasm which I, at the same age, had devoted exclusively to sexually precocious girls. The speed of their grasp was astonishing, fed I am sure by their dedication to a cause.

With some sixteen-millimetre out-takes I'd brought with me from Los Angeles, I was able to demonstrate most of the moviola's functions. 'Okay. Sound tracks on the left for dialogue, music or sound effects. Viewer on the right. You can sync a beat of music to the exact frame you want.'

'*Sacre du Printemps*,' Aaron said under his breath.

'Stravinsky's *Rite of Spring*. I'm going to use it for a couple of scenes. To the exact frame.'

'Stravinsky? Will it fit?'

'Perfectly. It's based on savagery,' he smiled, 'and it will be used exactly the way the title suggests: the origial rite.'

The remainder of the class period evaporated. When the moviola bulb blew out, there was some brief swearing, but then the questions overflowed.

'How do you freeze a frame?'

'How do you get slow motion?'

'Can we skip-frame?'

'Should dissolves be plotted before or after shooting?'

The more questions they asked the more curious I became about *The Bridge of Erieview Lake*. Their questions were not being asked in the abstract. They had very specific applications.

When the buzzer sounded, there was a whispered chorus of disappointment. I had dented. Aaron was the last to leave, and turned around at the door.

'Thank you.'

I shrugged. 'My job, right?'

'No, really. I mean it. We . . . we need you.'

'My pleasure.'

He started to leave, then stopped, thought a moment and turned again. 'My mother's coming in tomorrow for the parent-teacher meetings.'

'Right. I saw her name on my list.'

'She's . . . ' he shook his head, looked at the script in his hand.

'What?'

'I don't know. I don't even know why I'm standing here trying to tell you something. You'll find out soon enough for yourself. She's . . . different.'

'How different?'

'I'm not sure. Maybe she isn't different. Maybe she's just like the other women around here.'

'She's your mother.'

'That doesn't made her different.'

'Sure it does.'

'Not objectively.'

'For God's sake, Aaron, who can be objective about their mother?'

'I will be.'

'Okay, okay.' I decided not to fight it.

'You've got to be able to do that, you know?'

'No, I didn't know. It's a tough assignment.'

'You're better off because of it.'

'I'm sure you would be. But don't you think trying to be completely objective about one's mother is like trying to bottle the ocean?'

'Meaning what?'

'Some of it's possible, but certainly not all of it,' I shrugged, convinced I wasn't being convincing.

'I'm going for all of it.'

'I wish you luck.'

'I've got to. She's not *clear.*'

'Who is?'

'Don't you see?'

'See what?'

'If you can't be objective about everyone, and particularly someone who . . . who isn't clear, it can really fuck up your head.'

'So? Welcome to the human race.'

'I can't let that happen.'

Sometimes it's unavoidable.'

'She's stupid!' he blurted. 'Jesus, can't you understand? Nothing's more wasteful then a bright person gone stupid. Charity luncheons here, PTA functions there, Symphony Association meetings everywhere, and bridge playing to make sure she fills the remaining holes. All waste. An example of matter over mind, of spinning wheels and going nowhere. Not dumb, mind you, just stupid!'

'Especially if that person happens to have a brilliant son who resents the association?'

'Oh, shit, don't you think I'm capable of examining the psychology involved? That has nothing to do with it.'

'Then what *aren't* you telling me, Aaron?'

His look changed. The eyes went through me again. The voice went flat. 'Just be careful,' he warned. 'Don't get sucked in. She could take you with the rest.'

He walked off, hands hooked into his pockets. The stride was purposeful. The only sound as he went through the darkening auditorium was the rhythmic, squeaking echo of his crepe-soled shoes.

VIII: The Night of 12 September

Rod Angstrom sat alone in the small, formica breakfast room tapping a steel fork on the edge of his plastic plate. It was 8 p.m. He'd received the phone call at 6. Usually, he'd be given a couple of days' notice. Not tonight. Something was out of whack. Aaron plotted his moves with a chess master's premeditation. And he hadn't been called out on a reprisal since his blowup with Aaron back in July. So why the last-minute decision? Panic? Not likely. Aaron was cool. A shift in the Saddleford position? No way, considering the stacking of those cards, man! did Aaron have a lock on that *situation. So then, what? He didn't even know what was expected of him.*

Mother and dad at the Currys, sister asleep; the doorbell rang. Rod dropped the fork on to the plate snickering at the clatter. China was for Thanksgiving and Christmas. At the door, Murray, from East Chester High, skin like chalk, nicknamed Alby for albino. And Fuzz, who never shaved. Along with Dango, who got teased by the chicks because of his baby-soft, mink-coloured hair.

'Hey, babe. Ready?'

'Sure,' Rod answered, pulling on his denim jacket. 'What's up?'

'Guy at Erieview.'

'Packer? Already? On his first day?'

'Nope. You'll see.'

Alby had a car and a phony license to back it up. His parents were wise to it, but didn't like the eighteen-year-old driving law anyway. Figured it should be sixteen, and Alby being fifteen, they'd bend, especially since he'd put more restrictions on their lifestyle than they on his. Simply by being an offspring.

'Where to?' Rod asked.

'Dango's garage,' Alby answered.

'The dude there?'

'Not yet.'

They crossed East Chester Boulevard, rocketed at sixty for five blocks, then fishtailed right on Shropshire Place, a dimly lit street with only upstairs lights burning after eight. Braked to a halt in three hyphenated screeches. Got out, slam the driver's side by Alby, slam the passenger side by Fuzz, double slam the back doors by Dango and Rod; a souped-up, four-door, fifty-six Chevy Alby'd picked up for a song and a dance down in Century Park.

Rod checked the empty street in both directions. It was his way. 'No one here, Alby. We early?'

'Right on time. All taken care of.'

'Fuckin' crazy is what it is,' Rod said, hunching his jacket up around his neck against the Lake Erie wind, knifing in at a chill factor of freezing-your-ass-off.

Dango grabbed the latch chain, waist level, yanked. The door creaked open, a dangling light on the far side throwing long-handled, garden tool shadows like bars around the walls of the garage. Rod stepped in. The others entered quietly, quickly, pretending busyness with crates, chains, clearing an open space beneath the A-frame beams supporting the roof.

Rod picked up a Sears manual on home improvement lying on the work bench, flipped throigh diagrams of wiring, plumbing and skylight installation; tossed it down. 'So, how long we gotta wait?'

Alby threw a rope over the centre beam. 'Not long, man, almost time.'

Rod watched the uncoiling, began to feel an impatience, the irritability of not knowing. 'I don't just mean when, I mean who?'

Dango, unseasonably large for fifteen at five foot eleven and two hundred pounds, threw the latch of the garage door from the inside, came and stood in front of Rod and shook his head, the shallow apology of not understanding in his eyes, the smug smile of not caring on his lips. 'You, babe!'

Rod instinctively summarised the room, measured his options. As Dango had spoken the words, both Alby and Fuzz had stopped what they were doing, turned to watch, arms loose by their sides, at the ready. They knew Rod well. They'd been in similar situations dozens of times before, together. It wouldn't be easy.

'Why?' Rod played for time. No windows. Door bolted. A tyre iron on the work bench. A pick hanging on the wall.

'Aaron,' Dango shrugged, as if that should be enough. Alby strolled towards the door, Fuzz moved to the bench.

'No reason?' His options were decreasing. He'd have to make a move.

'There's always a reason, babe, you know that.'

'So?' He settled on the pick.

'Seems you talked to Packer. Not wise *man, not wise at all.'*

Rod feinted towards the door, reversed as Dango bought the fake full price and slipped trying to shift direction. The pick lifted easily from the wall, and in the same fluid motion of bringing it down, Rod caught the approaching Dango across his left ear with the flat side, sending him sprawling into a pyramid of half-empty paint cans. Glimpsing Fuzz from the corner of his eye, Rod quickly swung the pick back up in time to catch him, mid-dive, point first into his thigh, just below the hip bone. Fuzz rolled away, clutching his leg, the embedded pick yanking free of Rod's hands.

But there was a blur of white that Rod didn't see. Alby, from behind, brought him down before he could retrieve the pick. And it was Dango who, stunned and bleeding freely down his left cheek, had thrown his two hundred pounds across Rod's chest and face enabling Alby to pin Rod's hands to the concrete floor, knees digging into his palms, smooth, tight and deliberate as a pestle in a mortar.

'Fuzz!' Dango shouted. 'Get the fuckin' rope.'

'Can't . . . '

'Do it!' Dango's voice garbled with pain and rage.

A shuffling across the floor, a pause, heavy breathing as Alby stomached towards the kneeling Fuzz.

It was only a matter of time. Of which there was plenty. And Rod was bound.

Words few. All in pain. A certain anguish. Eyes averted, as only friends turned enemies can do. A scene in pantomime.

They tied his thumbs. Knots turning the tips to purple. Rope over the beam. Pulled till his feet left the ground. Taped his mouth shut. Dango picked up the tyre iron. Alby and Fuzz turned away, pretending other chores. Dango swung at Rod's shins, once, twice, until the agains ran out, and he'd lost count, the perspiration and tears shellacked Rod's face and pain no longer registered when Fuzz finally turned and said, 'Christ, Dango,' without looking, 'enough's enough,' and Dango out of breath said, 'Right,' as he picked up the .22 rifle from behind a camping harness and looked into Rod's eyes for probably the first time that evening; briefly.

Nodded. Levelled at Rod's chest and fired once.

Walked to the garage door. Threw the latch. Tossed the gun in the corner. Walked out. It was his way.

7

I have a special respect for parents, in addition to sympathy. It is the only profession I am aware of that doesn't require specific training.

A parent must be able to operate at peak efficiency despite the offspring's refusal to acknowledge a fundamental fact of life: adult humanness. God help them, we are flawed. A parent should have tennis stamina and bridge playing intellect and the capacity to learn the delicate nuances and strange sounds of a foreign language. Don't get taken, but don't let on we knew we were about to be taken.

Parenting should be degreed or licensed. In which case Aaron and his cohorts would have had fewer complaints.

All this idealism filtering into me, along with the reality of broiling hamburgers. Margie taking her turn at the stove. Every third night. One for me, one for her, and one for both of us, as we take a break and eat out. Our cease-fires included not being in the kitchen on the other's night. Fridays we celebrated with wine.

'Ready?'

'Sure,' I sip my scotch and continue reading the evening paper.

'Well?' She stands there, hands on hips, giving me that look which means, 'If I've taken the time and made the effort to prepare it, you'd better move it.'

'All right, all right.'

'Rather eat in front of the TV?' she cocks her head.

'Unh-unh,' I sit down. 'Smells good.'

'Good as last week?'

'Better.'

'Why better?'

'I'm hungrier than last week. You know Aaron before we came back here?' I'm terrible that way. It's a parent trick. I sneak loaded questions into the middle of empty conversation.

'Pardon me?' she dodges, cutting up her hamburger so she has an excuse not to look at me.

'Oh, Margie, cut the stall! Answer the question straight.'

'Yes.'

One word answers catch me in limbo. Like standing next to your disabled car on an uncaring freeway. 'Yes, what?'

'Yes, I knew Aaron. But not in person.'

I liked that about Margie. Guilty as she often was when it came to the sin of omission, she never lied. Unless she'd become so adroit as to make detection impossible. Which I doubted. Honesty was important to us. It was the one area we still shared as neutral ground. 'Meaning?'

'Meaning we wrote a couple of times.'

'Oh? How did that all come about?'

'Aaron sent out a general letter to the four Los Angeles chapters asking if any of us had parents with a film background.'

'And you responded.'

'Right.'

'So how come you didn't tell me?'

'I don't know,' she shrugged. 'I guess I just figured if it worked out, you'd know about it soon enough.'

'Good God, Margie, that's not an answer. Not one word?'

'Daddy!' she threw back with equal exasperation. 'Do

you remember once, years ago, what you told me about studying piano?'

'What's that got to do with this?'

'You told me you wouldn't push it, remember? You were afraid I'd take a negative attitude towards anything you'd suggest, remember?'

'So?'

'So I didn't want you to take a negative attitude about moving to Cleveland just . . . '

'You're kidding.'

' . . . just because I'd suggested it.'

'You've got to be putting me on.'

'No, I most certainly am not.'

'All right, all right. Then what happened?'

'Aaron went in and talked to Mister Saddleford.'

'Now wait,' I shook my head. 'You expect me . . . you *really* expect me to believe a twelve-year-old student talked Saddleford into hiring me sight unseen? Especially since I *know* it was Bill Kasko who . . . '

'Mister Kasko didn't get involved until later.'

'Margie!' I put my fork down. 'What in God's name is going on here?'

'Politics.'

'Politics . . . ' I said under my breath. I put my elbows on the table and leaned forward. I was losing my appetite. It's a feeling I recognise at once, an insidious form of apprehension, because the threat is an unknown. Something sinister, yes, but without definition. 'Margie . . . listen honey,' I began softly. 'Do you mean Aaron's buttering people up?' I hoped it would be that simple.

'No, Daddy,' she chastised. 'That's not politics. Least not any more.'

'Is he setting Saddleford up?'

'Doesn't have to,' she smiled smugly.

'You mean he's already got something on Saddleford?'

'You'd better believe it.'

'Oh, no . . . ' I let my head rest in my hands and rubbed my eyes. What could I say? 'Oh, Margie. What can I say? That's really crummy, you know that? *Course* you know that. You *must* know that.'

'It's the way it is.'

'It's the way it is for a lot of grownups, love, but not . . . '

'It's the way it is for everyone, Daddy.'

'How do you figure?'

'Remember Aggie who lived down the street from us in Malibu?'

'Aggie? No . . . '

'The one with braces all over her teeth? The one you called, "Sparkly"?'

'Yes, yes, okay.'

'When I was six, I remember telling her she couldn't play with my shell collection unless she gave me a bite of her popsicle.'

'But, Margie, that's blackmail.'

'I seem to remember you calling it "clout".'

'It's not . . . the same thing.'

'She gave me half her popsicle, no matter what you call it.'

'What's Aaron got that Saddleford wants?' I watched her carefully.

'Some pictures.'

'Of what?'

'No, Daddy, please?' She shook her head. 'If Aaron wants to tell you, he will. He trusts me not to say anything. Okay?'

The sense of loyalty I'd instilled was working against me. 'Okay,' I said weakly. 'Okay.'

'You all right?'

'No, of course not!' I snapped.

'What is it?'

'I'm sick.'

'Oh, Daddy, that's silly.'

'Don't make it worse.'

'Would you like some coffee now?'

'I suppose.'

'It really is, you know.' She left the table.

'Really is *what*?'

'Silly.' I heard the cabinet open and shut, the cup placed on the counter. A slow and even voice from miles away as the coffee started pouring: 'After all, he has it coming.' Then again: 'It's deserved.' the sound stopped, and she stood facing me in the doorway. She didn't smile: 'It would appeal to your sense of fair play and poetic justice, I promise.'

I sat back, blinked my burning eyes. Let the air escape from my puffed cheeks. 'The price is too steep.'

'I don't understand.' She handed me the coffee and sat down.

'It's got something to do with meting out your own form of vengeance. And that can be as deplorable as the crime itself. Worse, considering you little vigilantes are only eleven and twelve. Worse yet, when I consider what your values will be at thirty and forty.' I got up and started pacing my side of the table. 'What's he got on Saddleford, Margie?'

'Daddy, please . . . '

'Margie!' I stood still and faced her. 'What are you involved in? I'm raising a sneak, you know that? By remaining passive and silent I'd be contributing to the delinquency of a minor.'

'That's not . . . '

'Margie Mata Hari!'

'It's not what . . . '

'Why don't you two go play Bonnie and Clyde together? Shoot up the PTA from coast to coast. Or is that too primitive a tactic for you intellectuals?' The room went silent. Margie's eyes reddened as she tried to hold back the tears.

The ringing of the phone jangled the emptiness. As I started for the other room Margie quickly brushed by me. 'I'll get it,' she said softly.

I sat back down and sipped my coffee. Closed my eyes. Wondered the same universal wondering all parents fall prey to: Where I'd gone wrong (for surely I had), how the hell I'd missed a signal telling me my daughter was getting sucked into an ugly business (for surely she was). Was it too late? Already? What kind of ugliness was going on?

There was silence from the next room. Briefly. Then Margie's voice, unexcited, even. 'Yes. No, I won't. Fine. Bye.' She came back into the dining room and sat down.

'And what, if I may ask, has your band of insurgents got on me?' the words came out through gritted teeth.

'Nothing, Daddy,' she said shaking her head, the tears beginning to fall, 'nothing, I promise. I'm so sorry all of this came out. I didn't . . '

'So am I. Who was on the phone?'

'Aaron.'

'Figures. What'd he want?'

'Rod's been hurt.'

'Rod?'

'Rod Angstrom.'

'Aaron booby-trap him?'

'No . . . '

'No, of course not. I suppose he has a hit-boy to do his dirty work.'

'That . . . that's not fair.'

The phone rang again. 'Mine! And as far as what's fair,' I said over my shoulder, 'I hardly think you're in a position to judge.'

I picked up the receiver, glanced at the clock: 8.45 p.m. 'What!'

'Matt?' A woman's voice.

'Yes.'

'Are . . . are you all right?'

'Course I'm all right. Who's this?'

'Peggy. Peggy Kasko. You sound so . . . '

'Oh, Peggy, I'm sorry. We've just been having a slight altercation over here. Didn't mean to snap at you. How are things?'

'Fine. Bill just telephoned from school and asked me to give you a call; wondered if you could take his first two English classes tomorrow morning.'

'Sure, but I don't think it'd do much good.'

'Oh?'

'It's parent-teacher day, there are no classes. I doubt if it'd help for me to take his parent meetings.'

'Grief, that's right. We'd both forgotten. Oh, well, excuse our absent-mindedness, and please don't mention it around the school; you *know* how those people talk, or perhaps you don't, it's the Erieview Heights way. Long as I've got you, though, have you made plans for Saturday night?'

'Not a one.'

'Good. We're having some friends in. About six-thirty. The kids will be shooting some film, I think. How they waste their time these days.' Then she treated me to her phony, tinkling laugh. I'd forgotten the trademark. Two years and Erieview Heights affluence hadn't mellowed her brittleness.

'Fine. Look forward to it.'

'See you then, Matt. Bye now.'

When I returned to the dining room, Margie was sitting at the cleared table, hands folded in her lap, staring straight ahead. She was a pretty girl. Particularly in that quiet time after she'd been upset and crying. I sat down opposite her.

'You all right now?'

'Yes. Who was on the phone?'

'Peggy Kasko.'

'The Lady Saccharin.' She spread her mouth, revealing all teeth and no smile.

'So how did Bill Kasko get involved in our coming back here?'

'Didn't really,' Margie shrugged. 'Mister Saddleford thought Mister Kasko might have worked with you in California. Turned out he had, that's all.'

'What if he hadn't?'

'I don't know. Probably would have gotten in touch with you direct.'

'Then why the interview?'

'Appearances. So it'd look okay to the school board. Formalities.'

'Just going through the motions.'

'Um-hmm.'

'Will you tell me any more about what's going on?'

'I just can't, Daddy.' She shook her head, looked down at her hands. 'It wouldn't be fair to the others, and I . . . I'd get in trouble.'

'Okay. Let's drop it. I'm glad to hear fairness is still a consideration. Even if it is limited to Aaron's disciples.' She rubbed her eyes. 'Sleepy?'

'I feel wasted.' She came around the table and hugged me. I felt the moisture in strands of her hair, the added warmth of emotion burning her cheek. She had a natural, little girl smell, fresh as following a lawn mower. 'Good night, Daddy.'

'Good night, love. Sleep tight.' I watched her unhappy walk to her room, the door closing softly with special care, as if a sharp sound might reawaken my anger. And behind that door, what? An entry in the club notebook which they all carried like battery packs to power their fanaticism? An entry incriminating her father for anti-children's lib activities? Like the Hitler Jugend? Turn in your father and win a medal?

I tiptoed to her door, squeezed the knob, pushed an inch. No sound. The soft glow of a reading lamp. Margie on her bed, face down in her pillow, the small of her back and roundness of her sides lifting and expanding in the uneven rhythm of quiet crying, the relief of having something over with, the recriminations of having hurt someone hurting you – the healing.

I closed the door, shut my eyes and stood very still. I understood why people wanted to become parents, licensing be damned.

IX: Later That Same Night

At precisely 9.15p.m., Bill Kasko arrived home, fed up with the adolescent antics and paper bureaucracy of opening day. Peggy pulled the souffle from the oven at 9.16, placed it on the table as Bill flopped into his dining-room chair, dropping his briefcase on top of the bin table. By 9.20 they were both sitting, eating without words, as was their custom. Finally, somewhere between 9.45 and 9.47, Peggy spoke:

'Harlan was here from Condor plumbing . . . said the disposal was fixed, which, needless to say, it isn't, and no, I did not fill it with the artichoke leaves from last night; it simply won't work, Bill, and I'm at a loss as to what to do, I ask you, call another plumber and pay another thirty-five dollars for inefficiency? You know I can't do that, so what do I do?'

'Tell me.'

'I just did.'

'So? What's the big problem? I'll take a look at it.'

'Well, I wish you would, I'm so sick of paying good money for bad work.'

'Chris home?'

'No. At Aaron's.'

'Still . . . miffed?'

'Oh, Bill, I don't know. I'm completely at a loss as to what

to do with that child. I don't think last night helped. I don't think physical violence helps at all. I think hitting him just inflames an already volatile situation, don't you agree?

'Could be.'

'Will you look at the disposal?'

'I have no plans,' he shrugged.

'Good. You know how at a loss I am without these conveniences. I wonder how the frontier women got along.'

'You don't have to tell me.'

'Bad day?'

'What else is new?'

'Cora-Louise has an abscess.'

'I asked, "What else is new?" '

'Bill! Be nice. She's very uncomfortable.'

'I couldn't have put it better myself.' He pushed away from the table. 'Better have a look at that disposal . . . otherwise you might have to take the garbage out.'

'Thank you, dear.'

Beneath the sink, Bill grunted into a position where he could see the red, re-set button, pushed, shimmied out. Threw the switch on the wall above, heard the hum of electrical effort thwarted.

'Still jammed,' he shouted.

'I know,' Peggy responded.

Bill turned the switch off, squeezed his hand down through the rubber mouth, groped for the obstruction. He felt the wet smoothness of heavy wire locked securely between the rotary blades.

'What the hell?' he mumbled.

'What's that, dear? I didn't hear you.'

'Goddamn wire in here. Feels like a coat . . . '

Peggy heard the whirr and a grinding. The chicken bones from the night before? 'Darling, thank you, what . . . '

But Bill's scream had cut her short. As she got up, she felt the nagging irritation of expecting something to be fixed which wasn't, after all, heightened, she was sure by the *typical result, that Bill had once again cut his finger and she would have to rush for the Mercurochrome and Band-Aids, not to mention unguentine and soothing words.*

With sympathetic smile fixed she entered the kitchen. Bill was doubled up on the floor, blood everywhere, his hands viced between his thighs.

She clutched her chest, closed her eyes. 'Oh, my God!'

8

The next day: 13 September. Homeroom period: quiet and without incident. The kids were looking forward to Special Projects. There would be mini-courses in psychic awareness, Zen, Balkan dancing, and others of equal eclecticism.

I slipped through the mustard cards with checks, asterisks and letters, where student histories were reduced to an academic credit rating. Two absences. One, Rod Angstrom.

Chris and Amy reviewed their knowledge of the moviola until a guide belt broke. Aaron was memorising the manual. The others read quietly and whispered occasionally.

I put down the cards and regarded my parent list. Not even my curiosity about the 'unclear' Sylvia Farrow helped abbreviate the list of seventeen.

The bell rang, funneling fourteen through the door. Aaron remained and approached my desk. 'How do I go about blowing up a bridge without really blowing it up?'

'This your day of the week for riddles, Aaron?'

'For my film, I mean.'

'*Your* film?'

'This your day of the week for communication difficulties, Mister Packer?'

'Not *our* film, Aaron? You squeezing out your production team, are you?'

'Our film,' he agreed sheepishly.

'You shoot it in miniature and overcrank your camera motion,' I said quickly to gloss the indiscretion.

'Slow motion?'

'Right. Looks less phony. Know anyone who can build you a model?'

'Robbie . . . ' He glanced at his watch.

Saddleford appeared in the door. 'Ah, there you are, Aaron, just the man I was looking for. Have a few items I'd like to talk over with you.'

'It'll have to wait, Mister Saddleford,' Aaron said, brushing by him. 'I'm late as it is.'

As the crepe-sole sound faded into the auditorium, Saddleford slowly came towards my desk, puffing on his pipe in quick, short draws, despite the fact that it had gone out. A school key dangled from his vest pocket, a Shriner pin pouted from his lapel. Rep tie, the right Brooks Brothers suit. What the hell could Aaron have on him? Couldn't be too serious. Drinking? A flirtation? Saddleford didn't really have the backbone for anything illegal, or the flair for anything juicy.

'Morning, Packer. Ready for the parade of mothers?'

'No, I'm not particularly up to it. I have a hunch it's going to be like advising a Beverly Hills matron about her toy poodle: she'll be into powdered bows and show cuts and I'll be into diet and exercise.'

'Oh, come on, Packer,' his blue eyes flashed suggestively. 'Consider the possibilities. Who knows? Perhaps a . . . liaison.'

I ignored the inference. 'Mister Saddleford, I suspect you are endowed with far more tolerance than I . . . or diplomacy. No matter, I'll give it my all.'

'I'm sure you will . . . ' the leer returned. 'Afraid Rod Angstrom won't be in for some time,' he said, taking a seat.

'Oh? I heard he'd been hurt. Serious?'

'Might say so,' the left eyebrow flicked up. 'Parents called in earlier. He's in the hospital.'

'What happened?' I sat up and leaned on my desk.

'Multiple fractures of both shins, a twenty-two bullet in his chest, two . . . '

'A *what*? A twenty-two . . . '

'Yes, yes, happens much of the time in lower income districts.' He shrugged, removing the pipe from his mouth. 'Angstrom's from East Chester, a bad neighbourhood. Parents sent him over here to avoid the baser elements. Would seem they can't be avoided. You say you'd heard about it?'

'Yes, last night. Aaron called Margie just after dinner.'

'Hmm, wonder how he knew so quickly.'

'You know kids. Word gets around fast.'

'Odd, though. Police didn't find him until after midnight.'

For what I suspected to be the same reason, neither of us was willing to discuss our mutual apprehension. We were both looking for answers involving neither Margie nor Camilla.

'Police know who did it?' I asked.

'Riffraff from East Chester High.'

'They sure?'

He nodded. 'Almost positive. Picked up one boy. Holding him at Juvenile Hall.'

'They find out anything more? Motives?'

He nodded. 'Another boy involved, though the little bastard in custody won't reveal his name. You know, that same old warped code of ethics. Don't be a snitch. Some kind of vendetta, I'd wager,' he trailed off. Then, without warning, 'Savagery! Do you realise what barbarians kids are?'

'Ah . . . no. Quite frankly, Mister Saddleford, I don't.' I could see a loathing, indistinct and filmy like heat waves from a desert highway. I was also observing the first layer of dirt beneath the asphalt. And I had the distinct feeling I wouldn't like what I'd find below.

'How can such beauty turn so ugly: hung him up by his thumbs! By – his – thumbs. From a beam in a garage. Then they cracked his shins with crowbars. Nine fractures. Two broken ribs. Then shot him point-blank.' There was a certain rolling of the words, I was picking up something vicarious – of pleasure, not horror.

'My god,' I whispered, ignoring the implications. 'It's a wonder he wasn't killed.'

'Packer.' Saddleford sat forward, removed his pipe. 'That's exactly what they were trying to do. Punish him. Then, kill him. They missed his heart by half an inch. He was left for dead. That he's alive is pure accident.'

'What the hell've they got over there, a collection of pubescent Hell's Angels?'

'The boy they're holding is eleven,' Saddleford said.

'You're joking.'

'My brand of humour doesn't run to the macabre or sadistic.' He got up and started pacing the room, glancing at me from time to time as if to drive his point home. 'Purely for your own edification, Packer, I'd suggest you take a personal field trip to the East Chester School District so you can compare the environment and facilities with those here in Erieview Heights. Pain and injury are commonplace. Gang wars are precipitated by lost football games. Death, accidental or deliberate, is regarded as casually as cutting classes. Cruelty is the norm. Saddest of all, I suppose, is the acceptance of such violence as the way it is, as it will always be, especially by children who have little or no chance to observe, much less experience, alternate life styles. Television is their reality, not our fantasy. They make a game show out of brutality; the more grisly the deed, the higher the degree of peer adulation.'

I was feeling lectured again. 'I've seen rough neighbourhoods before.'

'Since fifty-one, Packer?' he shot back.

'Since fifty-one, Mister Saddleford, though I grant you the . . . the thinking and motivation behind the violence seem to have changed.'

'I'm not sure I'm following you.'

'It's been my experience that violence in youth is spontaneous, disorganised, random and emotional.'

'It still is, with few exceptions..'

'Is it?' I sat back. 'Is it, Mister Saddleford? Perhaps you're right, but something doesn't feel like it to me.'

'I see. In other words, you believe they're out to do each other in premeditatedly.'

'It would seem so.' I was hearing a false note. Something wasn't fitting right. The words were coming out on top, but they weren't connecting to the thoughts below. What the hell was it with this guy? He made a move to leave, then turned around. 'Oh, Packer . . .'

Here it comes, I thought. 'Yes.'

'Mrs Farrow coming in?'

'I believe so.'

'She's a rather extraordinary woman . . . as you might surmise.'

'I hadn't surmised anything.'

'Well, she is. I'd appreciate it if you'd be on your best. Her husband's well thought of in the community – lawyer, politician, carries considerable influence with the school board. As does she. Trustee with the Symphony Association, docent at the art museum, that sort of thing.'

'Quite a schedule. Do they see their kids?'

'And something else,' he said, ignoring my question. 'She's very gracious, probably will offer you a social invitation. Done it in the past. Your former associate, Bill Kasko, others. Don't feel obligated to accept,' he gestured with his pipe. 'Well, fact is, I'd prefer you decline. Nothing personal, mind you, just that you're still an unknown quantity, and school-community relationships are particularly delicate here in Erieview Heights. I'm sure you can understand my position.'

'Mister Saddleford, I promise I won't say a word about being bussed in from Los Angeles. You have my word.' I smiled. The uninterpretive variety. Could be nice, could be shitty.

'Good,' he smiled fatuously and walked towards the door.

'Oh, Mister Saddleford . . . '

'Yes?' He turned around.

'Before you leave . . . ' I stood up, slipped my hands into my rear pockets. ' . . . Ah, it may be none of my business . . . but then again it might.'

'Yes?'

'I'm still not familiar with how things are to be handled around here. I don't know that much about your people . . . '

Saddleford glanced at his watch. 'Packer, I'm pressed for time. If it's all the same to you, I'd . . . '

'Yes, I'm sure you are. How well do you know Aaron Farrow?'

'Why?'

'Perhaps I should rephrase that. How well does Aaron Farrow know *you*?'

'As well as most other students,' he said flatly. 'why do you ask?'

I chipped some paint from the radiator with my thumbnail. 'I heard a rumour one of the libbers had something on you. I felt you should know about it.' I turned to face him, watched carefully.

'Bullshit!' he snapped. 'That's utter nonsense, Packer. You've been in Hollywood so long you're beginning to believe every sordid story you hear. Failing real scandal, you seek it out where it doesn't exist, which bespeaks, I might add, a certain depravity all its own. I'm quite sure there are already some saucy rumours circulating about you, despite the fact that this is only your second day. So! Where did you hear this one?'

'My daughter said she'd heard something,' I said quietly, realising by his agitation that I'd hit a chuckhole.

'Such as?'

'Wouldn't say.'

'There, you see? Common gossip.'

'Could be. Though I have reason to believe she's adhering to some code of silence.'

'A charade. A childish method of conjuring smoke where there's no fire.'

'I suppose. Sorry to bother you with it.' I wanted out of the conversation; it wasn't taking me anywhere.

'Hear me, Packer!' Saddleford's voice dropped ominously. 'Don't be so quick to assess. I don't know you. *Really* know you. And you certainly don't know me.' I was feeling on dangerous ground. 'I am what I am, and not that much different from yourself. If you think me pompous, I think you superficial; if you consider me pedantic, I regard you as banal. Conceivable misreadings on such short notice. Perhaps what I am is out of fashion today, and you – the film-maker – you are what's "in". But, remember: Tomorrow you, too, may be "out". Public opinion is ephemeral. History is a spectrum. The overview accepts all patterns and colourations. To take a stance above *any* way of being is intolerance.'

I felt seduced by his glibness – momentarily – but on closer examination, I came to the conclusion that, with a nod, I'd be condoning something I knew nothing about. 'Just . . . checking things out. No offence meant.'

'I hope not. You have your own vulnerabilities.'

'I'm . . . sure.' Fair enough for the present. 'By the way, is Rothermill Film Lab the best in town? I have some footage I'd like developed.'

'From what I've heard. Material you brought with you from the coast?'

'No. Something Aaron wants me to take in.'

'Matt!' Bill Kasko's shout echoed from the auditorium. Saddleford didn't turn around. I felt him studying my face. 'Down here!' I shouted back.

'I'm afraid,' Saddleford said evenly, 'it will have to wait until I can get budget approval. I wasn't aware anything had been shot.'

'Neither was I. How long will it take to get approval?'

'A month to six weeks ought to do it.'

'That long?'

'What's the rush?'

'Don't want to dim his enthusiasm,' I lied.

'Point well made. Though it will take considerably more than bureaucratic red tape to accomplish that.'

'Gabe!' Bill nodded a greeting. 'How's it going?'

Saddleford brushed by him and hurried off. Judging from his agitation, he evidently believed Aaron had more in his possession than I'd originally thought. Not even Bill's hand and arm in a canvas sling had slowed his hasty exit. 'What the hell's with him?'

'Not sure,' I answered, 'but I have the feeling Gabriel Saddleford is coming into difficult times.'

'Wouldn't surprise me.'

'Oh? And what do you know that I don't?'

'I know better than to ask, I'll tell you that.'

I glanced down at his lame wing. 'Even if I twisted your bad arm?'

'Not funny.'

'You always did have trouble keeping your hands to yourself, William.'

'Still not funny.'

'Oh, come off it, Bill. We all break a bone or two now and then. What happened?'

'Our plumber botched a repair job on the disposal yesterday, so bright Bill figured he'd give it a shot. Thing went off with my hand inside.'

'Good God!' I regarded his hand with a new appreciation. 'How much damage?'

'To the disposal?' he asked ruefully.

'To your psyche, asshole!'

'Two broken fingers, seventeen stitches.'

'Jesus, Bill, sue the plumber. That's inexcusable.'

'Perhaps I could . . . had it been an accident.'

Now I'd known Bill for the better part of seven years. Not only was he humourless – certainly a peculiar deficiency in a former comedy writer – he was literal to a fault and candid to an embarrassment.

Women were attracted to his square jaw, sandy hair, dimple chin, Kirk Douglas-style. Light brown eyes set into tanned skin, he looked as one-dimensional as a sepia-toned photograph. But so did his wife, Peggy. In the same room they could have been selected by an interior designer with a penchant for beige.

'You mean the guy from the plumbing repair . . .'

'No, no. I don't know who. I know *how*. The off-on switch had been tampered with. Than a piece of baling wire had been wedged between the rotary blades and casing – the way you'd rig a mousetrap. Remove the wire,' he lifted his hand, 'and snap.'

'Any ideas?'

'Not . . . really. But I think if I knew the why, I'd know the who.'

'Anything to go on?'

'Only this.'

He handed me a short typewritten note. It read: 'If thy right hand offends thee, cut it off.'

'Where'd you get this?'

'Came in the mail. The same day.'

'A quote, right?'

'Right. From the gospel of Saint Matthew.'

'Any idea how it applies in your case?'

'A hunch. Maybe a long shot, I don't know. Doesn't

even fit when I stop to think about it. But when I don't, something begins to work. It's sick, Matt.'

'Fire away.'

'Did you know Gabe was being taken to the cleaners by our resident genius, Aaron Farrow?'

'How so?'

Bill indicated the film equipment in the room. 'Ever wonder how all this was being paid for?'

'Taxes? Alumni? A philanthropist?'

He shook his head. 'So far your novice film class has the equivalent of two tennis courts originally earmarked for thr phys-ed department.'

'They must really welcome my addition to the faculty. How the hell is Aaron . . .'

Our heads jerked around as we heard the clicking of high heels coming down the auditorium aisle.

'I don't know how the hell anything. But I intend to find out. And when I do, I hope my hand's well enough to be used again.' He lowered his voice. 'Be careful, Matt.'

'Me be careful? You're the clumsy one, *you* be careful.'

'Margie one of the libbers?'

'Sure.'

'That's why,' he said quietly. '*That's* my hunch.'

Bill flashed a smile at the approaching mom and walked briskly up the aisle.

'Goodness!' she gasped. 'Poor dear. Was it a skiing accident?'

'No,'I answered. 'Disposal.'

'Oh.' Then she squeezed my arm and smiled. 'You *must* be Mister Packer. They told me you were a comedy writer.'

She said her name was Gloria Abigail Smith Hamilton. She was dressed in a wool suit the colour of an orange popsicle. I offered her a chair. She sat down and launched into the outline of the Hamilton history, ending fifteen minutes later with the eighth generation representative,

Bobby Hamilton, who smoked grass and watched his sixteen hamsters fornicate simultaneously. Blessed with the opportunity of saying nothing, I examined my new information, courtesy of Gabriel Saddleford and Bill.

I was not liking Saddleford. Principals who practise manifest snobbism in the guise of school-community relations are more repugnant than the stereotypes I'd left in LA. And why the 'coming attractions' for Mrs Farrow? The man was mericulously cagey. He could convince the unwary that true was false. I wasn't about to buy any of it. Including what I was sure was a creative interpretation of the Rod Angstrom hospital report, for reasons which would only be apparent to a principal being pursued by a precocious student. I wanted the story first-hand. From the boy himself: assignment number one. Assigment number two: develop Aaron's film at my own expense without Aaron or Saddleford knowing anything about it.

I had to take Bill Kasko's remarks with liberal sprinklings of salt. He was an alarmist. Always had been. I often felt he preferred it that way as a means of attracting attention. It was as simple as that. So. Pin Margie: assignment number three. Assignment number four: grill Aaron. What pictures did he have? How did he know about Rod three hours before the police discovered him? Find and read the script. Above all, don't forget about being careful.

X: Noon, Tuesday, 13 September

Having interviewed eight Erieview mothers, and feeling bored, incompetent and frustrated, Matt Packer went home for lunch, relief and a regathering of forces.

Originally, he'd been a trusting person. Born Matthew Jabez Packer, Jr, he'd been informed by his first wife, in a moment of pique, that Jabez meant, 'He who shall cause pain,' and that this represented some esoteric form of parental absolution; the basis for all the difficulties for which he, and he alone, was responsible, and which had destroyed their marriage. Divorce was inevitable by legacy. Guilt was his by name.

Initially he'd wondered about a person who would undertake such a concerted effort to find reasons for failure within a name. Now, after years of retrospect, he'd pinpointed her *need to shift responsibility. Nonetheless, a distrust of* all *persons and their so-called motives remained, regardless of their private launching sites, ranging from astrology to phrenology to just plain pass-the-buck.*

If he vacillated when confronted with the obvious, it was because of his original trust. If he concluded the worst after much weighing of contributing factors, it was a scepticism taught by the years, an intolerance which evolved through exposure to numerous disappointments. And, in the end, he still doubted his conclusions. Until this day.

On his way back to school he noticed his gas tank gauge flashing red. There was an Oxitron gas station at the corner of Colby and Van Dillon, where he'd turn left for the return to school. Certainly not enough fuel for the trip home that evening.

He pulled in next to the unleaded pump, turned off

the ignition, waited. A young boy with a blanched complexion stopped an older man, mid-stride and trotted to the car.

'Hi. Fill 'er up?'

'Please.'

Packer glanced in his rear view mirror to see if the boy had pink eyes or was just plain flu ridden. He heard the dinging of gas dollars registering on the face of the squat Star Wars *robot. He smelled the clean odour of raw gas.*

As he fished for his Oxitron credit card, he became conscious of the boy standing at the passenger window. He looked up just in time to see the spray of gasoline hit the front seat and splash across the front of his suit. 'What the hell . . . ?'

An 'Oh! Sorry, sir,' was tossed off as the boy returned the hose to the left ear of the robot.

Matt gingerly dropped his wallet on to the seat next to him, flicked his hands. 'Hope you guys pay cleaning fees.'

'Yes, sir.'

Matt looked up. The boy stood close, placed a cigarette in his mouth, stroked his lighter.

Matt started to open the door on his side, as he felt the cold moisture, the creepimg evaporation easing down his thighs. But the boy stood close, the door bumping his leg.

'Apologies, Mister Packer.' He was holding the lighter at chest level, puffing through a smile.

'Along with a towel, if you wouldn't mind,' Matt said unbuttoning his shirt.

'In due time,' the boy said, extending the lighter into the window.

Matt backed across the distance between the two seats. 'You crazy? Be careful with that thing.'

'Oh, no, Mister Packer, you *be careful.'*

Matt collected, watched carefully. 'What's going on here? How do you know me?'

'A harmless warning, sir,' the pale boy said, leaning on the

door, the lighter still lit. 'Stay out of things that don't concern you. Do I make myself clear?'

'I don't know what the hell you're talking about!'

'Be a teacher, Mister Packer, not a detective.'

'I'll be what I want, thank you, now get the hell off my car!'

'Margie's a libber too . . . right?'

Packer's breath caught. 'What's that got to do with . . . ?'

'So was Rod Angstrom.' The boy nodded and flicked his lighter shut. ''Nuff said?'

*As Matt started to get out of the car, the flame quickly reappeared, accompanied by a slight smile and a shaking of the boy's head. '*Please, *Mister Packer, don't make it easy. I'm into challenges, not foregone conclusions.'*

Matt slammed the door and started the car.

'Oh, by the way,' the boy smiled magnanimously, 'the gas is on me.'

As Matt drove away, the boy returned to the office. 'Mister Fenster,' he said to the older man at the desk, ''Fraid I have to quit. Just found out my Mom's ill.'

'But this is only your third day.'

'Sorry,' the boy shrugged. 'If it were anyone else, I might reconsider. We're . . . very close.' His voice trailed off. 'You understand.'

Mister Fenster smiled and nodded, pulled the chequebook from his drawer. 'I respect your concern, Alby. A rare commodity, these days, I don't mind telling you.'

9

I'm not a man who's quick to anger. It triggers instant irrationality and can sever relationships which, in calmer moments, would weather the most trying situations. This wasn't one of those moments. Nor was it one of those relationships. Without going into detail, let's just say I experienced a potentially inflammable confrontation with a libber employed at a local gas station on my way back to school from lunch.The outcome of the – shall we call it 'not-seeing-eye-to-eye?' – was that I got doused with gasoline. Let it go at that. I was issued a warning before there was anything to be warned about. The encounter boomeranged: I would now confront what I'd originally been trying to avoid in order to assure Margie's safety. I would now move quickly, for the same reason. In less than two school days, and on one night's sleep, I'd been goaded into action by a fanatical kid's cheap shot.

I made a fast trip home to shower and change my clothes. Arrived at school in time to greet Eloise Calder, who, along with five, possibly nine – one loses count – other mothers, came and went. They were impeccable, handsomely dressed women. The interviews were amicable in tone and superfluous in content. The mums were putting in a requisite performance, giving it their Sunday best.

A guy in coveralls and a pony tail burst into the doorway, a transitor radio firing The Sex Pistols from his belt.

'Don't tell me you're a mother.'

'Only on Tuesdays, man, my old lady's day off. You Packer?'

'That's right.'

'Hi. I'm Tornado. From Rothermill Film Lab.'

'Over there next to the radiator. In the totebag. Sixteen hundred feet of ECO and eight-hundred of Super-eight. Develop and one light print.'

He cradled the film tins under one arm. 'Later,' he tossed off and dashed out.

I was sitting in one of the student chairs at about mid-room, my eyes still resting on the open door where Tornado had blown through. In my line of vision were all the piles of books stacked on desk chairs, left behind by my homeroom students. On the arm of one near the door was a familiar-looking book, *The Home of David.* It was the libber's handbook. The lettering was branded on soft kidskin. A logo in the same umber was just below the title: a sling, beautifully rendered, delicate, graceful, yet all the more threatening because of the deliberate juxtaposition of its gentle appearance and its lethal purpose.

Although *The Home of David* was the club name, thay called themselves and were known to others as 'hods.' Even their T-shirts carried the letters and the logo of the sling across the front. When Margie had first mentioned the nickname the year before, I'd asked if she knew what a hod was.

'Of course,' she'd replied. 'A tray for carrying building materials. We all consider ourselves hod carriers, sort of the builders of the new world, you might say.'

'Don't you think that's a little pretentious?'

'No more so than "United Nations".'

'But they mean it.'

'Well, so do we!'

I'd seen the book in Margie's room on several occasions. She never made any attempt to hide it. None of the libbers did. No reason to. I'd known from the outset it was off limits to me. Even if I'd been a prying parent, any effort of demolition would have met with failure. The book was double latched and locked with two keys, reminiscent of fine diaries and Swiss bank deposit boxes.

When I'd inquired about the contents, Margie had volunteered specific answers. There was a declaration of independence, a constitution of sorts and a list of commandments. The remainder consisted of blank pages in diary format. As I understood it, daily entries were to be unemotional accounts of adult activities and attitudes contrary to the spirit of the club's charter and recommendations for action to be taken to prevent or inhibit recurrence. Adult 'indiscretions' were logged as they occurred, followed by adolescent 'votes of censure' recorded at their meetings. Unanimous 'convictions' resulted in a form of 'subpoena' being drawn up on club letterhead and later hand-delivered to the erring parent by the victimised child. Carbons were sent to school boards, church councils, private clubs and corporate personnel in positions superior to the offender. The reports said what they had to say and got out, without rancour, contrary to the natural inclinations of the age group.

As I stared at the copy of the book in front of me the old ambivalence returned. It was Aaron's chair. Absent-mindedness of the genius? Confidence of the man who has nothing to hide? Or the assumption that I simply wouldn't have the time to pry?

Perhaps nothing there in any case. Possibly everything. Maybe all the answers. My mind raced. No keys. Break the locks. A mother coming? Must know. Must find out. Two slips of paper as bookmarks protruding from one end. Accessible. Unnecesssary to break latches? Get up. High heels. Clicking echoes. Then self-conscious tiptoeing. Too late. Sit back down. Stare. Change focus back to doorway.

Mrs Farrow smoothed the front of her skirt before she spoke.

'. . . isn't it? Or do I have the wrong room?'

'Mrs Farrow?'

'Yes, I said that. You are Mister Packer?'

'Yes. Won't you sit down? Forgive me for fogging out.' I felt an immediate magnetism. Ineffable. As if her soul were a little closer to something than mine. Call it charm, charisma, magic, whatever. In some cases it's just good, old-fashioned sex appeal, which in this current age of promiscuity seems well along the road to extinction along with other endangered species of human behaviour.

'Was it a place or a person' She smiled and sat down.

'A little of both, I'm afraid.'

'Why, Mister Packer,' she tilted her head. 'Only the students are supposed to daydream on spring days.'

'Ah, but this is fall, you see.' I hadn't played the flirtation game in almost a year. It felt good.

'Same affliction, isn't it?'

'Not quite. There's considerable difference between spring fever and fall.'

'I wasn't aware of any.' She slowly removed her gloves, dropped them in her lap.

'Yes, the latter's much more . . . discriminating.'

'Oh, but I've found quite the opposite to be true. The older we grow the more casual we become. Middle age is fickle, not youth.'

'You may have a point.'

She shrugged. 'Perhaps we both do.'

She gave me one of those penetrating looks that, without warning, set fantasies skip-framing through my imagination.

One aspect of Sylvia Farrow disturbed me: she moved her body a lot, arching her shoulder forward, then up and back, slowly and languidly, so her bra strap would adjust subtly without the use of hands. Or, lifting slightly out of her chair as if fabric folds were crimping. I was hopelessly distracted. Even if I had succeeded in getting around her body language, I would have been stopped by either the colour of her hair or the sound of her laugh. She was a rainbow blonde. Full strands of sienna and caramel, gold and cocoa splashed to her shoulders and scattered down her back. Her laughter was half suggestive, half chaste, midway between Jodie Foster and Melina Mercouri. She had light green eyes, the colour of new lemon leaves, exactly the colour of her jersey blouse. She had a delicate way of teasing with her eyes. My ruination.

Sylvia glanced down and broke the moment. When she looked back up, she'd formed new boundaries. 'Aaron is very excited that you're here.'

'I'm delighted to hear that, Mrs Farrow, I'd . . . '

'Sylvia,' she corrected matter-of-factly. 'Please. I have

the feeling it's going to be a long and complicated year. I'd like to dispense with formalities as quickly as possible. Do you mind?'

With a smile like that at the end of a question, what could I say? 'What can I say?'

'Anything you want.'

'I don't mind a bit.'

'Matt, isn't it?'

'Yes.'

'Bill . . . Bill Kasko spoke highly of you, said it would be a marvellous opportunity for the kids.'

'In all honesty, I believe it's a great opportunity for me.'

'Aaron said he liked your forthrightness. So do I.'

'With Aaron, one is given very little choice.'

'Do you find him abrasive?'

'I find him challenging. He is brilliant, as you know. He is also wilful, which I'm sure you also know.'

'There are many intricacies to be aware of in dealing with a genius, Matt, as you might well imagine – particularly the psychological.'

'I wouldn't know, but it certainly makes sense. I don't see how they could be avoided.'

'Do you like him?'

'I'm . . . sure that will come with time. Right now I'm fascinated by him. I'm boggled by him. I think I may also be a bit afraid of him.'

'Oh, but that's nonsense. Why on earth should you be afraid of him?'

'It's war, isn't it?'

'War? I'm afraid I'm not understanding you.'

'Aaron versus the adults?'

'Oh, Matt, come now. That's just a childish phase, and you know it. Generation gaps have been around for as long as generations. Aaron's is no worse than our own.'

'Then let's just say I'm a little apprehensive about his . . . fervour.'

'Matt,' she leaned forward. 'I'd be apprehensive if he *didn't* have it. Think of the waste. I applaud the enthusiasm. I try to feed it. And I should think you'd welcome it.'

'Oh, I do, I do. Don't misunderstand. Only obsessions worry me.'

I could almost hear the attitude shift: a dropping down from second gear charming to first gear defensive. 'Aaron's not obsessive, you're just inexperienced. Forgive me, I don't mean to be condescending, but one day in school doesn't make you a teacher, much less a child psychologist. Especially regarding someone of Aaron's complexity.'

I held up my hands. 'Whoa. Pass. You're probably right, and certainly, you're in a far better position to judge.'

'Of course, I'm right. But only because I've lived with him for twelve years. It has nothing to do with your ability to teach, I assure you.'

'I hope not.' I put aside the temptation to point out that distance provides perspective. I had no doubt as to my motives. 'By the way, have you read his script?'

'No. Not as yet.'

'Has the opportunity been offered?'

'No, but it can't be too nuch longer. I supposedly have a featured role.'

'Does he discuss it?'

'No more than to say it has elements of Lewis Carroll, Thorton Wilder and Dante. I think it all sounds fascinating, especially if I get to play Alice. I know the book by heart; my escapist tendencies.'

'*Wunderkind in Wonderland*,' I mused, staring beyond her at the forgotten copy of *The Home of David*.

'Now then!' she slapped her hands on her legs and sat up straight. 'What's a good day for you to come over to the house after school? I'm sure my allotted quarter-hour has all but dissolved. Unlike most mothers, I insist on being a participant in my son's education.'

I glanced at my watch. 'Two more minutes.'

'There, you see? What would be a convenient day'

'Sylvia . . . to quote Aaron, let me be forthright.'

'By all means.'

'I have been instructed by my superior to decline parental invitations. Especially, I might add, those offered from your quarter.'

'Ah, yes, yes, yes,' she said, lightly tapping her lower lip with her gloves. 'Methinks I detect a note from that old Gabriel Saddleford melody.'

'I'd prefer not to be around for the lyrics.'

'Ignore it, Matt.' She stood up and straightened her skirt. 'His suggestions are based on deep insecurity. Simply consider it sad,' She tossed off the words as if she were emptying ashtrays.

'If I didn't work here, I'd have trouble considering it at all.'

'I assure you,' she said, crossing to the door, 'visiting me will not jeopardise your job.' That teasing look again. 'How about next Tuesday?'

'Tuesday's fine.'

'Three-thirty?'

'Three-thirty,' I nodded, as she turned to leave. 'Oh, Sylvia . . . '

She stopped. 'Already change your mind?'

'No. Was Aaron home last night?'

'Yes, why?'

'The whole evening?'

'Of course, it's a school night. Matter of fact we played piano duets for a couple of hours after dinner. That's when . . . why, it was your daughter, Margie, that called.'

'Margie? You sure?'

'Yes. About nine-thirty, quarter of ten. Aaron had called her earlier. What's all the mystery?'

'You wouldn't know the parents of Rod Angstrom by any chance, would you?'

'No. Rod used to be a member of Aaron's lib chapter,

but I never met his parents. They live in another section of Cleveland.'

'Used to be?'

'Yes, why?'

'Why not any more?'

'Oh, Matt, I don't know. Maybe they had a falling out, maybe it was internal politics. Perhaps, God forbid, he turned fourteen. Why the worry?'

'I don't know,' I said quietly. What the hell was I trying to alarm her for? 'I don't know.'

'Tuesday, then.' She smiled and started up the aisle.

'See you then,'

Her high heels made dungeon sounds. I thought I heard the tinkling of keys. Or was it wishful thinking, as my eyes again fell on Aaron's locked club book?

This time I didn't hesitate. I knew there was no way to pick the locks without being a professional. I stood there looking down at it. Helplessly.

The two slips of paper serving as bookmarks. Perhaps a clue. I pull them out. Hands shaking. Speed reading. A newspaper clipping datelined New York City. The date and paper added with a Pentel, fuzzied on the porous news stock, but legible: New York *Daily News*, 9/3/76. A year and two weeks ago. A one column, two-inch item:

2 ALARM BLAZE
1 FOUND DEAD

William Penn Robinson was found burned to death in his fourth-floor apartment last night following a two-alarm blaze. The top three floors of the tenement structure, located at 112th Street and Lenox Avenue, were completely razed.

Other occupants were evacuated to the Saints of Our Saviour Church two blocks away, where they waited the arrival of relatives and shelter for the night. Robinson, 34, an unemployed ex-convict, is survived by his wife, Annalie, and a son, Peter, aged 11, both of Staten Island.

Funeral arrangements pending. Chief Charles (Cazzy) Brooks of the 143rd Division of NYFD indicates arson is being investigated.

I quickly go on to the second slip of paper, the clipping making absolutely no sense at all to me, even if Peter Robinson of Staten Island was not of Erieview Heights. Why the hell would Aaron be keepimg an item from the New York *Daily News*, browned with the year of exposure, about a man four times his age and five hundred miles away?

The second slip is much simpler to decipher. The handwritting is familiar: Aaron's. The few pencilled words are clear. The message can have but one meaning.

> Enter page of 9/12/77. 9.51 p.m. Margie just called.
> Packer suspects Rod truth.
> Also looking into Saddleford matter.

I hear the squeaking of running steps down the auditorium aisle. Panting. It sure as hell isn't a mother.

> Kasko bears continued observation. He'll never learn. Shit! Didn't want it to be that way with Packer. He's just another. No choice. Now he's got to go with the rest. As might I, now, as might I. Time is running out.

The panting closer. The slips not fitting back into the book, jamming up, crumpling. Slips into pocket. Put down book. Turn around. Sit. Chin in hand. Relax. It is Aaron.

10

Standing in the door. His eyes flick around the room, come to rest on me.

'Mister Packer . . . ' A wary greeting.

'Aaron . . . ' Ditto the response.

'Everything seems in order here.'

'Why shouldn't it be?'

He walks towards me, picks up his lib book on the chair to my right. 'I left my book.'

'I don't believe that would incite a riot. Perhaps . . . an investigation.'

A quick glance. 'I'm late for the genetics lecture.'

'Aaron?'

He stopped at the door, turned. 'I said I'm late . . . '

'What happened with Rod?'

'He was hurt.'

'I know. How?'

'Couple of hoods from East Chester.'

'You knew before the police.'

He smiled. 'So? The tortoise knew about the hare.'

'Meaning?'

'The police spin their wheels all over town. I reason in one place.'

'You have anything to do with it?'

'I wasn't there.'

'That doesn't answer the question.'

'Mister Packer,' he smiled again 'it has everything to do with it. Ask the police.' He started to leave.

'Should I also ask them about the pictures of Saddleford?'

He stopped, spoke with his back to me: 'Mister Packer . . . why are you doing this?'

'A need to know. I'm concerned about Margie.'

'Pursuing this tack will increase your concern. Otherwise, you have no cause for worry.'

'I can't buy that.'

He turned to face me, his eyes riveting. 'Your worry is prompted by what you don't know. I guarantee her safety.'

'I consider that the guarantee of a weatherman.'

'I consider your analogy the result of panic.' He tilted his head slightly, the voice softened. 'Please don't underestimate what we are doing, Mister Packer, nor the good that will come of it.'

'Then *enlighten* me, Aaron! Alleviate my concern. Help me to understand. Let me . . . ' He started out the door again. 'Aaron!' I shouted. He stopped. '*Listen* to me, please. I . . . I'm a great fan of Thomas Mann. Somewhere, I forget exactly where, he once wrote, "Order and simplification are the first steps towards the mastery of a subject – the actual enemy is the unknown."' I paused, hoping reason would sway his obstinacy. 'I don't want you as an enemy, Aaron.'

'Leave it alone, Mister Packer. You will know in good time. You are not an enemy of mine.' He turned once more to face me, an open smile filling his face. 'And to paraphrase Thomas Huxley, a favourite of mine, "A little bit of knowledge is a dangerous thing." Once you know more, you'll be convinced of Margie's safety. I'm late.'

The departing echoes. My room silent. Barely left with crumbs to tempt a cockroach. 'Slippery bastard,' I said to no one.

The next morning, Wednesday the 14th, I stopped off at the Oxitron station on my way to school. Eight o'clock a.m., and the attendant was asleep in the office. I slowly rolled across the hose next to the pumps on a diagonal. Watched him lurch four positions into full upright in time to the bell clanging over his head.

'Mornin',' he smiled at my window.

'Hi, I'm Matt Packer, teacher over at Erieview. Your

assistant here? The kid who helped me yesterday?'

'Alby, no. His mom took ill, and he quit. Nice boy.'

'Right. Too bad, though. Said he wanted to transfer to Erieview for their drama programme. Told him I'd see what I could do. Got his address?'

'Hang on.'

The slip of paper with pencil scrawls and a greased thumb print said, 'Alby Crothers, 137 Pierce, Old Mill Station; 555–7809.'

I called the number and was not overly surprised to hear, '. . . and please make sure you are dialling correctly.'

It took thirty minutes to reach Old Mill Station, another ten to find 137 Pierce, site of a deserted cafeteria with a weathered sign announcing 'For Lease.'

Later that afternoon, after school, I called East Chester Memorial Hospital, asked about the condition of Rod Angstrom.

'Still in intensive care, Mister Packer,' the brusque voice announced, 'and a police watch around the clock. Suggest you try Friday or Saturday.'

'May I leave word for him to call me?'

'Mister Packer, have you laid eyes on that boy? It's difficult enough getting an EKG reading, much less . . . '

I slammed the phone down, called Rothermill Lab. A printer breakdown would delay delivery of Aaron's footage by two, perhaps as many as five days. It was indeed a Kafka world. Tough enough to live in, why in hell would anyone want to write about it?

That evening, just prior to dinner, I got hit with a bug, clocked in with a temperture of 102. Swollen glands, a knife in my throat and a basketball in my head: it was my old nemesis, strep, a semi annual visitor who always sought me out since I'd never had a tonsillectomy. Margie nursed me through Thursday and Friday, pressing a gentle, cool hand to my lips when I'd whisper abbreviated, unintelligible questions, and she'd reply with bromides such as 'Anger will prolong the fever,' and 'Anxiety increases bacterial propagation.'

On Saturday morning the fever was gone and so was Margie. It was the libbers' prep day for that evening's shoot. I vindictively hoped she'd pass around my illness with the shot list.

'Balance' was the word I kept repeating through the day's convalescence – 'balance' along the thin line between investigation and discovery, between friend and enemy, between Mann and Huxley. But the bottom line, I reminded myself as I prepared for Peggy's dinner party, was being a father: my greatest advantage. Should the balance fail, I would kill without pause or remorse for the safety of my daughter. A parental instinct. An edge a twelve-year-old prodigy could neither comprehend nor anticipate, much less have access to in his emotional vocabulary.

TWO

I: Four o'clock, Saturday Afternoon, 17 September

A young boy from East Chester High unfolded a piece of paper in the crawlspace beneath the house at 682 Collingwood Lane. A wiring diagram was meticulously drawn, with a step by step list of instructions beneath. An itinerary of the activities of the occupants above was printed neatly on the reverse side.

He heard stumbling and raucous laughter through the floorboards, held his breath, doused the flashlight. As the steps faded to a far corner, he once again aimed the beam on the time schedule:

4.00 p.m.—Drinking begins.
Commence rewiring.
4.30 p.m.—Noise increases upstairs.
5.00 p.m.—Finish preparations.
5.15 p.m.—Thermostat thrown.
5.30 p.m.—Check pilot.
Wait for main burners.
Get the hell out when functions confirmed.
9.00 p.m.—Call police.

The boy smiled, began working on the furnace, turned the pilot valve to its off position. He'd been told only what he needed to be told when given the assignment by phone. The occupants were parents of a student at Erieview High. They were guilty of repeated physical abuse to the child. Their drinking habits were legendary to the point where next-door neighbours could set their mantel clocks, either to the opening tumult or the closing silence. The time lapse and distance from start to finish, were as accurate as highway speedometer checks from mile one to mile five.

He checked his watch: 4.10. Pulled the shield from the burner section, located the wire leading from the pilot, removed the housing plate stamped with the logo of Southwestern Furnace Corporation.

At first he worked quietly, but as the racket above increased he ignored the precautions: the scraping of the file, the tapping of a ball hammer, the tamping into place of the shield.

At 4.55, he was finished. Waited.

At 5.10, he heard the electric tick of the thermostat being thrown. Needlessly, he glanced at the pilot to assure himself it was out and would not magically reappear.

The gas, like a low and steady wind, began. The burners were operational. To his specifications.

As he crawled towards the grate, he imagined the final activities of the couple above. The wife removing her shoes as she fell on top of the bed. The husband, incapable of locating a shoelace, flopping down beside her, one leg left dangling over the side. A duet of deep breathing, quickly lowering into clogging-throat, uneven snores. They lay there like rumpled bedclothes. Coughing their bodies' complaints. As they always did. Unseeing. Insensate. Smelling nothing unusual, nothing at all.

The boy's imagination left nothing to illusion.

1

I enjoy parties and detest socials. Peggy Kasko 'threw' detestable socials which she referred to as 'wing-dings.' I was sorry I'd accepted. There are better ways to spend a Saturday evening, such as at home with a book. Or Sylvia Farrow. Who just happened to be one of two reasons for not cancelling. She ran a close second to Aaron's filming.

When I arrived, Bill answered the door and flashed his photogenic grin. The living room was brimming with tipsy occupants, the noise level indicating that elbow bending was already releasing hostilities.

Through the sitting, standing, weaving guests, I picked up jigsaw pieces of Sylvia on her way to the bar. Margie and Aaron were already huddled over a camera and assorted gear along with Chris Kasko, Camilla Saddleford and Amy Witt. I headed for Agatha Wickware, who seemed to be enjoying her temporary role of barmaid. Sylvia was unaware of my approach.

'May I have another, Agatha?' she asked, putting her empty glass on the serving table.

'Hello, Sylvia.'

'Matt . . . how nice.'

I moved in beside her. 'Hoped you might be here.'

'Another *what*?' Ahatha asked, a suggestive smirk crossing her face.

'Drink,' Sylvia answered.

'I meant what kind of drink, Sylvia,' she smiled.

'Scotch mist, Agatha.'

'Oh, of course, how silly of me. Mister Packer?'

'Oh, I think I'll have . . . '

'Not at all, Agatha,' Sylvia interrupted. 'I could hardly have expected otherwise.'

Agatha glanced up quickly, beginning to bristle.

' . . . a scotch and water, please,' I said, turning to Sylvia and breaking the moment. 'Appears as if Aaron and crew are about ready for their first setup.'

'Have you been entrusted with a scenario?'

'Not by my definition. You?'

'A brief, one-liner.'

'Ah, yes,' Agatha winked, handing us our drinks, 'The Aaron Farrow specialty: speak little and say nothing at all.'

'Oh, Agatha, *please*,' Sylvia heaved a sigh. 'I suspect you mean well, but what appear to be abstract dialogues are only Aaron's efforts at sparing your feelings – his realisation that you wouldn't begin to comprehend his meanings the first place.'

Agatha idly mixed a drink for herself. 'I sincerely doubt that, my dear.'

'That is a shame, Agatha, for to doubt it must inevitably lead one to mistrust your objectivity. Matt, I'd like to sit down.'

'Exactly what I had in mind.'

We crossed the room to a window bench in a bay, overlooking a carefully laid-out garden of azaleas and privet, flagstone paths and a cherub peeing in a bird bath.

'So, what sort of one-line scenario did Aaron give you?' I asked.

'He describes it as a film about athanasia.'

'I don't know the word,' I said.

'Deathlessness.'

'And he's shooting scenes at an Erieview Heights cocktail party?' I smiled. 'Isn't that . . . curious?'

'Well, I must say, it's one of the few times recently that I can recall Aaron displaying a sense of humour.'

'I'm not so sure humour is what he has in mind.'

'Did he say anything to you?'

'I'll give it to you *exactly* as he gave it to me: "We will stage it, but they won't know they'll be following a script. To them it will be spontaneous. But we know them well – they'll say and do the same things they always say and do." '

'That's it?' she asked.

I nodded. 'Isn't that enough?'

'I don't understand. You mean we're . . .'

'He means we *know* the scenario, if we stopped and thought about it for any length of time.'

'Hmmm, deathlessness. I've always been aware of Aaron's fondness for opposites; love and hate, war and peace. He once told me they were all the same. When he was nine. Erieview Heights parties, Erieview heights funerals; glaciers and deserts. He called them molecules of the same atom. Perhaps I do know some of it. Friends and . . . enemies,' she drifted.

'Well, I certainly don't.'

'You didn't grow up here.'

'Is that a prerequisite?'

'Or a similar environment, yes, I believe so. I keep hoping it'll be different somewhere else . . . but, of course, it isn't.' She stared across the room. 'Time doesn't pass here, Matt. Perhaps Aaron is simply looking for a way to start it up again. Either that or to make us realise it is just the way it is – a youthful blend of Camus and Sartre.'

'Mom? Mister Packer?' Aaron stood in front of us, camera resting on his shoulder.' Mind if we shoot your scene first?'

'Not at all, dear,' Sylvia answered, turning to me.

'Might as well.' I put down my drink. 'Nice back lighting here in the window seat.'

'It's good for another twenty, thirty minutes. Amy, would you attach the mikes, while I set camera position?'

Amy Witt clipped Sylvia's mike under the collar of her blouse and hid mine under my tie. Amy looked schoolgirl fresh in her plaid jumper and pony tail tied with a yellow ribbon.

'Any script suggestions, Aaron?' I asked, 'such as limiting ourselves to the usual ageist propaganda?'

'Whatever seems natural, Mister Packer,' Aaron answered, eye pressed into the camera. 'Whatever level your relationship with my mother may have reached by this time.'

'Tenuous,' Sylvia smiled.

'Thanks a lot,' I whispered. I was having trouble with her barbed restlessness.

'Then remedy the situation. Be daring.'

I watched Aaron and Amy carefully. 'Not on your life.

Not for the purposes of this film, whatever they might be.'

Aaron flashed me his smug smile. 'Precisely, Mister Packer. Exactly what I had in mind.'

'Fine by me,' Sylvia shrugged, 'though I doubt people will shell out good money to view such nonsense.'

'They will, Mother I assure you. Amy, the Nagra hooked up?'

'Any time you're ready, C.B.,' Amy smiled.

Camilla helped Amy plug a small tape recorder into the camera. I continued to watch the preparations, trying to spot a clue to Aaron's plan.

'What's the matter, Matt?' Sylvia asked.

'Roll sound!' Aaron ordered.

'I'm not sure. I don't like the not knowing.'

'Sound speed!' Amy looked at Aaron.

'No one does, Mister Packer,' Aaron said quietly. 'Camera rolling. Mark it, Chris!'

Chris Kasko held the slate in front of Sylvia's face and clapped it shut.

'Action, please!' Aaron barked.

Sylvia recrossed her legs and smoothed her skirt, sat up and moistened her lips.

'Action, *please*,' Aaron urged.

Sylvia took a sip of her drink and smiled at me. 'Well, Mister Packer, we're delighted that you decided to come to Erieview Heights for your first teaching assignment.'

'It's a pleasure to be here, Mrs Farrow.' Jesus! What a shot this was going to be.

'I'd be interested in hearing about your first impressions of the community . . . the school, the students.'

'Well, Mrs Farrow, so far I find myself most impressed with the relaxed atmosphere and quick friendliness of the people in the community. The school is smoothly run and the students courteous and enthusiastic.' My mind raced. What idiocy!

'Tell me, Mister Packer, do you find it easier or more

difficult to make friends here, I mean in contrast to Hollywood,' she chuckled, 'the purported flesh capital of the world?'

Come on, Packer! Give it some polish. 'Oddly enough, Mrs Farrow, people here seem to be more accessible. As far as the transient way of life you correctly infer exists in Los Angeles, I am delighted to find that people here are more concerned with *real* values, *real* relationships, an emphasis on intellectual development.'

'Mister Packer, thank you for your time.'

'It's been my pleasure, Mrs Farrow.' Enough! I made a slicing gesture across my neck to Aaron.

'Cut!' Aaron said, pulling away from the camera.

'What bullshit,' I mumbled.

Sylvia touched my hand. 'Maybe it's a travelogue.'

Before Amy could finish removing the mikes, my attention was drawn to Aaron. I quickly turned to Sylvia, hoping for some rational explanation. Her expression was bemused at first, the faint beginnings of a smile, the slow shaking of her head, as she watched Aaron leaning against the camera, convulsed with laughter. But then she looked to me for an answer to his hilarity, as if I, an outsider, could divine reasons within Aaron somehow beyond her reach. Camilla watched silently. Chris looked at Sylvia, then me.

'Matt? What . . .?'

'Don't look at me, Sylvia, he's not my kid.'

'Were we that bad?'

'Or that good.'

'Aaron!' she snapped. 'What's so damn funny?'

'No, Mom . . . I . . . you don't understand.' He came towards us.

'Then help us to understand.'

'You . . . you were perfect. Both of you. Perfect.'

'Enough of this! You may go home. Now!'

'Oh, Mom . . . ' The laughing subsided. 'Really.'

'I want to know.'

'But I can't explain. Not until the film's cut. Then you'll see. It's the juxtaposition of two scenes.'

Sylvia turned back to me, helpless. 'I need another drink, Matt.'

'I should think so.' I took her empty glass. Aaron stood waiting. 'I'm afraid we'll have to wait to get this footage developed, Aaron. I'm sorry.'

'How come?'

'Saddleford claims budget approval will take four to six weeks.' I patted him on the back. 'Like being at the mercy of the Hollywood moguls. Nothing to do but hurry up and wait.' I was grateful for the legitimate excuse. It would give me plenty of time to view the film unencumbered.

Peggy Kasko walked briskly up to Chris and yanked the slate out of his hand. 'Didn't I ask you to help serve the hors d'oeuvres?'

'We just finished shooting the first scene, Mom.'

I left for the bar hoping to avoid one of Peggy's snits, but she was still going strong whan I returned.

'Listen to me, my friend, it's bad enough having all these toy-things strewn about without having to put up with your unreliability. Oh, Lord, my heart will never stand it.' She grasped her chest. 'You'll be the death of me yet, Chris Kasko, and all for a silly school film.'

'It's *not* a silly school film,' Chris insisted.

'Don't you talk back to me! Making film *is* silly.'

Aaron moved in next to me and tapped Peggy on the back.

'What do *you* want?' Peggy snapped, bumping into me as she spun around.

'Just getting Sylvia a drink, Peggy. It's Aaron who's trying to get your attention.'

'Oh. Yes?'

'It's not silly, Mrs Kasko,' Aaron said flatly.

I handed Sylvia the drink.

'Thank you. I'm needing this.'

'Aaron, be careful,' Amy warned, tugging his sleeve.

'Now you listen to me, Aaron Farrow, you're only here with all your tomfoolery because Bill and I try to be of some help to you kids.'

'*It's not silly*, Mrs Kasko,' Aaron pressed.

'And then you have the unmitigated gall to send us one of those insulting club letters.'

'Now *that's* serious,' I tossed in, trying to relax the tension.

'You're . . . you're no better than a juvenile delinquent,' Peggy continued, ignoring my effort.

Sylvia stood up. 'Come along, Peggy, I'll help with the hors d'oeuvres.'

'You'd be the most help, Sylvia, if you'd exert some influence on this impudent son of yours.'

Sylvia took a count-to-ten breath and sat back down. 'In that case, I doubt if I can be of any help at all.'

Peggy huffed off towards the kitchen, Chris in tow.

'Son of mine,' Sylvia said quietly to Aaron. 'I believe it would be most appropriate at this time if you and Amy quickly and unobtrusively set up your next scene.'

Aaron shook his head slowly and rurned to me. 'See what I mean, Mister Packer?' He turned to leave without waiting for a response. Amy detached the tape recorder and began to remove the camera from the tripod. Margie and Camilla, knowing their exact duties, picked up extraneous pieces of equipment and carried them off to the next setup. Sylvia lit a cigarette and let out a cloud of relief.

'Your husband here?'

'Michael's over on the couch between Gabe and his wife. The one in the camel's hair sportsjacket.'

'The cast for Aaron's next scene by the looks of it.'

'Gabe and Michael! Now there's a combination.'

'What does Michael do?'

'Lawyer. Criminal law.'

'Political aspirations?'

'But, of course,' she winked elaborately.

'Is your cynicism directed at politics in general, or your husband's in particular?'

'Both. But then Michael wouldn't excel in anything. Call it a private stumbling block.

'I see.' I looked at the remains of my drink. It was obvious I'd chosen a lousy subject.

'Don't be embarrassed, Matt, please. Michael and I haven't been close in seven years.'

'Why do you stick it out?'

'It's easier,' she shrugged. 'I don't have the stamina to go out and find something better.'

'Ever try counselling?'

She blurted out a laugh. 'No. Ours is a situation where counselling would be a total waste of time.'

'Then there's no point . . . '

'Well, well, what have we here? Sylvia, Mister Packer, see you two have become quite chummy over here. An incipient liaison . . . ?' Gabe loomed over us before I'd seen his approach, but I'd recognise the suggestiveness anywhere.

'Ah, Gabe,' Sylvia smiled benevolently and turned to me. 'Meet the real Mister Saddleford, Matt, the one who prefers scotch to schooling.'

I nodded once. As did Gabe. As if we'd passed each other on a busy street, but couldn't place the name.

'Have some good news for you, Packer.'

'I'm not being transferred?'

'Course not. Just thought you'd like to know I've been given budget approval for that film you wanted developed.'

'Oh? That was quick.' I studied the man closely. No hints Either too drunk or too clever to reveal anything but polish.

'Just want to make you feel right at home.'

'Home was never like this,' I said quietly.

'Oh-oh, look out, Matt,' Sylvia warned. 'Me thinks the gentleman is leading up to something.'

Saddleford glared at Sylvia. 'Must there always be an ulterior motive, Sylvia? Can't anything be taken at face value with you any more?'

'But, of course, Gabe. That's precisely what prompted the observation in the first plae.'

Gabe turned to me and shrugged. 'Sylvia's become our resident cynic, and contrary to the rule, her bite is far more damaging than her bark. Be warned.'

'The world of the bitten, dear Gabe,' Sylvia sighed, 'is occupied by those who take relish in biting. Which reminds me, I'm famished. Excuse me, gentlemen.' She stood up. 'You're both quite safe.'

'Hang on, Sylvia, I think I'll join you.'

'Oh, one last thing, Packer.'

'Yes?'

'About your request not to grade the students in your film class . . . '

'Yes.'

'I assume the initiator was Aaron?'

'Not . . . entirely.'

'I see. Well, I think it can be arranged. Consider it done.'

'One other last thing,' I said, 'as long as we're on the subject of Aaron.'

'The subject never ends.'

'What's *The Rite of Spring*?'

'A concert piece by Stravin . . .'

'I know that – I mean what was the original rite.'

Saddleford looked at me quizzically. 'Why do you ask?'

'Aaron mentioned he'd like to use it as background music for a portion of his film.'

'Oh, that's different. He'd have a helluva time shooting the original rite, I can assure you.'

'Which was?' I pursued.

'On one particular day every spring in ancient Greece, the entire population got tighter than ticks – a national bacchanal. At a predetermined time, the women were sent running into fields; about fifteen minutes ahead of the men, I believe. Then the men took off after them.' His voice took on a nostalgic quality. 'Running over rocks, scrambling through briars, panting, sweating, bleary, finding the women huddled in caves, hiding in gulleys and thickets, then violating tham, the most monumental mass fornication the world has ever witnessed, the countryside heaving, writhing, grunting beneath hundreds of thousands of copulating savages.'

'Savages?'

Saddleford came out of his fantasy, but too late to cover a twitchy smile. 'Why, we're all savages,' he recovered, 'whether we build Parthenons or Apollo spacecraft.'

'Why did they do it?'

'It was a fertility rite. They believed that in the planting of their own seeds *en masse*, their fields would flourish with bountiful crops.'

'Did they?'

'Does it matter?'

'As long as they believed it . . . '

'As long as they *enjoyed* it,' Saddleford corrected.

'Ass!' Sylvia snapped.

'Of course,' he toasted her tipsily. 'And why ever else would we be quite so fond of each other?' He staggered off towards the bar.

Aaron had already wrapped his Gabe Saddleford-Michael Farrow sequence. During dinner we were interrupted twice, once when Sylvia played a caustic scene with Saddleford, and once when she participated in a self-conscious vignette with Bill Kasko. Then Michael came towards us with a wired smile and furtive eyes. Odd sort of guy – hiding from something.

'Matt, what a pleasure to meet you.'

'Thank you, I'd . . .'

'By the way, before I forget, I have some books for Margie. She'd asked some old codger, name of Ozzie Witherbee, if I'd pick them up. Know him?'

'Never heard of him.'

'He's got a small office in my building. Retired from practice some years ago. Didn't know your daughter had an interest in law.'

'It's always been a fancy, not much more.'

'Oh? Extraordinary.'

'How so?'

'Because she's chosen some rather complex cases and opinions on juvenile law. Let's see,' he looked skyward, '"*In re Gault*," Supreme Court Decision of Nineteen-Sixty-Eight; "*Juvenile Delinquency Its Prevention and Control*," from the Russell Sage Foundation . . . ah, "*Fairness to the Juvenile Offender*," by a guy name of Paulsen; "*A Juvenile's Right to Counsel in a Delinquency Hearing*." Like that,' he nodded matter-of-factly.

'Like that,' I repeated, feeling left out. 'Like that and what else?'

'About eight other books.'

'That is odd.'

'Yes, well . . . but I thought you knew about it, you see. I didn't foresee any objections.'

'No, of course not. There are none.'

Michael smiled and nodded a departure.

Saddleford, after avoiding a head-on collision with Michael, pulled up short at my feet and stared down at me. After a long pause, either by design or alcohol, he asked, 'What do you think so far?'

'What do I think so far, *what*?'

'Of Erieview Heights.'

The problem with pot smoking and too much booze: the cosmetics are cold-creamed off. 'I like it all right.'

He smiled, shook his head. 'Hollywood never was known for its eloquence.'

'What do you want, Yeats?'

'No. Packer will do.'

'It's a game of hide-and-go-seek.'

'Quaint. Not Yeats . . . perhaps Thurber. How so?'

'Everyone's hiding, and I've got to go seeking.'

'Suggestion: don't!'

'Response: out of the question.'

'Why?'

'My daughter's involved.'

The words came slurred, but with clear meaning. 'Listen, Packer . . . in the great scheme of things, there's not much that matters here. I do my job, you do yours. My daughter, your daughter, all daughters come and go. They'll make their way: it's part of the discovery. Let it alone.'

'Wish I could be that blasé.'

'Not blasé,' his eyes narrowed, 'inevitable. Keep your fucking predilections to yourself. You're an interloper, a cinder in a Cyclops' eye. Accept and be accepted. Otherwise . . . '

'Otherwise?'

He smiled. 'What's your definition of "normal"?'

'I don't have any.'

'Good. In that case we may get along. Otherwise you might find yourself with a . . . serious problem.'

'My job?'

'Oh, no, not so paltry a consequence.'

'Then what?'

'You shall see. You shall see.' He wandered off, leaving me as I'd been found – bored, confused and angry.

The attrition of coats from the bedroom began, a jamming up at the door with goodnights lingering in the room like the drone of a TV.

Phone rings. Seven of us left. The Kaskos cleaning up, Michael Farrow still pontificating, Sylvia still reaching for something inaccessible, the Saddlefords still laughing over a parlour game where two chrome balls slap three others.

Seven, not including the children, Camilla Saddleford wrapping the sound gear, Chris Kasko marking film tins with scene numbers, Margie and Amy Witt checking off pages in a script, and Aaron packing his camera. All very efficient, all very mysterious. Because inside those tins are adult panoramas as viewed by children.

The phone rings again, and Peggy in her sweet apron and sour manner answers. 'Yes, yes, hello?'

The room listens. The two balls keep click-click-clicking.

'Yes, she's here.'

I put down my drink and get ready to leave.

'Are you sure?' Peggy says into the phone and looks around the room.

Michael stops and turns to watch.

'I . . . I don't know what to do,' Peggy says softly to the room.

The balls stop clicking. I stand still.

'We . . . we can keep her here for the night,' Peggy offers, her voice gentle.

'What is it?' Sylvia whispers.

Peggy shakes her head and puts a finger to her lips. 'All right. Yes, I'll do that,' she says and hangs up.

The party murmur is gone. The children stop what they are doing. Because Peggy is still. Peggy who is never still.

After a moment's hesitation, she came and stood in front of me, Matthew Packer, man in the street, party irregular.

'Amy Witt's parents have been killed,' she whispered.

I didn't say anything, just stood there unblinking.

'You should be the one to tell her,' she continued. 'A terrible accident.'

'How?'

'Gas. The furnace pilot went out. At their house. Accident.'

I took a cigarette from Sylvia's pack and lit it. 'You sure?'

'Police say it must be an accident, but . . .'

'But what?'

'Something wrong about . . . wiring. You'll tell her?'

The children watched. All except Aaron, who latched the camera case.

'Yes. All right.'

I watched her closely, then looked at Amy, Amy in her plaid jumper and yellow bow gathering her eleven-year-old hair into a pony tail. Amy.

'I'm sorry,' Peggy repeated.

I looked at Peggy again and shook my head. I felt as if I'd lived too long. 'Are you, Peggy? Are you really?'

II: Five-thirty p.m. Sunday, 18 September

Aaron checked his watch, nodded. His parents would be home in thirty minutes.

'Half an hour more,' he announced.

Chris Kasko finished sealing the double lenses into the fireplace aperture, gently closed a hinged painting to hide the chamber.

Amy Witt taped the final strip of magnesium to the bottom of the last throw rug.

Cammie Saddleford corked two bottles of colourless liquid and turned to Margie Packer. 'Fill each reservoir to the brim, then moisten the surrounding fabric.'

'Won't it evaporate?'

'Right. Has to be dispensed no earlier than five in the afternoon before the viewing.'

Robbie Farrow sat in a corner with electronic gadgetry spread like broken clockworks on the table in front of him.

Peter Robinson checked and re-checked two 16-mm Bell and Howell cameras. 'All set Aaron. We can install them whenever you'd like.'

Aaron smiled. 'We're six days ahead of schedule.'

The others completed their chores, turned to him in unison. Chris spoke: 'Want to move up the viewing date?'

'No,' Aaron answered. 'Don't want to arouse suspicion. And there's a couple of things I haven't figured out yet.'

'Like maybe Packer?' Peter asked with a curious smile.

Margie glanced at Aaron. He held her gaze. 'Maybe . . .'

'What's the other?' Amy asked.

Aaron smiled. 'Me.'

2

I don't believe even the most imaginative of my former Hollywood colleagues could have fabricated a fictional counterpart to the Witts' death. On being told, Amy had been impassive. I had expected an outburst. She had shown equanimity. I had anticipated tears. She had responded with practicality. I had told her gently, then held her. She had allowed herself to be held, but her arms had remained limp at her sides. When I looked at her again, expecting to see the beginnings of grief, she had asked a simple question, in an even voice.

'Will you tell me what to do, Mister Packer?'

I had talked to Michael Farrow on Monday morning. He would handle the legal aspects and make the funeral arrangements. Amy would stay with Bill and Peggy Kasko, until a more permanent situation could be found. She didn't want to live with her relatives in New York; she wished to remain in school. By Tuesday afternoon,

September twentieth, she was shooting scenes with the libbers and looking forward to her class picnic on Thursday.

Tuesday afternoon. Finally. Sylvia's Tuesday. Our appointment at her house. I was feeling ambivalent: attractive woman in an unattractive situation. Yet she might answer a few questions. And fulfil a few fantasies, who knows. Providing she could get behind her unrealistic expectations of life which, I suspected, were feeding a severe depression.

'Sorry I'm early.'

'Better than late.'

She took me on a tour of the house winding up in a basement recreation room fitted with built-in benches, a pool table, its own brick fireplace and heavy, wrought-iron bars around the windows. I ran my fingers over every surface. It was like a magnificent, old yacht. I stopped at the used brick.

'Odd. It's wet.'

'One of Aaron's projects.'

'Masonry?'

'I think he and Robert were hoping to find a secret passage,' she nodded.

'On the physical plane as well?' I quipped.

'That's where most of us stop.'

We returned to the warmth and deep cushions of the living room, and sipped our scotches in front of a fire. The weather had turned raw, matching my disposition. I assumed it would soon snow.

'You seem down, Matt. Bad day?'

No worse than the last few.'

'Anything specific?'

'Ever have the feeling something was about to happen over which you had no control?'

'At times I've felt that way about my entire life.'

'No, I'm serious.'

'So am I.'

I eased back into the overstuffed chair and smiled at her. 'I like that about you, Sylvia. You always say what's on your mind.'

'Perhaps it's just overflow, a need to relieve the pressure.'

'Perhaps.'

'What is it you're not saying, Matt?'

I stood up and went to the mantel, turned around to face her. Time to gamble. 'Oh, I have lots to say, Sylvia. It's just that I'm not so sure you're the person I should be talking to.'

'Who else?'

'I don't know.'

'Try me. You can't afford a psychiatrist on your present salary.'

'I noticed the bronze plaque on the corner of the house as I came in. "The Bridge"?'

'Yes.'

'You put it there?'

'Heavens no. The previous owner was a commander in the navy. Career man. Had his own carrier during the last war. Couldn't stand it when they retired him, so the house became his bridge. He used to pace from room to room, peering out the windows, trying to spot un-neighbourly periscopes.'

'Jesus, insane!'

'No, just bored.' She lit a cigarette. 'What's that got to do with what's bothering you?'

'Nothing, maybe.' The mantel clock read 3:15. 'Most of what I'm thinking concerns Aaron.'

'I suspected it might.' She sipped her drink, the glass shaking slightly.

I downed most of mine. 'Were you aware that Aaron knew about the attack on Rod Angstrom three hours before the police?'

'No, but he was home that night. We talked about that.'

'Don't you find that odd?'

'Probably a phone call from one of the . . .'

'Who else called, besides Margie?'

'I have no idea. He has an extension in his room.'

'How many calls? Don't the other extensions ring?'

'There were several, Matt, but I don't see . . .'

'Doesn't it strike you as peculiar that ten minutes after I told Aaron we didn't have the funds to get his film developed, Saddleford staggered over to inform me the money was available? Immediately?'

'That could be coincidence.'

'The coincidence being that Aaron is blackmailing Saddleford.'

'Who told you that?' she asked quietly.

'Margie. And what about that charming description of *The Rite of Spring*?'

'What about it?'

'To quote Aaron: "It will be used in the film the way it was intended to be used, the original rite."'

'That's impossible, Matt, and we both know it. Perhaps it's . . .' she stammered, 'an . . . an allegory?'

I began pacing the far side of the cocktail table. I had to break through. 'And Margie's sudden and insatiable appetite for juvenile law? Find me the allegory there.'

'I . . . I'm not sure.'

'Show me something allegorical about these.' I tossed Aaron's two book markers on to the table.

She picked them up. 'Two-alarm fire? Means nothing to me.'

'The other one?'

'". . . he's got to go with the rest."' She whispered the words. '"as might I . . . as might I." Where did you find these?'

'In Aaron's lib book.'

'Last night . . .' she started, stopped, tried again, '. . . last night I read to him.' I could see the beginnings of tears. 'He asked me to read from *Alice in Wonderland*, as he did when he was younger and wasn't afraid to show he loved me.'

She glanced down.

'Asked if he could record me. I said yes, that would be nice. You know, where Alice finds the bottle with the words "Drink Me."'

She looked back up at me.

'"It was all very well to say, 'Drink me,' but the wise little Alice was not going to do *that* in a hurry,"'

I watched her, damning the fact that the hurt was necessary, searching for a mislaid piece.

'". . . a red-hot poker will burn you if you hold it too long."'

Her words faded off.

'I always read it to him when he was younger. I'm sorry, Matt.' She pressed the corners of her eyes with a cocktail napkin. 'I am sorry. I don't know what's going on. I'm afraid of what's going on. It's beyond me, and I'd just as soon it would stay there. It would kill me if anything happened to Aaron.'

I went to her and put my hands on her shoulders. 'No, Sylvia, *I'm* sorry. I didn't want to upset you. There was no other way.'

She put her forehead against my chest and closed her eyes. Closed it out. Whatever it was she was avoiding.

'Can't we forget it, Matt? Just let it alone?'

I put my arms around her. 'I . . . I can't, Sylvia.'

'Why?'

'Because . . .'

'Because you're afraid something terrible will happen?'

'I'm afraid something terrible has already happened.'

'I don't want to know about it.'

'You'll have to.'

'I know, I know, but not now.'

'You can't close out life.'

'Yes you can. Parts of it.'

'Not this part. I'm sorry.'
'For now.'
'You can't walk away from it.'
'For now I can.'
'I have to leave,' I whispered, wanting to, yet not wanting to, fed up with my ambivalence, loosening my arms as a question.
She put her arms around my waist in answer. 'Touch me a little first. I need the closeness. Something close.'
'Sylvia . . . I'm not good at one-night stands.'
'Neither am I.'
'Then why?'
'Your honesty. Your gentleness. The quality Aaron finds in you, the quality he displays: His affection, his respect. In knowing you, I know a part of Aaron I've never known. In being close to you, I become closer to him. And understand better.'
I shook my head slowly. 'Too soon . . .'
'There is no too soon or too late. I've been alone since last year. I don't have the time, youth or inclination to follow the usual courtship pattern.'
'I don't mean that . . .'
'And I don't have a husband. I have a person living here, who never touches me, never cares. I never see his eyes because he never looks at me. He looks through me, and what I do see is repugnant, deviant. I don't know how to describe it or what to call it, and perhaps my attraction to you is only half that and half my repulsion from him, I'm not sure. Is that so bad? Can we stop talking now?'
'All right.'
'Can you stop thinking? I don't want to think about anything for a while, a long while.'
'I can try.'
'You're real. God, you're the only real thing around here.' Her head still down, I could see her smile. 'Thank you for that.'

I took her face in my hands, gently. 'There's nothing to thank me for, Sylvia.'

'Yes there is: moments.'

'Do you only live for moments?'

'Where would I be without them?'

'With the rest of us.'

'The rest of you need moments.'

I nodded, paused. 'Yes, I suppose we do. I'm sure we do.'

'Would you like to stay?'

I looked at the mantel. The clock said 3.35. 'Yes, I would.'

A laugh caught in her throat, she looked up at me shaking her head. 'Perhaps some day I'll meet a man who doesn't care what time it is.'

III: Tuesday Afternoon, 5 p.m., September Twentieth

Peggy Kasko prepared for her daily bath. She'd been working in the backyard most of the day and felt grimy. Dirt packed her nails and the stench of insecticide stung in her nostrils. Bill would be home at 6.00. She looked forward to a leisurely hour of scrubbing and primping; shaving her legs and plucking her eyebrows. She considered it a form of penance, absolving her of aphid genocide and the mass murder of slugs and snails. Perhaps even the hard, back-handed slap she, not Bill, had inflicted across Chris's mouth the day before, cutting his lip with the diamond in her engagement ring. It had been a first. She'd felt better because of it. Deserved or not at the moment, her anger had been welling since the party. He'd had it coming.

She smiled as she opened her medicine cabinet, removed the Q-tips from the first shelf, the dental floss from the second. She pulled a clean Maxi-Pad from the box neatly secreted behind a large bottle of blue mouthwash. The body lotions, face creams and bottles of youth recapturers were already arranged like a pharmaceutical display across the side of the sink.

She tested the water in the tub with her wrist. Tepid, to her liking. Shampoo at one corner, a clean towel in the other, she dropped her robe at her feet and stepped in. Eased down till her toes touched the foot of the tub and the water level turtle-necked around her chin. Felt the bath-oil permeate her pores, loosen the tension in her shoulders. Ran her hands down her belly, between her thighs, around her hips. Mentally skipped from a momentary derision of Bill's physicallity to Chris's stubbornness to Matt Packer's eyes. She felt untapped and was not beyond caring.

Ran the pumice stone across her palms, the razor up her legs. Scratched the shampoo into the very roots of her scalp, bent deep between her legs and scooped handfuls of water through her hair.

Eyes closed, head tingling, she gropes for the towel. Finding it, she unfurls the clean scent of fresh laundry around her head. And something else, something light and tickling like threads or fur or dandelion fuzz. She quickly drys her eyes open. Her breath catches. A scream locks in her throat. Her hands freeze in front of her, quivering involuntarily. Her body wrenches, once, twice, her breath returned, but in short, staccato gasps.

Spiders large, spiders small, smooth and furry, brown and black, tumble down her shoulders on to her breasts into the bath water, then frantically scamper back up her sides to her arms, climbing free of the pool, reaching for the safest peak above the thrashing water, on to her face and into her matted hair, only to be violently brushed down once again, but having sighted the island off her body they return and scurry northward with renewed panic.

The movement subsided, then ended. Peggy lay still, eyes

closed, the water's surface calming once again around her chin, as the sodden spiders pulled themselves wearily on to the shores of her arms and began the long climb to higher ground, dragging their way up the steepness of her neck, picking their way along the sudden undergrowth of disarranged hair where they'd find a bridge to the edge of the tub and drop to the floor.

Bill arrived home promptly at 6.00. Knocked on the bathroom door, opened it a crack. Noticed a cricket cage on the floor in the far corner. Odd. 'Peggy? You all right?'

3

From the lab, to the school, to a phone – a fast but rather maladroit bit of detection. I checked my watch after dialling Sylvia: 5.30 on the first ring. An hour since I'd left, but a lifetime of discovery. I'd gotten lucky.

It rang a second time.

'Yes?'

'Sylvia?'

'Hello, Matt.'

'I've got to come over. Is it all right?' I tried to keep the panic out of my voice.

'Of course. What is it?'

'I've been to the lab. The film's gone. Aaron picked it up. Had written authorisation from Saddleford . . . which is hardly surprising under the circumstances.'

'Oh, no, Matt.'

'So I came back to the school and broke into Aaron's locker. Had to. No choice. I had to find out what the hell's going on.' I gripped the receiver in both hands.

'Well . . . ?'

'Oh, Christ, Sylvia, I found out what he's got on Saddleford. Why didn't you tell me?'

'Matt, I don't know what you're talking about.'

'Is Aaron there?'

'No, he's come and gone.

'Oh, shit, no!'

'What is it, Matt? For God's sake . . . '

'I'll be right over.'

It took ten minutes to get to the house and ten seconds to reach the front door. Sylvia answered, looking frail and white.

'Anybody else home?' I ask.

'The maid. Betty Sue.'

'Where?'

'Kitchen.'

I brush by her and take the stairs three at a time. Sylvia follows quickly. By the time she catches up I an standing in her bedroom, having already pulled the mattress half-way on to the floor. I stare down at a small metal plate resting on the inner springs. An attached wire disappears between the bed and the wall.

Sylvia peers over my shoulder. 'What is it?'

I pull the bed from the wall, yanking at the wire. 'Your son,' I say between breaths, 'is diabolically clever.'

The wire disappears under the carpet. I tug at it slightly, look to the other side of the room. In four strides I cross the room and pull the bureau away from the wall. The wire briefly emerges from the carpet, then disappears into a hole in the baseboard.

'For God's sake, Matt, what is it?'

'The gadget under the mattress is a pressure-sensitive aluminium plate.'

I look at the mirror on the wall above the bureau, then back to the bed.

'What's behind this wall?'

'My dressing room . . . and closet.'

'Figures.'

I enter the dressing room, glance around, open the sliding door of the closet. I sweep the clothes to one side revealing built-in storage drawers and a cabinet on the rear wall. Open the drawers . . . full. Open the cabinet . . . full. I pull out the shoes, scatter the sweaters on to the floor and step back. The cabinet is empty.

'What do you see?' I ask.

'An . . . an empty cabinet. Shelves. Shelf hooks. Ventilation holes. Nothing.'

'Your genius son saw something more.'

I removed the adjustable shelves, one by one.

'A lot more.'

I put my index fingers into the top holes of the wall and tug slightly. The back panel comes forward and is easily removed; revealing another six inches in depth: a chamber, padded with sound proofing. The wire reappears.

Sylvia sits down on the dressing table bench. Shaking. Quick breaths. Speechless.

I wait. Our eyes rivet to the small, Nikon still camera.

'It's what I think?' she asked.

'It's what you think,' I answered.

I handed her two black-and-white prints. Saddleford and a boy. From another time. Michael Farrow watching. On Sylvia's bed. Locked. Saddleford's face contorted in rapture, the boy grimacing in pain.

'There are probably others,' I warned.

She stared at the photos. 'Marty Kyle . . . my God, it's Marty Kyle.'

'The boy?'

'Yes. It continues . . . '

'What?'

'The repugnance . . . grotesque . . . ' she drifted off, returned in waves, 'twisted, ill . . . it's better not to see, not to feel . . . ' She ran her finger slowly across the boy's face, again, caressing, consoling. 'Better to pretend, stay inside, like a radio . . .'

'These . . . these were the only ones I could find in his locker.'

'Yes . . . yes, of course.'

'He's got the negatives somewhere, and protection prints . . all over the place, God knows where.'

She nodded, unhearing.

'You'd probably have to tear the house apart to find them.'

'Probably.'

'And that's a chance, they could be anywhere.'

'Anywhere.'

I began a slow, quiet, and deliberate teacher's explanation, more to take her mind off the horror than to inform.

'When activated, the aluminium plate became sensitive to the weight of a human being on the bed, automatically triggering a picture-taking cycle by the Nikon. The hole in the wall is large enough to house a wide-angle lens which shoots through the two-way mirror. There is an automatic timer and light meter attached to the camera so that at specific intervals, say every sixty seconds or so, the shutter is touched off.'

It wasn't working. I was beginning to feel as sick as she looked.

'Simple as plugging a percolator into a clock radio,' I continued. 'Complicated only by the mind that devised the system, and how he planned to use it.'

I slowly replaced the panel, the shelves, the shoes and sweaters. I was operating by rote. Muffled sounds knifed the stillness. The air was numb. My mind wasn't functioning. I thought of Margie. The horrible, crushing thoughts. The inevitable conclusions: She was part of the corruption and decay. Anger, horror, grief, revulsion, but always and helplessly, the return to numbness.

I slid the closet door shut, sat down on the floor and closed my eyes. 'I think I know what you must be going through, Sylvia.'

'Do you?'

'I have a daughter. She's involved.'

'Not . . . not like this.'

'No, not to this extent.'

'How did this happen? What . . . didn't I do?'

'I don't know, Sylvia.'

'Tell me what you did. I've got to know.'

'The same things we all do.'

'Then why Aaron? Why not Margie? How is it . . . good between you?'

'We're open, most of the time. We're close.'

She stared off, whispered, 'Why not Margie?'

'She's *involved*, Sylvia.'

'Then how do you answer yourself?'

I shook my head. 'I don't try any more.'

We were like two people whispering in the back of a church.

'I've tried to understand, Sylvia,' I continued. 'Sometimes I try to figure out what kind of chemistry makes things happen the way they do. A measure of this, a measure of that and suddenly something starts to blister and turn ugly. It's delicate. It's me, it's my wife, it's the world, but I'll never know what measure of which tipped the balances the wrong way. No, I don't try any more. It's a gamble, Sylvia. Always a gamble. I don't hold myself totally responsible. I simply try to work with situations the way they are now. Adjust the scales if I can.' I looked up at her. 'That's all we can do. That's all anybody can do.'

'I feel dizzy, Matt. It's gone too far. It's too horrible.'

'Nothing's too horrible. Not after the first moment. Then we start again.'

'Too late. Now I know a "too late."'

'*Not* too late, Sylvia. Let's try.'

'How?'

'Begin with what we know.'

'Oh, God, Matt, do you realise how much more there probably is that we don't know?'

'We have to start somewhere, Sylvia,' I said quietly, firmly.

She rubbed her forehead. 'No, no. Not today.'

'We have to: now. It may not be as bad as we think.' I took the prints from her hand. 'I'll hang on to these. We may need them later. In the meantime, you've got to tell Saddleford that we know. Assure him we won't . . .'

'Oh, my God, Matt! Can't you see?' she shrieked, jumping to her feet.

'See what?'

Standing over me: 'He may have a whole drawer full of pictures. Locked and double locked. We don't even know where to begin. He's been . . . maybe he's been at this for two years.'

'And?'

'And? And! Is that all you can say, when there are probably other shots of Gabe and . . . and of Bill, and . . .' she stopped and looked directly at me. ' . . . you?'

'There's no reason for him to need something on Bill and me.'

'Are you sure, Matt? Are you so very sure? Your own daughter probing through tomes on juvenile law, Amy Witt happy as a lark three days after her parents are killed, Bill's hand mutilated, are you so very sure?'

'No. No, I'm not.'

'Listen to me, Matt.' She crouched in front of me. 'Listen because I know Aaron. I know once he begins to pursue something, he does it with all his might, with every breath he takes. There's a *reason* for everything. He needs these photographs to hold over you and Gabe and Bill so he can get whatever it is he wants and needs for his film. And Matt . . . *that's* what's so frightening. Because if he can do this . . . this little sample of homespun porno as . . . as a dalliance, then can you imagine what he's got in mind for his masterpiece?'

She stood up and went to the closet, faced it, as if trying

to see through it, as if on the other side she might discover some clue.

'This is just a toy of his,' she said softly, touching the closet door. 'A set of building blocks. I want to know about the Stonghenge he's designed.'

I rubbed my eyes, got up. 'We've got to find the script.'

'He wouldn't be foolish enough to put the design in a script. We'd find some words and scenes, maybe a line or two, but not the grand design, not the finale. That's in his head,'

'Well, Christ, Sylvia, we've got to start somewhere.' I walked into the bedroom and sat down on the edge of the bed. 'I'll have to confront him with what we know.'

'And what good will that do?'

'It'll force the . . . '

'Let him know how naughty you think he is?'

'I'll just come right out and ask him.'

'And he'll just come right out and tell you?'

'All right, Sylvia, all right! Then *what*?'

'Let me talk to him my way. I'm familiar with the double language. I've learned some of his glossary.'

'Meanwhile, I stay out of it, right. Just go on giving him all the information he needs to make God knows what kind of film. Ignore who might be next on their hit list. Pretend they had nothing to do with Bill Kasko and the Witts.'

'Talk to Margie. She may be willing . . . '

The phone rings. Sylvia answers it quickly. 'Yes? Yes, he's here, just a minute.' She put her hand over the receiver. 'It's Bill. Margie said you'd be here.'

'Yes, Bill?'

Sylvia wandered about the room.

'When did it happen?'

Touching the walls.

'Will she be all right?'

Staring into the mirror.

'Can I help?'

Turning slowly towards the bed.

'Fine. Take care.'

Sensing a child's seeing of an animal world.

I drop the receiver into the cradle, absently pick up the aluminium plate from the bed, rub my thumb across it. 'It was Bill.'

'Yes, I know.'

'He wants me to quit sniffing around; stay out of the libbers' way. Says I'm endangering their lives.'

'That's absurd.'

'Is it?'

'I think so, yes.'

'Peggy's been taken to City Hospital. She's in intensive care.'

'What happened?'

'Heart attack.'

'What she was always afraid of. When did it happen?'

'This afternoon.'

'Will she be . . . '

'While taking a bath.'

'How could the libbers be involved when . . .'

'Reached for the towel on the edge of the tub.'

'What is it, Matt?'

'Wadded up. When she opened it to dry her hair, dozens of trapped spiders fell out on to her head . . . '

'Oh, God.'

'. . . and chest and shoulders. Frantically trying to escape the water.'

'No, please.'

'Crawling up her arms on to her neck and face.'

'Stop, Matt.'

'Perhaps I *should* stay out of it. Peggy received a note from them in the morning mail. Bill read it to me. Not easy to forget. Seems they've changed their literary style. As well as their reprisals. Guess they didn't feel they vere getting the intended response. The note said:

Be kind to children and animals, the small beings of your garden. They mean you no harm. The only injury you will suffer is inflicted by the fear within your own mind.'

4

We sat silently for what felt like several minutes, as if we could suspend the compounding horrors. Then Sylvia stood up and walked quickly to the bedroom door.

'It has to stop!' she said, her back to me. 'It's time to examine Aaron's club book – time to stop . . . avoiding the truth.' She turned around. '*My* problem, Matt.'

'How soon will he be back?'

'Another half-hour, possibly less.'

'Let's get on with it.'

Aaron's door was the first at the top of the stairs. Shut, but unlocked. Sylvia opened it.

'We're not a prying family. Until today.'

'It would seem Aaron never shared in the understanding.'

'No . . . I suppose not.' She turned on the light. 'Aaron's lived in this room all his life.'

I went to a bookshelf on the far wall. It contained a year-by-year chronology of Aaron Farrow; a teddy bear, a music box, roller skates and a music school diploma, all critically placed like some esoteric form of punctuation between Carroll, Salinger, Poe and Tolkien. A special section on the top shelf held four books: *Lord of the Flies*, *Childhood's End*, *The Midwich Cuckoo*, and *The Home of David*.

The room was impeccable. Beds made, desk clean, not a piece of thrown clothing in sight. A casette tape recorder rested on his bedside table. I started to turn it on, stopped. The tape would be fragmentary at best. We had too little time before Aaron's return. I took *The Home of David* from its altar and followed Sylvia back to her room.

There wasn't a moment's hesitation as she picked up the pinking shears from her sewing table. 'I've always had the opportunity,' she explained, as if needing further justification for our intrusion, 'but I've always respected his privacy. Particularly since he's never made the effort to hide anything.'

'None of them do. It's deliberate. One of the methods they employ to discourage spying.'

Sylvia wedged the shears as far as they would go under the first latch. There was a momentary hesitation before she forced it open. The second latch broke more easily.

We sat down on the edge of the bed and I quickly began leafing through the pages. Once inside I had the strange feeling of visiting a foreign land where mores and customs and dress are totally unfamiliar; a different rhythm of speech, a tilt in thinking.

The first page was a preamble of sorts, a handwritten introduction in Aaron's precise lettering:

> DEAR MEMBER:
> This is your personal copy of *The Home of David*. It is a brief history of where we have been; it is our projection for the future. Our most important asset is dedication; our most significant goal is sustained growth; our operational imperative is confidentiality. Our present existence and future growth depend on allegiance to this imperative. Breach of this rule will result in immediate expulsion. Further disregard will result in consequences to be determined by each local chapter. Every member must be informed of this mandate and the steps to be taken should it be violated.
>
> The growth projections contained herein may seem unrealistic at this, the infancy stage of our brief life. They are not; and dedication to this growth will result

in the bargaining power which, until now, has been the exclusive domain of the adult world, the sole instrument of change wielded by the ageist forces.

To this end we must be willing to give our lives; for to stand by and do nothing is to accept our deaths.

The contents were thorough and voluminous. We would never have time to examine them in their entirety. There was an hour-by-hour activities calendar, minutes of every club meeting, and copies of all letters to erring adults.

There were drafts for a constitution, a bill of rights, a declaration of independence, and a plank to be submitted to a party platform committee at some future political convention.

There were ledgers, graphs, demographic breakdowns, possible geographic locations of communal farms to be run by juveniles, a listing of likely corporations and ad agencies who might secretly hire children as marketing, design and sales consultants.

With each new discovery my uneasiness grew. What I had correctly assumed to be a protest movement with a smattering of chapters was, in fact, the embryo of an eventual worldwide organisation.

I began to feel sick as I multiplied the blackmail of Saddleford several thousand times. I was stunned when I came to a page listing projected dollar goals to be accumulated over a period of five years: one millon dollars. I wondered how much of the total would come from membership dues as opposed to hush money.

We skimmed the rough draft for their declaration of independence:

We hold these truths to be self evident that *Whereas*: Everything in our society discriminates against children; and *Whereas*: Parents are isolated with them and assume, without question, the awesome and questionable responsibility of raising children; and *Whereas*: Schools have rules and regulations that students had no hand in setting up; and *Whereas*: Juvenile laws discriminate: There is no trial by a jury of our peers, a right adults have; and *Whereas*: The system discriminates so that children will have no skills, and therefore are unable to secure work, and consequently are dependent on their parents for support, *We Therefore* do solemnly publish and declare that all children are, and of right ought to be, free and independent; that they are absolved from all allegiance to their parents, and that all familial connection between them and their parents is, and ought to be, totally dissolved; and that, as free and independent children, they have full power to levy war, conclude peace, and do all other acts and things which independent human beings may of right do. We mutually pledge to each other, our lives, our fortunes, and our sacred honour.

We urge that all members immediately become *Emancipated Minors* by retaining a lawyer and, with their parents, sign a document which will give them the freedom to live where they choose, and keep any wages they earn.

I skipped back to the plank to be submitted at a political convention, target date: 1980.

Assault Against Ageism

We demand all age requirements on voting be eliminated.

We demand all juvenile laws and the juvenile legal system, which denies young people equal rights under the law, be eliminated.

We demand that young people shall not be compelled in any criminal case to be witnesses against themselves.

We demand an end to job discrimination and discrimination in wages for young people and senior citizens.

We demand that a student not be required to attend a specified number of hours a day at school as it doesn't allow him adequate time to support himself.

We demand that a student not be oppressed regarding his sexuality.

We demand that young people be accorded the right to be secure in their persons, houses, papers and effects against unreasonable searches and seizures.

We demand a review court (to be known as The Student Staff Court) of our peers at all academic institutions for suspensions and expulsions.

We demand a national switchboard for children, which will make referrals with respect to sex information, legal aid and act in an advocacy role.

In skimming from page to page, I was able to define why I was finding the book so chilling: The juxtaposition of adult documents composed by a youthful idealist. The restraint of age versus the raw passion of youth. The power Aaron had tapped contained passion *and* thought, zeal *and* organisation. Capable of any horror? Of course. Because what is more imaginative than the mind of a brilliant child? He could summon the collective energies of his contemporaries in the tick of a clock. He could execute his fancies in the picking up of a telephone. Most frightening of all, he had not only reasoned this out, he was capitalising on it.

Towards the end of the book we found carbons of the threat letters. I quickly flipped to the last few, finding the one to Peggy Kasko. The second to last was addressed to the Witts. It was dated a week prior to their death. It read:

> Freedom is the house of life. Bondage is the domain of death. Only in suffocating others do you smother yourselves.

I turned to the last. My breath caught. I stood up, wanting to yell, beat the hell out of someone, anyone. I was appalled by anything which could eavesdrop on lives with such dispassionate precision. The note read:

> Those who have need off prying into the lives of others have found their own life wanting. And when one finds his own cup empty, he must replenish from the wells of others. It is this same man who cannot bear to see the butterfly fly, but rather must pin him into stillness, exchanging the sun for electricity and the sky for glass. In putting bars around others, he seeks only to escape the prison of his aloneness.

The date was the day before: September nineteenth.

It was addressed to me.

I sat back down on the edge of the bed, the book in my lap, the onion skin carbon fluttering in my hand. 'Lovely. Just lovely. Sounds like a Kung Fu reject.'

'What now?' Sylvia took the book and flipped to the last section.

'I'm not sure. I'd hoped to find something more concrete.'

'Here's a list of chapter addresses.'

'Useless.' I started to get up.

'Wait. Look at this, Matt.'

My eyes fell on the blold print heading at mid-page:

Inter-Chapter Responsibilities
All Chapters Participate in the Actions of Others

I read what followed. It was a piece, an answer to what had been happening. I knew how, and I knew why. But, I still didn't know what would happen next. Nor did I know how it would happen. And, God knows if there was any way I could prove it once it had happened.

I heard the front door open and close. A conversation from downstairs. Betty Sue's voice. And Aaron's.

'That must be what happened to Rod,' I whispered. 'Another chapter . . . . where there wouldn't be any suspicion, no reason to suspect. No apparent motive.' I closed the book. 'Better put it back. Fast! I'll detain Aaron. Then I'm going to East Chester Memorial Hospital.'

'Why, what's there?'

'Rod is what, and now is when. It's time he talked about who and why.'

THREE

1

I sat on the edge of the empty hospital bed and dialled Sylvia's number. A nurse appeared and disappeared at the door in the flick of a smile.

'Sylvia? Everything all right there? Good, wish I could say the same. No, it couldn't be worse. He's dead.' Static on the line, muffled voices, then clearing. 'I said, Rod's dead. He died about four hours ago.'

I was feeling homesick again. At least most of the mysteries and melodramatics in Southern California had occurred on film.

'Yes, I got the original of the warning note. It was in my car when I left your place. Aaron must have slipped it in with his set of skeleton keys. These kids could open Fort Knox with their Alpha waves.'

I glanced at the clock on the far wall, white on white, black hands directing lives in and out at a hundred a day.

'I don't know what I'm going to do. Right now it's ten o'clock and I'm tired. Maybe just home to bed. Maybe a talk with Margie. Maybe a talk with the police tomorrow, though God knows what I'd say. How about, "Wealthy kids run amok?" You ready to have me do that?'

I heard muffled voices as she spoke to someone in the room, her hand over the receiver.

'What? Well, tell Betty Sue you don't have time to plan next week's menu right now.'

She continued to whisper, but she wasn't panicking.

'Sylvia, you don't have to have a confrontation with Aaron. He doesn't know who broke into his book. It could've been me. Don't talk to him until we have more to go on. So far we've only scratched the surface. OK? Good. I'll talk to you tomor . . . I *know* he's your son, Sylvia, but right now he's more into brotherhood then motherhood. You're an outsider, an adult. You're on of *us*. All right?'

I lowered my voice and tried to locate some mislaid gentleness. 'Sylvia, you're . . . for me, you're Gilda. I know you don't know what that means, but it's nice. I'll tell you tomorrow, OK? Good night.'

The hospital room returned to soundless white.

I uncrumpled the note Rod had scrawled that morning. I'd crushed it into a ball after one reading, damning the fact that he had died, damning that I had been partially responsible by alluding to my role in *The Bridge of Erieview Lake*, damning anything around to damn. The note affirmed the inter-chapter reprisal participation. It went on to say there were five chapters in the Cleveland area with a combined membership of forty-three, over two hundred nationally. So where do you start?

'Mister Packer, I presume?'

I jumped half-way off the bed. Standing in the doorway was a gnome of a man, well into his seventies, cherubic as Edmund Gwenn in *Miracle on 34th Street*. He carried a tattered fedora in one hand, an umbrella in the other.

'Yes, that's right.' I stood up.

'I'm Dexter Witherbee,' He walked over, hand outstretched.

'Mister Witherbee,' I shook his hand.

'Call me Ozzie,' he chuckled. 'My friends do.'

'Ozzie?' I smiled. 'How do you go about getting that out of Dexter?'

'The Wizard of Oz,' he explained, patting the two chins which overflowed his collar. 'I've been told I can hoodwink pearls out of clams, and they'd be so much the happier by losing the lumps in their throats. Tell me, Mister Packer, did you know the departed well?'

'Matt,' I corrected. 'No, I knew him for two days. I was his homeroom teacher.'

'I see. Of course. Then your visit must be of a practical nature, how silly of me.'

'And yours?'

'Also practical,' he nodded and smiled.

'How so?'

'I'm a retired attorney, sort of the Grandpa Moses of the legal profession; like to putter around my . . . '

'For the family?'

'Oh, my, no. Are they . . .'

'Then, for whom?'

'Why, the children, Matt, the members of that little club you have over there, The . . .' he looked heavenwards.

'. . . Home of David.'

'That's it. Lovely children, don't you agree?'

'Of course,' I smiled. 'But I'm not too clear as to why they'd feel it necessary to engage your services.'

'Only my advice and counsel,' he corrected, 'I'm not practising. Why, Matt,' he shook his head, 'they've come through some nasty moments this last year. In Ohio alone, five youngsters were kept all night in juvenile detention, five outstanding young minds subjected to round-the-clock grilling. Can you imagine your own daughter put through such an ordeal?'

'I'd heard from Michael Farrow that Margie'd been in touch with you.'

'Yes, and what a bright young lady she is. You must be very proud.'

'Of course. And were these five youngsters you mention also libbers?'

'Oh, yes. It would seem our judicial system has it in for them.'

'Might they have grounds, Ozzie? A boy's death is a pretty rough form of reprisal.'

'I'm surprised at you, Matt. Rod was simply the victim of a gang war in a deprived neighbourhood.'

'Ozzie, my friend, the soldiers of your so-called "gang war" have formidable IQs a sling tatooed on their souls, and ruthlessly wipe out anything that gets in their way.'

The twinkle left Ozzie's eyes. 'Mister Packer,' he shook his head, 'the thought is insulting to your powers of reason. Is it possible your Los Angeles lifestyle has infected your grasp on reality?'

I walked to the door and turned around. 'In the very near future, Mister Witherbee, I hope to grasp enough reality in my hot little hand to completely dismantle *The Home of David.*' I started to leave.

'To what end, Packer?' The voice was different. As if Jekyll had just given way to Hyde. 'To have your daughter face prosecution as an accessory after the fact?' The look was four aces in the hand of Paul Newman. 'On a first-degree murder charge? Or, do you find "party to the obstruction of justice" more palatable?' He smiled benignly. 'Good night, Mister Packer.'

The short walk from the hospital to my car was endless. I was numb. Numbers flicked off apartment buildings promising rooms for deviant appetites. The smell was cold. I was in a strange town. Steam from sewers, glow from neon.

Margie, suntanned.

A hooker smiles. Touches her ratted hair where spiders live.

Margie running down a freshly washed beach.

An ambulance screams by, smearing red streaks deep into musty shops. Muffled music and a sawdust floor. Stale beer and curdled bodies.

Margie, hair blowing. She was of the sand and water. She was lovely. I thought I'd done well.

When I reach the car my eyes are burning. The enemy anger. Angry at the way it is.

I put the key in the VW handle and turn. No resistance. Yet I'd locked the door. I slowly put the key in my pocket and whisper, 'Shit!' at the sky, and 'Shit!' again. It had been unlocked. Again.

I feel my throat tighten. I am tired of having my life broken into.

'No,' I mumble at the sky. 'Please, no more.'

Cars drive by in red and white streaks. I get inside and rest my head against the steering wheel, the plastic cold pressing back the ache.

'OK?' I whisper. 'No more? Promise?'

I sit up, take a deep breath and look around the car for a second warning note. Nothing. Odd, though. Cigarette butts in the ashtray. Messy kids. Nothing else out of place. I put the key in the ignition switch and start the car. I engage the clutch, but the pedal remains flat against the floor when I remove my foot.

'Bastards!' I am in no mood for middle-of-the-night harassment. As I reach for my automobile club card, I am quickly aware that I am in for far more than a student prank. Without being touched, the transmission shifts into first gear. Yet the handle doesn't move. I grab it and it dangles loose in my hand. The steering wheel begins to turn, lurching the car into traffic. I seize the wheel with both hands. It moves right and left under my tightest grip, freely, unhindered, darting through traffic, picking up speed. I feel like a kid in an amusement-park bumper car. I'm not amused.

I quickly turn off the ignition and pull out the key. The engine continues to run. I hear the gear change into second, automatically the car accelerates. I reach for the trigger door handle and pull. It has been disengaged. I try the passenger side. Same result. Back to the driver's side, I rotate the window handle. It spins and comes off in my hand. I hear the quick grind into third. I glance down. Forty miles per hour. Check the rear windows. Clasps removed. Jam down on the brake pedal. Flat to the floor with the clutch. Increasing speed, a red light rushing at me.

I brace, legs stiff to the floor, hands tucked beneath the dashboard. The intersection already clogging with cross traffic. As I tense for the collision, I hear the down-shift and feel the car brake for the light, as smooth as if I had been driving myself.

Next to me at the light, a woman with a red hat in a Buick. Her husband driving. I slam my fists against the window. 'Hey! Hey, you!' She turns to look at me. 'Yes, you, get . . . get the police.' I point at the steering wheel, shake my head. 'I . . . I can't control it,' I shout. She turns to her husband. He looks over suspiciously, listens, frowns. 'It's remote controlled. Call the police!'

He smiles, shakes his head. His wife waggles her fingers bye-bye at me, as if I'm some lunatic drunk, and she's safe and warm in her locked Buick.

The light changes, and I'm thrown back against the seat. Suddenly I am aware of something else. A smell. Like exhaust fumes, yet somehow different. Close enough to sense new danger. I turn around and see thin, hazy trails of smoke coming from beneath the rear seat. I lie on my back, bracing myself against the seat, and kick at the windshield. It frosts but won't shatter. The car turns down a side street. The lights are fewer outside. I use the heel of one shoe, kicking at a spot near the centre. Chips splinter away. A small hole appears. Cold air pours through. I stop, put my nose to the hole.

The street darkens, a residential area. I sit back and force my heel into the small hole, pieces falling away. My foot breaks through. I feel the glass tear my pants, slice into the back of my leg. I pull it back inside, the hole larger. The car heads for the rear end of a truck parked under a tree. The houses are dark, a street light reveals an empty sidewalk. As I brace myself, I see that the back of the truck is open. There are ramps leading inside. Before I can kick out the remaining shards of windshield, the car bounces up the ramps and into the truck. The car stops but the engine continues to run. I look out the back window in time to see three kids, unsmiling, dressed in black windbreakers and ski masks, pushing the ramps inside. They have the quickness and precision of a highly trained guerrilla unit. The doors slam, a metal bolt bangs into place. A cross bar whacks into its slot, the sound echoing in the vault of the truck.

As an involuntary reflex of the mind, I marvel at the preparation and execution. Am I now in Robbie's hands? But, of course.

Except for my headlights, it is dark. I begin to enlarge the hole in the windshield, using my jacket as a glove. The truck engine starts. My headlights go out. They've thought of everything. So far. The VW rolls against the back doors as the truck begins to move. I speculate how much time it will take before carbon monoxide fills the van. I squeeze through the hole, fall on to the hood, cutting the palms of my hands. Impossible to unlock the doors. Must get to engine compartment. Rip off spark-plug leads. Feel my way along floor. Touch back of car. Press hood latch. Locked. Grope my way back for keys. Find them inside on floor. I begin to cough. Crawl back. Put key in latch. Turn. Still locked. Turn again. Still locked.

Must have missed something. Think. Think! I damn my dumbness. I know little about cars. I feel around walls for an object, any metal object to pry open the hood. Nothing. A rope. A dolly. I fumble around on the floor. Moving blankets. My coughing heavier. Relax. Don't breath so hard. A roof hatch. I climb wood rungs along the side. There must be a roof hatch. I feel for an indentation. The truck jolts to a stop. I fall to the floor, dizzying, weakness seeping into my limbs.

Why, Margie, why?

Crawl to back door. Stand on knees. Feel for latches. Truck starts again. Stops again.

You knew about this, Margie?

Time jamming up. Car horns in far distance. A hell of a way, a hell of a way. *O brave new world, that has such people in it*. It's all yours . . . baby!

2

Regaining consciousness. Blinking. Again. Several times. Thinking about that. Because it is next to impossible that I am sitting here conscious, blinking.

Slowly now, cautiously. Take it a step at a time. I am sitting in my car. I turn to the right. The car is parked in front of my apartment building. Turn my head back again. Look out the front window. The windshield is intact. My keys are in the ignition. I pull the door handle, the door opens. I turn the window handle, the window rolls down. I step on the clutch, the brake: functional. A piece of paper flutters under the wiper blade. I start the car, turn it off. Think about this.

I look at my hands. The cuts are there, the blood dried. I feel the pain in the back of my right leg. Touch it. Not a dream. I look at my watch. Four in the morning. Six hours since I left the hospital. I touch the seam where the windshield slots into the frame. Dry. Impossible! You can't unrig a car in that span of time. Clutch, engine, transmission. I spin around; rear window latches in place. Brakes, door handles, steering mechanism. Impossible!

My eyes fall on the closed ashtray. I pull it open, empty. Pull it out of the dashboard, spotless. Smell it, not a trace of tobacco. It had never been used. It begins to fit. Of course. They used a substitute car. Same year, same colour, same model. Took all the time they needed to rig it, hauled mine away from the hospital, substituted their mockup, then dropped me back into the original. And here I sit, cut, bleeding, having come within seconds of death, and nothing to show for it. Not a pinhead of evidence. Nothing to relate but a nightmare.

The flutter again caught my eye. I reached out the open window and grabbed it. Same paper as before, same typewriter, one line:

> Butterflies caught and released fly higher than those that have never been caught at all.

I folded the note neatly, twice, and slipped it into my pocket. I felt the old, helpless desperation returning. 'Goddamn,' I whispered through a breath. 'Goddamn fortune cookies.'

What now? Where to begin? Margie? Damn right. But it would depend on how much of her was still mine. If I could walk out with her, I would. If not, I'd stay. I was now much more concerned about her safety and well-being than mine. Those who live by violence die by violence. Today the perpetrator, tomorrow the victim. If spared, the law would step in and levy the same end result.

When I closed the apartment door behind me, I looked around and smelled the air. I would be very cautious from this moment forwards. I'd underestimated them. A clock ticked, the kitchen light glowed, lighting the living room. There had been a fire in the fireplace. Shadows on the ceiling from street lamps. If it hadn't been for the pain in my leg, I might be coming home at seven in the evening, looking forward to a drink and the evening paper.

The door to Margie's room was partially ajar. I went to her desk and turned on the reading lamp. She was asleep, her hair wisping over her face. As I was about to touch her shoulder, something moved at her waist. I recoiled, prepared for a new horror. 'Mew,' and again, 'Mew.' The small head of a yellow kitten looked up at me, head unsteady, the eyes reflecting the light in a tortoise-shell glow.

'Daddy?' The covers moved. The voice was sleepy. I

rubbed my eyes, the same implausibility of natural beauty aligning itself with grotesqueness: How could this, my daughter, be of blackmail and injury and killing?

Her small hand had fallen limp outside the covers. She was asleep again. 'Margie?'

Her eyes opened, blinked. 'Is something the matter?' She sat up, awakening quickly. 'What happened, Daddy?'

I stood up and walked slowly about the room. The kitten mewed again, wobbled to its feet and arched its back in a Hallowe'en stretch. 'Where'd you get the kitten?'

'Cammie Saddleford. She has lots. Is it all right to keep her?'

'I thought Cammie's speciality was chemistry. Is she going to start raising piranhas, too?'

She looked at me oddly. 'No.' Then quickly started petting the kitten. 'I can tell you don't like Muffin.'

'Who said I didn't like Muffin?'

'You did. By the way you sound.'

'The way I sound has nothing to do with Muffin. I just got worked over by your charming brothers, that's all.' I sat down at her desk and stretched my legs.

'That's why you sound upset?'

'That's why I sound upset, That's why I *am* upset,' Easy, easy, don't startle.

She picked up the kitten and rubbed noses. 'Can we keep her?'

'Can we talk?' The evasiveness was all too familiar.

'Sure.'

She put the kitten down and folded her hands in her lap. The look was expectant and willing. I knew better. As I related my terrors in Robbie Farrow's dream machine I watched for moments of concern, expressions which might offer some indication of how much care remained. But she had learned well. If there were such feelings they never surfaced. When I finished the story I waited for a response. There was none.

'Why, Margie, why?' The question was becoming a household idiom.

She looked down.

'You knew about this. Margie?' As if I'd asked the same question many times before.

Then, in a voice I could barely hear, she said. 'They didn't mean to have you hurt, Daddy. They just wanted to scare you.'

I gritted my teeth, closed my eyes. Keep the anger down, it's your only hope. 'They succeeded. *You* are succeeding.'

Head still down, she picked at a hangnail. 'I didn't have anything to do with it.'

'But you knew about it.'

'I knew something would happen. But none of us are allowed in on cases involving our own family.'

'You had nothing to say about it?'

'No. It's put to a vote. I'm disqualified from discussions and voting. I'm not allowed in the room.'

'How about Rod Angstrom? And the Witts? Were you in on those votes?'

She looked up. Her voice was flat, her expression unyielding. 'I don't have to talk about this, Daddy.'

'I know you don't, Margie.' I watched her carefully. Control. 'I was hoping you might.'

'It doesn't have to be this way at all.'

'If what? If I pretend nothing's going on?'

'Just leave it alone,' she nodded.

'Ignore it.'

'That's right.'

'Stand by and watch people maimed and killed.'

'Do you know how how many children are maimed and killed every year?' she snapped, breathing faster. 'Do you?'

'Margie, I'm not . . .'

'Try ten thousand!' Her eyes glistened. 'In this country alone.' She pointed at the stacks of books on her desk. 'And do you know how many cases of child abuse are brought to trial? Actually get into court? And of that number, do you know how infinitesmal the number of convictions is?'

I sat forward in the chair. 'No, Margie, I don't. But then again, I don't know anything that justifies taking the law into your own hands.'

'Oh, spare me, Daddy!' She bounded off the bed. 'You sound like some ancient tyrant.' She jerked on her robe and sat facing me.

'Spare *me*, you're beginning to sound like Aaron. And what's that got to do with . . .'

'Every time the colonies tried to be reasonable, they got their faces shoved in it. And if those renegades Franklin, Jefferson and Hamilton hadn't taken the law into their own hands, where do you think we'd be today?'

'Oh come on, Margie,' I rubbed my head, sick of the same old rhetoric, 'that was seventeen seventy-six.'

'So? How about the *nineteen*-seventies version of Portugal and her colonies, Russia and Czechoslovakia, and for that matter, the United States and Chile?'

'You're not going to convince me you're a country struggling for independence.'

'Yes we are, Daddy,' she smiled. '*A people!* Same thing.'

'And looting and blackmail and killing and . . .'

'Do you know any other way to win a revolution?'

'Oh, my God, Margie, this is *today*!' I stood up and paced, aching with frustration, losing what little patience I had left. 'This is the United States. These thing just don't happen any more.'

'They're happening. And they're increasing.'

'They're preposterous! All seven of you are going to be on trial for your lives.'

'All two hundred?'

'And if your father just happens to get killed somewhere along the way, so be it.'

'Dad-dy . . .'

I stopped pacing and looked at her. She was shaking her head sadly. 'Well?'

'You're not going to be killed,' she said softly.

'What do you call exhaust fumes with carbon monoxide?'

'It wouldn't have been carbon monoxide. It was probably a mild derivative of ether and Cammie added the odour to frighten you.'

'How about the Witts?'

'Continued to tie Amy with electrical cord, beat her with belts, burned her with cigarette tips, forced her head under water, gagged her with . . .'

'Why didn't she go to the proper authorities?'

'She did. But the Witts promised to be good little parents, so they got off with a scolding. When they got Amy home, they told her if she ever reported them again they'd tie her in her room for good.'

'And Rod?'

'Neville Chamberlain. An example.'

'An example of cruelty! Show me where it says revolutions are fought hanging people up by their thumbs and pummelling their shins with tyre irons. I call that an example of Aaron's grisly imagination.'

'That wasn't Aaron's doing.' Margie lowered her head. 'When he heard about it he had two of the three East Chester members expelled. He was extremely upset.'

'Well, bully for Aaron. That makes up for everything, I suppose.'

'Oh, Daddy, none of us are idealists to the point of proclaiming the purity of our group. Judas, Chamberlain, Brutus: There have always been betrayers . . . always been those who act outside the true spirit of the group.'

'Oh, come on, Margie, come off it. Quit making excuses for him.'

'Aaron is *not cruel*!'

'I don't believe this is happening; I simply do not believe this is going on.'

'You *won't* believe it's going on. Can't you look at the other side, Daddy? A little bit?'

'Margie, Margie . . .' I sat down on the bed next to her. I was hearing a sincere 'please' in her voice. 'I know you mean well,' I sighed, 'but you're heading for a heap of trouble.'

'We're prepared for that possibility.'

'Look, I *know* there's justification on your part. I know kids have been oppressed and abused. I know your position is valid. There's much good in what you're trying to do, I . . . I just can't approve of your methods. I don't want you hurt.'

'I'll be all right.'

Deaf ears. 'Listen, I'll tell you what.'

'What?'

'I'll make you a deal. You give up the libbers, and I'll give up teaching. We'll move back to Malibu.'

'We haven't even been here a month.'

'It's been a lifetime.'

'After the film's finished.' She glanced down and suddenly seemed very sad. 'Aaron needs you.'

'Well, he has a funny way of showing it. When's the film supposed to be completed?'

'Another two weeks.'

'What's so important about the film?'

'It will show the truth by showing the lies. Our statement. And if enough adults with open minds see it, then perhaps changes will be made by working within the system.'

'Sounds reasonable.'

'It will also be shown to students everywhere, to encourage membership, to make them aware of the way it is. A print will go to all the chapters.'

'Then Malibu?'

'If you still want to go . . . after you've seen the film.'

'What about Aaron?'

'What about him?'

'Won't you mind leaving him behind?'

'Aaron will be leaving too.'

'Do his parents know?'

'No.'

I shook my head. 'I'll never understand.' I walked to the door. 'Better get some sleep.'

'Daddy?'

'Yes.'

'Please don't interfere any more.'

'I can't promise that, Margie.'

'*Please*, Daddy.'

'I'm afraid not.'

'Then I can't promise . . . '

'I realise that.'

'Daddy?'

'Yes?'

'There's a preview showing of a portion of the film at Aaron's house on Monday.' She was working the hangnail again, having already returned to another time and place. 'He'd like you to be there.'

'Is it safe?' I smiled, trying to make light of it.

'Yes.' She didn't look up.

And the voice was detached again.

3

I suppose I could be accused of wasting Wednesday. I was a physical wreck. And there are times when, after grappling with a crossword puzzle for hours, I put it aside and busy myself with other projects, hoping that answers in eclipse will be revealed at a later time, when the shadow passes from my memory. It was time to do some careful plotting, stretched out in a hot tub with Agatha Christie.

On Thursday my pampered body felt ready to function

again, yet my mind had not been visited by any of the revelations I'd hoped for. I began an effort to appear 'cured'. I let the libbers alone, taught what they wanted to be taught, and kept my sardonic ad-libs to myself. I caught Aaron watching me on occasions, as if to make sure I'd learned my lesson.

At noon I called Jim Bagley's furnace repair. Asked Jim to examine the Witt's unit. Yes, he also did appraisals, and he'd check it out. I was to meet him at 3.30 after school.

His shop consisted of a long closet housed in the brick buildings on Erieview Square, a shopping centre with white-peaked roofs off a Tyrolean postcard. Had I been in the right frame of mind, I might've liked it. Today it was Hansel-Gretel, cookie chic.

'Jim?' I called out from the front counter.

'Be right there.'

He came out wiping his hands on a cloth which was offering more grease than it accepted.

'I'm Matt Packer.'

'Right.' He shuffled some invoices, his hair stringing into his eyes. He looked like Oscar Homolka with a hangover. 'Here it is, right here. That'll be twelve dollars.'

'Well, what'd you find?'

'Nothin'.'

'What do you mean, nothing? The thing malfunctioned and killed the occupants?'

'Safety froze up.' He stood there staring at me, as if that should explain everything.

'Does that happen often?'

'Not hardly.'

'How does it happen?'

'Mostly people tamperin' with things that don't concern 'em. Looked to me like that guy Witt put the whole thing together with cornstarch and undershirts. Messiest thing I ever seen. Wonder it didn't blow up.'

'Let me get this straight. You mean the whole system had been tampered with, not just the safety?'

'I mean, whoever's lived in that place for the last ten years has tried to do the whole thing himself; why there's rags wrapped around the ducts that just go to dust between your fingers.'

'But had the safety been tampered with?'

'Why, course it had, sonny, but the whole . . .'

'When?'

'Hard t'say. Like lookin' at an old Model-T left out in the rain, all rusted up and rotted like that.'

I felt like an ass. Detectives I'd read about never got answers like that. They'd get clues. They got results.

'Thanks, anyway,' I said, and turned to leave.

'Hey, sonny, how 'bout m'twelve bucks?'

I returned, wallet in hand, and offered an apologetic laugh.

Then I went home and poured a drink. Ruminated: I was wasting my time – let it alone – make a preposterous call to the police – demand a special meeting of the libbers and have it out. I concluded with a vow to return to the hunt the next day by paying a visit to East Chester High School for a close look into the HOD chapter at that institution.

I called Sylvia and found she was tied up at a museum function. Margie was off on an all-afternoon war dance with Aaron. Muffin climbed the draperies and urinated on my pillow. Odd cat. She always stopped what she was doing when I entered a room. I was sure Cammie Saddleford was responsible.

Left to such fancying, one of the shadows lifted: An underlined book I'd seen in Margie's room the night we'd talked. Convinced my clues to the past had been deftly removed, my main concern was to find a trail to the future. I was positive something major was about to happen, probably in conjunction with the showing of the film; some symbolic demonstration to bring nationwide attention to their cause. I was also sure it wouldn't be anything as harmless as draft-card burning. The symbol would mean business. The more spectacular the better.

When I entered Margie's room, Muffin followed. She would report my indiscretion. The books remained stacked, some closed, some open, all over the desk. My afternoon was cut out for me. As I reached for the first book, I caught sight of a legal tablet buried beneath the stacks. I pulled it out. Margie's writing, quotes, it appeared, from many sources. Though I was unfamiliar with a lawyer's brief I would be hard pressed not to assume that this was precisely what I was holding. Furthermore, with each successive paragraph, I became convinced that what I was reading was a prepared defence for a crime not yet committed. From these excerpts my apprehension mounted. I sure as hell had found my trail.

> *Haley* v. *Ohio*, 332 US 596, 92 L ed 224, 68 S Ct 302 (1948), involved the admissibility, in a state criminal court of general jurisdiction, of a confession by a fifteen-year-old boy. The court held that the Fourteenth Amendment applied to prohibit the use of the coerced confession. Mr Justice Douglas said, 'Neither man nor child can be allowed to stand condemned by methods which flout constitutional requirements of due process of law.'

> The early reformers were appalled that children could be given long prison sentences and mixed in jails with hardened criminals. They believed that society's role was not to ascertain whether the child was 'guilty' or 'innocent,' but, 'What is he, how has he become what he is, and what had best be done in his interest and in the interest of the state to save him from a downward career.'* The child – essentially good, as they saw it –

*Julian Mack, 'The Juvenile Court,' 23 Harv L Rev 104, 119–20 (1967).

was to be made 'to feel that he is the object of care and solicitude,' not that he was under arrest or on trial.

> The idea of crime and punishment was to be abandoned. The child was to be 'treated' and 'rehabilitated,' and the procedures from apprehension through institutionalisation were to be 'clinical' rather than punitive. (Re Gault 387 UL 1, 18 L ed 2d 527, 87 S Ct 1428.)

The words stuck in my mind: 'What is he . . . how has he become what he is, and what had best be done in his interest?' My guilts began to surface. Did I intend to become executioner or child welfare worker? The next quotation had me pretty well convinced.

> In *Haley* v. *Ohio*, 332 US 596, 92 L ed 224, 68 S Ct 302, where this Court reversed the conviction of a fifteen-year-old boy for murder, Mr Justice Douglas said: 'What transpired would make us pause for careful inquiry if a mature man were involved. And when, as here, a mere child – an easy victim of the law – is before us, special care in scrutinising the record must be used. Age fifteen is a tender and difficult age for a boy of any race. He cannot be judged by the more exacting standards of maturity. That which would leave a man cold and unimpressed can overawe and overwhelm a lad in his early teens. This is the period of great instability which the crisis of adolescence produces. A fifteen-year-old lad, questioned through the dead of night by relays of police, is a ready victim of the inquisition. Mature men possibly might stand the ordeal from midnight to 5 a.m. But we cannot believe that a lad of tender years is a match for the police in such a contest.

Mr Justice Douglas hadn't met twelve-year-old Aaron Farrow!

> No lawyer stood guard to make sure that the police went so far, and no further, to see to it that they stopped short of the point where he became the victim of coercion.

'Victim of coercion.' The phrase bothered me. How could anyone be the victim of coercion before the fact? I skimmed the other cases Margie had outlined:

> The body of a ten-year-old girl was found. She had been strangled. Two neighbourhood boys, aged thirteen and fifteen, confessed to the police with vivid details.

And again:

> Two twelve-year-old boys were taken into custody for the brutal assault and rape of two aged domestics, one of whom died as the result of the attack.

And yet again:

> A boy of ten-year-old was convicted on his own confession of murdering his bed-fellow, there appearing in his whole behaviour plain tokens of a mischievous discretion.

All released. Yet all involving murder. They had all been freed on legal loopholes. In some cases, justified, to be sure. But what about kids who study the loopholes and plan to capitalise on them *before* committing the crime? Hardly what I'd call 'mischievous discretion.'

Sure, I'd found my trail, with roadsigns every step of the way. All that was missing was the victim. Unless they had been anticipating trouble over Rod Angstrom. I'd check it out, but it wasn't jelling for me. I was guessing Aaron had hatched a super plot, was going to get it on film, and had his defence prepared to the letter.

4

Friday morning, the twenty-third, Margie left for school without me. I had used extra work as an excuse to be late. The moment she was out the door, I was dialling the East Chester Police. After ten minutes of being shunted from extension to extension, I finally ended up with the guy who had been on the Angstrom case from the beginning, an Inspector Falzone of the homicide department.

There are times when the phone has an advantage over face-to-face encounters, particularly when you want to dispense with pleasantries. I explained who I was and why I was interested in the progress that had been made. But, not the whole why. He was most co-operative and unstintingly honest. Described how his department had interviewed eighty-four students from East Chester High and had come up with zero. They were on the brink of writing it off as an unsolved homicide, explaining this had been particularly true of the age group, not only in the Cleveland area, but nationwide. He compared the situation to the Mafia and to the Tongs in Chinese communities.

'Self-preservation, Packer. They know goddamn well if they snitch, their number might be up next. Particularly with kids. They got a vengeance streak a mile long. And they run in packs. It's not that we haven't tried, it's just that we know what we're getting into before we get started. Add to that their abiding suspicion of cops, and what've you got? Silence. Sorry I can't be of more help, Packer. Maybe next time.'

'Hope there won't be a next time.'

'There will be.'

'By the way, anybody else not associated with the family been asking questions?'

'Yeah, some guy named Witherbee. Looks like Santa Claus, but I think he's an attorney. Pretty shifty character.'

'Thanks, Inspector Falzone.'

'Don't mention it.'

I hung up. Another dead end. Of sorts. The preparation wasn't for Rod. I dialled operator and asked for the Erieview Heights Police. Another ten minutes of jumping voices, and I landed on a Captain Schumaker. I was getting up in the world. I asked about the Witts. His voice must have been produced by IBM.

'Open and shut. Accidental death.'

'How about the safety on the furnace freezing up?'

'You see that place, Packer?'

'No.'

'Thought so. Can I help you with anything else, Mister Packer?'

'Not unless you know anything about juvenile detention.'

'It's here. Same building. What's up?'

'Ever hear of a children's lib organisation called The Home of David?'

'Nope. What is it, a high school fraternity or something?'

'Something like that. Do you provide counsel for juvenile offenders when they're brought in?'

'If counsel's available, why?'

'Do me a favour, Captain Schumaker, play it strictly by the book for a while. If you get any students from Erieview High in there, have counsel on hand, *and* the parents. Don't get sucked into a harassment or grilling charge so that a shifty lawyer I know can get his clients off on a "victim of coercion" defence.'

'What's going on, Packer? You sound like you know something we don't.'

'Not much. Not enough, anyway. Just keep it in mind.'

'Where can you be reached?'

I heard the scratching of pencil on paper. 'At the school.'

'I'll relay your message.'

'Kid gloves, Captain . . . please.'

'That's one way of putting it. Goodbye.'

When I hung up and went to re-dial, there was static from the earpiece. I tapped the cradle buttons several times before it cleared, then made my appointment with the principal at East Chester High that afternoon. Somewhere along the way I was going to get the co-operation I needed.

I spent the remainder of the day being Johnny Goodguy with my students and fellow teachers. Bill Kasko was his mellow old self, Peggy was at home and recovering, Amy was being a delightful companion to Chris. Even some smiles from Aaron attested to the success of the 'cured' me. Until Saddleford stormed in the door following my last afternoon class. 'What in hell are you trying to do, Packer?' he seethed.

I pushed back from my desk and folded my hands in my lap. 'Must be mighty wrong, whatever it is,' I smiled.

'What in God's name prompted you to call the police?'

'Oh, that.'

'Most decidedly that! Are you out of your goddamned mind? What's possessing you?'

'They . . . called?'

'Goddamn right they called. Wanted to know what the hell I knew about some trouble brewing around here.'

'And you, of course, said, "Why, nothing at all, everything's just dandy," right?'

'Christ, yes! What did you expect? This is not the tacky, sordid community *you're* accustomed to. The people here have breeding! They have heritage! In my eleven years as principal, we've never had need of the police. Now pack up your tawdry, dirty imagination and take it back to Hollywood where people thrive on prurience.'

I got up, crossed the room, paused, then came back and stood in front of him. I put my hand on his shoulder.

'My dear, Mister Saddleford,' I said softly, 'at my apartment, safely tucked away in the far recesses of a closet shelf, I have two photographs, pictures of unquestionable authenticity, which depict – without much artistry, I grant you – *you*, Mister Saddleford, in the altogether, working out your feverish passions in unimaginative positions of cohabitation with – dare I say it? – one Marty Kyle. Now, Gabe, if I may assume the familiar just this once, despite the lack of camera technique, the photographs demonstrate beyond any question of doubt, not so much that you're perverted, God forbid, but that Erieview Heights, prize community that it is, is just as "tacky", just as "sordid", just as "tawdry", and perhaps just a bit "dirtier" than Hollywood. Do I make *my*self clear?'

His face drained of colour. 'Well . . . you . . . you seem to be holding all the cards.'

'Is that the best you can come up with?' I watched him with a sense of pity. He was stumbling badly.

'All right. What is it you want?'

I caught the drift and shook my head. 'No, Mister Saddleford, please don't be insulting. I'm not bringing this up out of self-interest. Blackmail and extortion aren't included in my credentials. I'd hoped you'd realise that by now.'

'You *are* a self-righteous bastard, aren't you! Never got mixed up in anything socially unacceptable, I suppose. Not once yielded to . . . appetites frowned upon by your standard, one-to-one heterosexuals.'

'No, can't say I have, prosaic as that may be.'

'The Greeks loved boys . . . '

'I'd . . . heard something like that, though I'd be willing to bet their definition of love differs somewhat from the . . . current example.'

'It was common practice during the Golden Age,' he said, ignoring my remark. 'Acceptable! *Not* deviant. We weren't tagged with whispered words like pederast, sodomite and such during those years.'

'I'm not judging you, Mister Saddleford.'

'Then *what*?' The voice remained tight, unrelenting.

'I'm trying, as best I can, to prevent something from happening.'

'Such as?'

'I . . . I'm not sure.'

He guffawed. 'Is that the best you can come up with?'

'I'm afraid so, for the time being. In the meantime, you're being blackmailed.'

'I can live with it. His demands aren't that great. He'll move on. I'll be here.'

'Is that so? Well, I believe he's got something else in mind.'

'It's up to you, Packer.' He took a deep breath. 'I'd wait until you had something more to go on before involving the police. I think you're asking for trouble you've never dreamed of.'

'Undoubtedly. I've already had a sampling of their methods.'

He turned and stared out the window. 'I'd prefer you leave well enough alone.'

'I know you would.'

'Stay out of it, Packer!' his head snapped around.

'No . . . I won't.'

'It could unleash an incredible scandal. Many fine people will . . .'

'I know all about your fine people.'

'Yes,' he paused. 'Yes, I suppose you do. So, then. I'm in the middle. If I try to stop you . . .'

'The pictures go to the school board.'

'I let you alone?'

'I do it my way, without implicating you.'

He shrugged. 'A Hobson's choice.'

'So it would appear.'

My afternoon at East Chester High was wasted.

Saddleford had been right. The grounds made the Erieview campus look like a botanical garden: all brick, asphalt and chain-link fencing. The remaining students complemented the granite atmosphere. Two toughs practiced Kung Fu, while the onlookers shouted for blood. Couple of others played mumblety-peg with a switchblade. It was a backdrop for Studs Lonnigan: leather and chrome, beers and limp cigarettes, eyes following my walk to the front door, challenging my trespass. I felt genuinely threatened. I did not doubt for an instant that this group would not only be capable, but be more than delighted to do me in for kicks on a dull afternoon.

The principal was a sprite of a man named Corcoran, with grey eyes, sunken and tired, but a spirited manner. He was much more co-operative than Saddleford, but then he probably didn't have an Aaron Farrow taking candid shots of his sex life. He assumed the libbers were much more constructive within his own school, because of his extremely liberal handling of student demands. They were involved with student government and spearheaded school events to raise money for an advanced audio-visual teaching facility. They had been instrumental in persuading the City Council to designate a rundown building as a city-funded museum of science and industry, devoted exclusively to the latest designs and accomplishments of the student body. He assured me they were harmless, as I alluded to my joy ride in Robbie Farrow's automated car. He advised me to leave them alone, and urged me to help, not hinder.

'How many members in the East Chester chapter, Mister Corcoran?'

'Five.'

'Hmm, not as many as I'd expected.'

'There were only two last spring. They're very selective, you know.'

'No, I didn't. As long as you brought it up, how do they go about lining up their prospects?'

'Several sources: the dockets at Juvenile Hall, lists from

the county's Parental Guidance Centres, the Children's Home Society, Big Brothers Incorporated. The screening process is meticulous. They deliberately keep their numbers small. It ensures confidentiality as well as loyalty.'

'I should think so. In short, they look in all those places where they'd be most apt to find children who have been victimised by adults in one form or another, deliberate or accidental.'

'Absolutely. And in so doing, I might add, they have earned the utmost respect of these institutions.'

'Oh? How so?'

'By instilling a sense of purpose in each child where none had existed before – even in hardship cases.'

'As well as loyalty to the cause, out of gratitude.'

'Oh, by all means. Fierce loyalty. They'd do anything for their club and never breathe a word of it. And small wonder, considering the distance they've travelled from hopelessness. Wouldn't we have done likewise in similar circumstances? A quite human reaction, I believe.'

I glanced out the window and traced the ingredients through my mind: gratitude, loyalty, secrecy, fervour, determination, youth. 'Ah, yes, Mister Corcoran – what more could one ask for in assembling an army of unified dissidents to do battle against a common enemy?'

'Oh, come now, Mister Packer, after all, they're still just kids,' he smiled.

In point of fact, the East Chester unit did appear to be more constructive, despite my well-founded suspicion of how they spent some of their evening hours. With the pride of a father, Mister Corcoran ushered me to a special room where the libbers had set up their own lab. It looked as sophisticated as the one I'd seen at Cal Tech, where I'd shot a documentary. A couple of students remained, including one freckle-faced boy who had popped his head into the office as we were talking. My only astonishment was at no longer being astonished. They were working with lasers, one of which was already functional. My stomach dropped as a piece of steel was neatly cut in half. It crossed my mind that if this was an example of progress in East Chester, Ohio, what might I be apt to find in a city like New York? An atomic energy reactor?

As we left, the boy with freckles smiled and handed me a programme from the local museum, in which I'd find the details and simplified explanations of their work with lasers and other projects. I thanked him, and Mister Corcoran, for their courtesy and tour.

When I reached the car, I checked it out, looking idiotic I am sure to any passers-by, doors open, hood up, windows down. It wasn't until I got in and started the engine that I noticed a small slip of paper extending from the centre of the museum programme.

I shook my head. How silly of me to assume I'd be spared more poison-pen notes. I turned off the engine, making sure it would turn off, before reading my next clue.

> Stone walls do not a prison make
>   Nor iron bars a cage;
> Minds innocent and quiet take
>   That for an hermitage;
> If we have freedom in our love,
>   And in our souls are free,
> Angels alone that soar above
>   Enjoy such liberty.
>
> – Richard Lovelace

MISTER PACKER:

> Surely, sir, you jest! A call to the police is but the hare mocking the tortoise when the race is done, the ridicule of Goliath as he whispers to David from death. As you are about to find out, Mister Packer, as you are about to find out.

5

Driving home I did not look for hidden lasers peeking through privet hedges. Which does not mean I wasn't taking the latest warning seriously. But I had learned that, as a group, the HODs were not a snowball throwing, short-sheeting breed. They were far too proud of their imagination and intellect. They were like chess masters, delighting in the moves of their adversaries which showed style and cunning.

When I arrived home, it was just past five. My first priority was to get rid of some anger. I picked up the phone and dialled one digit so the tone would disappear.

'Fuck you! you bunch of dumb-dumb, elephant brains; this is an illegal wire-tap and you're all as good as in jail!' I whistled through my fingers, hoping I'd burst an eardrum, then slammed the phone down.

I settled back on the couch with my evening's scotch and water. I felt better. They could have their fusty intellects; I'd take good, old, four-letter emotionalism any time. I sipped my drink, contemplating my next move. Sylvia had called the school earlier. Couldn't trust my own phone, so I'd see her the next day. A confrontation with Aaron? Possibly, though probably futile. Perhaps not. Saddleford? That was a loss. How would it look to the community if he exposed them? They'd just turn around and expose him, in all his pleated nakedness.

I began to feel drowsy. No wonder; half a drink can have the effect of four if the day's been bad. I put it down. It wasn't until I tried to pick up the newspaper that I knew there was far more at work here than the drink and the day. I say try, because the best I could do was to slide it into my lap. Turning the first page was impossible. My arm lay at my side, numbed, in-operative. My feet began to burn. Then I knew. The drink. They'd spiked the scotch. A

Camilla Saddleford mickey. I tried to reach the phone, but fell on my back, helpless as Kafka's beetle.

This isn't happening, I thought. *I'm no goddamn secret agent. I'm just a lousy school teacher.*

That my body had somehow become completely anesthetised didn't bother me, until I began to feel my insides follow suit. My pulse became slower. It was becoming impossible to breathe. I panicked. Camilla had gone too far. A slip of the hand: O.D. Like the coleus. Not yet perfected. I tried to scream for help. My throat and vocal cords were cut off. I was totally immobilised, but conscious. My breaths became shorter.

My God, I thought, *I'm going to die, I'm actually going to die. They wanted to drug me, but they botched it.*

My breath was running out, as if someone had removed all the oxygen in the room. Small panting. Shorter. Vision going grey.

I heard the key in the lock. Margie home? I couldn't move my head. Quick. Margie. Must know what to do. Must have told you. Standing above me. Not Margie. Three boys, tall as sky-scrapers. Grotesque ski masks. Wool gloves. Boy over my head, upside down, smiling, says, 'We came to watch you die, Mister Packer.'

I don't recognise the voice. From East Chester? Chicago? New York?

Another boy near my left leg says, 'He doesn't do it very well. He's not even moving.'

I want to scream, 'I can't.'

A boy with albino skin peeking through mask holes: 'Need our help, Mister Packer?' The gas station boy?

I want to scream, 'Yes, Jesus Christ, yes, you've overdone it.'

Upside-down boy: 'Poor Mister Packer.'

The others shake their heads. I feel my breath stop, a brown haze fills the room.

'Time,' I hear. From somewhere. A black, plastic scoop

is lowered on to my face. I hear hissing. Hands press on my chest. Something cool into my nostrils. I begin to breathe. Faster, deeper. The shape of a respirator and tube appear as my eyes begin to clear. Deeper breaths. Greedy, as if drinking water. My insides throb, my heart picks up. I am breathing, I can see, I think. But I cannot move.

Upside-down boy: 'We've saved you, Mister Packer.'

Albino boy: 'He appears to be grateful.'

Left-leg boy: 'Perhaps he's fooling us – again.'

I want to shake my head. Oh, my God, if I could just shake my head. I feel the respirator being taken away. I can't grab it back. The scream comes out in silent breath.

Albino boy: 'He looks frightened.'

Left-leg boy: 'Nah, he's kidding again.'

Upside-down boy: 'You puttin' us on, Mister Packer?'

Breathing shortens up, no way to say, 'No.' I flick my eyes, but can't tell if they move. They don't see.

Albino boy: 'It's a hype, Doug.'

Left-leg boy: 'Let's leave.'

Breath gone. The plastic scoop appears. I gulp as much as I can for next time. Cruelty belongs to people who don't feel.

Breathe.

It has no meaning to them.

Breathe.

Beyond their grasp.

Upside-down boy: 'We have more in store for you, Mister Packer, much more.'

He leans over, puts his hands on his knees. His head becomes oversized, as if connected somehow at mid-chest. 'There are worlds you know nothing about, places you've never been. This is just one of our many strengths, Mister Packer, the pooling of knowledge from two thousand minds. We have given you curare, a poison indigenous to Brazil. Possibly you know curare by its synthetic analogue, succinyl choline. Probably you don't. *Now* you do, however. Right, Mister Packer? Suffice it to say, you have not had a lethal dosage, though without the respirator you would have been long gone.'

Albino boy: 'It's time.'

Upside-down boy: 'Just a few more words, Mister Packer. Then we must leave you.'

The albino boy pulled a hypodermic from a small case in his pocket.

'We really don't care if you understand us or not, Mister Packer,' continued the upside-down boy. 'It ceases to matter. We're disappointed in you, but we've been disappointed before in trying to bring sight to the blind. Remember "Tommy", Mister Packer, the deaf, dumb and blind boy? He saw. The seeing didn't. Perhaps in order to see, you must first be blind. Perhaps in order to live, you must first die.'

The respirator was removed. My breathing continued without assistance. I began to feel sensations in my limbs. I moved a foot.

'Ready?' asked the albino boy.

'Yes,' answered the upside-down boy.

I feel the needle puncture my right arm. There is still not enough strength to stop them.

'We'll leave you now, Mister Packer. And probably you'll be leaving us. Frankly, we're not sure. But that also ceases to matter.'

The faces disappeared. I heard the door shut. Not a word was spoken between them during their departure. In a few moments I could sit up. With considerable difficulty I made it to the couch. I sat back and took deep breaths. My body seemed to be recovering, yet they had just given me a shot of something else. But then, I had no way of knowing what to expect.

At that precise moment, looking at the phone with the intention of calling a doctor, whatever it was began to take its effect. I sat perfectly still, because I suddenly realised it was pointless to make the call. I knew full well that no matter how fast I could summon a doctor, it would be too late. I knew, without any doubt, that as alive as I was at this given moment, I would be dead within a matter of minutes. The knowledge and acceptance were so complete, so irrevocable, the only feeling I had was one of terror. My last question was not if; it was when.

I had been in situations before where I'd faced death. At those times the life force, the will to live, the determination to fight had never left me. The closer the final moments had come, the harder I'd fought, the more instinctively predatory I'd become.

I now knew I'd never reached the final moment. My body growing weaker, a dryness in my mouth, my heart giving bursts instead of beats, as if two internal hands were squeezing out the last, exhausted muscle contractions. I'd never experienced absolute hopelessness. I'd never accepted my own mortality. My one last hope was that Margie would walk in, because no matter how hard I tried in these last moments, I could not bring a picture of her to mind. There was no vindictiveness. Only the honest wish for a last look.

I sensed my falling over on my side, a drifting away, something of fog and drums, wind and umbrellas, veils and a black horse. I remembered crying in the middle of crying, but not having begun. My last conscious fragment was wishing I'd done better, then seeing myself smile in the dark: It didn't make a bit of difference anyway.

Cold on my head. The touch of an icy cover. Pulled up from my feet to cover my face. Sounds without words. A cloud of blood red over my eyes. It is the going through. There is a something. Or is it only the hope there is a something?

FOUR

1

Cold on my head – a washcloth. The touch of an icy cover, a linen sheet. Sounds without words; Margie's voice. And someone else. The cloud lifts – my eyelids. A bed . . . mine. A room . . . mine. Night in the windows now. Margie's face close, red and tear-streaked. Man in the chair; Ozzie Witherbee.

'Daddy . . . ?'

'You're . . . you're kidding.'

'You all right?'

'No. I've . . . I've been dead.'

Ozzie comes over, his voice gentle. 'No, Mister Packer, it just seemed that way. You're quite all right.'

'You knew about this?' I looked at Margie.

She shook her head. 'I didn't know what they were going to do. They were just supposed to warn you again.'

I nodded, shut my eyes. 'They did. Warning heeded.'

'No child is ever aware of the specifics relating to his or her parents, Mister Packer. It would be unwise; it would cause unnecessary emotional upset, particularly in a case such as yours, where there's been absolutely no child abuse or cruelty, and the relationship's quite close.'

'I understand. What was it?'

'The drug?'

'If that's what it was.'

'It's called psycho-hexamine, Mister Packer. It's only in the experimental stage just now.'

I pushed my fingers into my eyes. The fear was still very close. 'Good God, what will the end result amount to?"

'An ego-destroyer. A total release from the will to live. It is intended to give one the fully conscious sensation of dying. It affects exclusively that specific part of the brain.'

I opened my eyes and blinked. 'It's in the wrong hands, Ozzie.'

'Any hands would be wrong, Mister Packer. But what would you prescribe to bring a halt to technological development and experimentation?'

I shook my head. 'Movies.'

Margie took my face in her hands. I could see the tears returning. 'Don't joke, Daddy, please don't joke.'

In that moment, all that I cared about was that she was caring again. The spell had been broken.

'OK, Margie.' I sat up, and she put a pillow under my back. 'And OK to you too, Ozzie, but I'm not joking. I think we'd all be a lot better off if you'd respectfully suggest to these kids that they take up necking in the balcony of the Bijou. Why this obsession with changing the world? Why can't children just enjoy their childhood the way they're supposed to?'

'They *will*, Daddy. That's what it's all about. Perhaps we won't, but the next generation will.'

'*I* did.'

'To quote Aaron, Mister Packer, "You weren't aware."'

'OK, OK,' I held my hands. 'I'd like a glass of water. This resurrection stuff is exhausting.'

'I'll get it.' Margie left the room.

'Well, Ozzie – friend Ozzie! – what now?'

'Correct me if I'm wrong, Mister Packer, but I believe the next move is up to you.'

'Terrorising *is* illegal, you realise.'

'I imagine that with ample proof these . . . caprices might be considered indictable offences.'

'As their spokesman, Ozzie . . .'

'Oh, my dear, no, Mister Packer, you flatter me. I'd never assume to be their spokesman. A legal advisor, yes.'

'Then, as their legal advisor . . .'

'I cannot and will not advise you.' He gave me that benign smile just as Margie returned with the water.

I gulped loudly. Margie smiled. The kitten jumped on to the bed. It felt good to be alive.

'All right, Margie, what do you think?' I asked. 'What do we do now?'

She shook her head. 'Whatever you want.'

'Whatever . . . ?'

She looked frightened. 'Don't . . . don't do anything more, Daddy. Please?'

'Little lady, there is one thing I value more than the fate of the world. My own neck. And that's more than I can say for some groups I know. As a history freak, you know all too well there have been movements, revolutions, wars and terrorising since the beginning of time. I have no further intention of stopping or starting any idiots who want to waste their lives on causes. They face futility. And that's been made abundantly clear on every page of recorded history. In short, I'd like a quick dip in the ocean off Malibu to wash myself clean of this whole mess. Please tell Aaron the world is his, but if he ever comes near our beach house, I'll shoot him on sight.'

'There's one problem, Mister Packer.'

'Just one?'

'Saddleford's gone to Aaron. Wants him to get the pictures back, by any means. Or he'll stop co-operating.'

'Then I'll go to Aaron.'

'To what end?'

'To assure him I will have nothing further to do with his club and school politics. He can have the goddamned pictures and good riddance.' Both Margie and Ozzie looked at me peculiarly, a tinge of disbelief. 'Hey, really. I mean it. I've had it. Jesus, what do you two want, an affidavit?'

Ozzie smiled and patted my hand lightly. 'I'm glad I was able to be of some help here. I was just dropping Margie off after going over a brief with her. I'll be on my way.'

'Thank you, Ozzie.'

'Not at all.'

Margie walked him to the door. There were some mumbled words. I was still beyond caring. When she came back, the kitten was nuzzling my hand. 'Nice kitten. What time is it?'

'Eleven.'

'Better get some sleep.'

'You sure you're all right now?'

'Better than before. Better tomorrow.'

'When do you want to go home?'

'Tomorrow. But I'll wait until tomorrow to decide.'

She hugged me and went to the door. She stopped and turned around. 'Daddy?'

'Yes.'

'Please don't go to the film showing Monday night.'

I tried to see her face, but she'd turned the light off. The silhouette was expressionless.

'Trouble?'

'I . . . I think so, I'm not sure.'

'How come you don't know so?'

'Because Aaron's changed his mind about something. He won't tell any of us.'

'That's a bad chink in the armour, sweetheart. Once you start being divided, it has a way of snowballing.'

'I know. I know . . .'

'Something I did?'

'I'm not sure. Perhaps something you didn't do.'

'I'm not sure either . . . about Monday.'

'I . . . I'd rather go home now than take the chance.'

'I know. We'll see. Get a good night's sleep.'

She shut the door partially. The living-room light went out. I *was* sure about Monday. I'd be there. But I wasn't ready to say it out loud. To anyone. I was even afraid to say it to myself.

2

Saturday I stayed home in bed; not that the drugs were still overly active in some residual capacity, just that I felt emotionally and physically hung over. At midday, I called Sylvia to say I'd drop by at some time the next afternoon, providing her Sunday wasn't booked. The conversation was surprisingly bland. At one point I assured her my interest was purely academic, that I was no longer to be considered a participant, and that she should go ahead and act independently, contacting any authorities of friends she might feel could be of help. I apologised. It was no longer my war. Her reaction was mixed – a certain disappointment, yet not at all what I'd anticipated – and a hint of relief, which I must say came as a surprise. So much so, that I became suspicious.

I then called Saddleford at home to say I'd be resigning at the end of the semester. He issued some hollow regrets. In passing, he mentioned the initiation of a new programme involving student teachers. Amy Witt and Peter Robinson would probably be able to handle a class in film techniques the following semester.

'What about Aaron?' I asked.

'He declined. Said he wouldn't be back.'

'Any reason?'

'None.'

'Odd.' I felt disappointed. As if I'd somehow failed to reach the unreachable. I'd gone through a war and had nothing to show for it.

That evening I bought a paper, a new bottle of scotch and returned to bed. Margie fixed dinner, and we played two games of chess. I chalked up my losses to convalescence, but she knew better. By 10 I was feeling fully recovered and ready for a good night's sleep.

*

I arrived at Sylvia's just after four on Sunday. The sky had become overcast and a thin, stinging sleet had begun to fall. Her fire was blazing, and Betty Sue had a drink in my hand before I could sit down. It was good to feel comfortable again.

'What happened, Matt?'

'What happened what?'

'Why are you backing out? You never struck me as one to give up easily.'

'Hey,' I reached over and touched her hand. 'How are you, the inside you?'

'Hey,' she smiled. 'All right. A little shaky, but better than Tuesday.' She looked down.

I scanned the walls, the painting over the fireplace, the myriad of objects scattered about the room in standard, acceptable-marriage collage: wedding picture, anniversary clock, paintings of the children and pristine, cutglass bud vases. I was seeing microphones, Nikons and pressure-sensitive plates. It was a stage set for self-consciousness.

'Ordinarily I don't give up, Sylvia. It's very simple. They're playing for keeps. I'm not. The future of the world isn't that important to me. *Margie's* future is.' I shrugged. 'What more can I say? I'm sorry.'

'So whatever's going to happen, you've decided to let it happen.'

'I didn't have much to say about Hiroshima and Vietnam either. We survived.'

She tapped the ice with a fingernail. 'Probably just as well. I think I understand.'

'No, I'm not sure you do. But, that's OK, too. What are you going to do now?'

'Let it go, I suppose.' She didn't look up.

'Sylvia, listen, I'm no hero. Grandstand plays bore me. I'm more interested in sticking around to be a father to Margie, than getting wiped out and leaving her with the memory of a mediocre martyr.'

'I gather you assume those are your only options.'

'Those are my only options. I guarantee it.'

'What happened, Matt? Something awful must have happened.'

I sipped my drink, put it down and leaned forward. 'I got the shit scared out of me.'

'Aaron?'

'Indirectly.'

'Always indirectly, isn't it,' she said quietly and stood up and got her purse from the cocktail table. She removed two pieces of paper and handed them to me. They were charred. 'I found these in the basement fireplace yesterday. Aaron burned both his book and the script. This was all that remained. Doesn't mean anything to me. I thought . . . I just thought you might want to see them. Do the names mean anything to you?'

It was a casting sheet and character description. 'Possibly.' The type that remained legible read as follows:

Sylvia Farrow: Dona Maria. An idolatrous love for her son. Cold and intellectual. Alcholic. A 'let me live now, let me begin again' kind of woman.

Michael Farrow: Esteban. 'I am alone, alone, alone.'

Bill Kasko: Brother Juniper. Love of God never waned even as he burned to death.

Peggy Kasko: Pepita. No life of her own, not even her death.

Gabe Saddleford: Uncle Pio. A woman's maid, errand boy and coiffeur. Always near beautiful women, of whom he was always in the best and worse sense, the worshipper. A ruse. Tormented.

Aaron Farrow: Jamie. Would anxiously estimate the approach of a cloud.

Matthew Packer: Captain Alvarado, the traveller. Blackened and cured by all weathers. He had one daughter: 'It sometimes seems to me that she is away upon a voyage and that I shall see her again.'

My crossed-out name struck me as peculiar. I didn't know whether to feel relieved or victimised. On the next page was a quotation:

> Universal experience and eternal return. Everything that happened might happen anywhere, and will happen again.
>
> – Malcolm Cowley
> *Saturday Review* 10/6/56

'Possibly. I think these are the characters from *The Bridge of San Luis Rey*. Not sure. Haven't read the book in twenty years. Where did you say you found these?'

'In the basement. The recreation room.'

'Mind if I take a look?'

'Not at all.'

When we entered the room, the stench was pungent enough to close my throat, a cross between urine and formaldehyde. 'Good God, what is it?'

'I don't know . . . I don't know.' Her voice trailed off.

She wandered about the room slowly, absently, speaking in fragments, as if she were leading me on a tour through the museum of her mind.

'I like to wander through the house, Matt. Like the commander, I suppose,' she smiled self-consciously. 'Into attic closets where I can touch the loneliness. Where I find ancient clothes with my father's smell. And my mother's warmth.' She turned to face me. 'It's like a reunion, in a way. Cameos and closed-eyed dolls. Browned letters from my grandmother. A pearl hat pin from sunday school. A button box. I laugh a little, cry a little . . . you know. There is so very much past, Matt, and so very little future.'

'If you choose to look at it that way.'

'Is there a choice?' She began walking again, trailing her fingers across the furniture. 'This room . . . I don't like this room, its insistence on maleness. Emerald green of pool table, walnut brown of panelling. Ox blood-red of leather chairs. All male. There's a presence here – do you feel it? Something new and foreboding.' She continued without waiting for my reply. 'Something of Aaron and Robert.

'I come down here because this is where they've been spending their time. This is the auditorium where they'll show a section of the film. I'm afraid to see it. Different now, Matt, this room.' She turned to look at me. 'It has a consciousness – self-protective, threatening. That smell, sickly. It burns my eyes. Something's wrong. It's not like Aaron. He's feeling pursued. Otherwise he wouldn't have burned his books. He's afraid of something. You must have found a key.'

'Not that I'm aware of. All right if I have a look around?'

'Please.'

I touch the cement around the massive fireplace. Still not dry. Above, a picture of hunting dogs and dead quail limp from their mouths. I try to remove it from the wall. Firm. Then it opens, hinged on one side like a medicine cabinet. Behind, another eye, blue and deep. It feels alive. I close the picture quickly, glance around. Other pictures in the room. How many cameras? Why are they here? What the hell are they looking for?

I cross the room, absently running my fingers along the back of the couch. It is moist. I stop. A choking smell. Dizzying. On my hands. Now burning.

Sylvia moves to my side, touches the couch. 'What is it?' she whispers.

'I don't know.'

Suddenly the door of the room slams behind us. I involuntarily rush to it, grab the handle and turn. It opens, no one beyond. I turn around and look at the windows.

One open, the sound of wind breathing through the window well.

Sylvia comes to the door and removes my hand from the knob. 'It's new, Matt. He's replaced the original.'

'Who?'

'Aaron . . . perhaps Robert.'

'How do you know?'

'Must be . . . must be.'

We move to the outer hall as the door again begins to close, more quickly now. It slams. We are outside. It is just the wind on the other side, just the wind.

Standing there. Sylvia in front of the door, close to it, touching it. She speaks as if it would hear, as if it were an extension of Aaron. 'Whatever he is, Matt whatever he devises, is also of me.'

'Not necessarily.'

'If there is fault, it is mine as well, if there is good, it is mine to share.'

I put my hands on her shoulders, turn her around. 'You're not making sense, Sylvia,' I say gently.

'There's more money in this house than can be spent in the world, Matt.' She smiles quickly, her eyes glassy. 'But not enough to buy back a button. Aaron is my legacy, Matt, my career. My statement. He is what I leave behind for the world to remember me by, isn't that cruel? But it is just. And I don't know, will never know, what I did. I can't leave him behind . . . ' She looks up and smiles again. 'I have a box of buttons, did I tell you about the buttons?'

'You mentioned them.'

'They are my closest gifts. And there's no one to receive them. My mother was killed. In a car accident. My father driving. I was asleep in the back seat. He put me in a boarding school. So he wouldn't be reminded. He wouldn't come to watch me in plays. He wouldn't let me write. I'd come home for Christmas, and he'd go to bed early. That's why I like to stand between their clothes and shut my eyes and breathe. It's the closest I can be. It's warm up there.'

'Let's go back upstairs, Sylvia.'

She started up the stairs. 'If I could just be comfortable with my withouts.'

Once back in the living room Sylvia sat down opposite me and picked up her drink. 'Enough of that,' she laughed nervously, casting off the episode like a bad weather report. 'I'm sorry. I get carried away.

'Can you stay?'

'Yes . . . ' I hesitated.

'*Will* you stay?'

'I'd rather do the Saturday we missed yesterday. We may need it after tomorrow night.'

'You mean you're coming?'

'No,' I lied.

'Just as well. It's only a preview of one segment. He'll be shooting at the same time.'

'Movie within a movie.'

' "Curiouser and curiouser." '

'I'm clean out of curiosity, thank you.'

'I doubt that. And anyway, after tomorrow night, they're through shooting.'

'I think I'll be able to stand the suspense.' I got up to leave. 'Good night, Gilda.'

'Gilda?'

'An old Rita Hayworth role.' I glanced ceilingward and whistled, went to the front door.

I felt sick to my head on the way home. I don't like to fib and appear to be something I'm not. My therapist in L.A. had put it best: 'Lying fucks up another person's sense of reality.' And Sylvia's appeared almost irretrievable, without any further contributions from me. I labelled my present falsehood as precautionary. If I was very lucky, the libbers couldn't read minds.

I would keep Aaron after school the next day and try my damndest to make him talk. Nothing, including physical violence, would allow him to escape that classroom. I was still bigger than he was. It was high time for the proverbial spanking, intellectual or otherwise. Within Aaron's oceanic brilliance had to be an atoll of common sense. If not, I'd try to interpret the language of a psychotic kid and pass the translation over to the police. Either way, I was looking forward to an orderly finish.

3

The sleet turned to snow flurries on Monday. It hadn't snowed as early as September twenty-sixth in fifty-two years. Radiators clanked throughout the school. Attention spans were short, imaginations packing snowballs and sledding. As three in the afternoon approached, I became more apprehensive.

'He's just a kid,' I kept telling myself.

'Yeah,' I corrected. 'Just a kid who can wipe you out with a telephone call.'

The libbers were more preoccupied than the others, that night's preview being the prime object of their distraction. When the bell finally rang, the children gathered their books and filed towards the door. I was about to summon Aaron's attention, but noticed he had remained behind.

The door closed. There was silence except for the radiators, crescendoing from pings to clangs, then diminishing to subdued hissing. Aaron was still, watching me stack my notes and papers. The light was penumbral, the exclusive wardrobe of deep, winter days.

'Thought it was time we talked, Mister Packer.'

I was dumbfounded. No one can convince me he hadn't read my mind. 'I'd been thinking the same thing, Aaron. Let's do it.'

The roaring of hopped-up cars skidding out of the parking lot rattled the windows.

'Where do we start?' he asked, perfectly composed, hands folded in his lap.

'Be my guest.' We had now advanced our pawns.

'I have photographs of you, Packer.'

I nodded once. 'So?'

'Do you know of what?'

'I know what of.' I rested my feet on the desk.

'That doesn't bother you?'

'That doesn't bother me.' It would be a long match. 'For *me*.'

'Then for whom?'

'For your mother.'

'It has nothing to do with my mother.'

'It has everything to do with your mother.'

'If you wish, Mister Packer, we are both quite capable of obscuring the real purpose of this entire dialogue with psychological allusions.'

Boy's voice from outside: 'Hey, Bob, we're goin' over to Valerie's.'

'I thought the purpose of psychology was to clarify.'

'In the right hands.' His black eyes riveted through the blond fineness shadowing his forehead.

'Psychology aside, then, your mother was hurt. To put it mildly. That means nothing to you?'

'No. It only means she has *allowed* herself to be hurt. She is seeing only through her eyes: her hurt, her humiliation, her disappointments, her life. No one else matters.'

'When you really get down to it, Aaron, isn't that true of us all?'

'No, Mister Packer, it isn't,' he smiled slightly. It was time for the Queen's initial move. 'That's a point most people reach early in life. With age it simply becomes more firmly embedded. Very few go beyond. There are those few.'

'For God's sake, Aaron, it's your *mother*!'

He shook his head. 'It's another human being, Mister

Packer. We come through you, we don't belong to you.'

He got up and walked to the window. His voice became soft and distant, as if muffled in the falling snow.

'We are not beholden to you. We are not in your debt. We owe you no allegiance.' He turned to face me. 'We won't spend the remainder of our lives apologising for whatever pain and discomfort we may have caused because we were growing, because we were young. In essence, that apology is fulfilled when we rear children of our own.

'We have much to learn from other species, Mister Packer. When the fawn is ready, he is nudged from the thicket. When the wings of a bird are ready, he is pushed from the nest. Not the man-child. He is imprisoned, living with probation officers who occupy positions titled "mother" and "father" to legitimise the power structure. If he is good, he reflects the good of the parents. But, if he is bad, he is the recipient of their shame, for surely they are not bad. Never is it the man-child's own good or bad, for his own better or worse. He is a reflection, nothing more.'

As he returned to his seat, I leaned forward on the desk. 'And so in the name of eatablishing self-image, for the purpose of destroying that reflection, you justify any and all means to accomplish those ends: blackmail, injury, terrorising, killing.'

Two snowballs thumped the windows in quick succession. The radiators clanked in irritation.

'Mister Packer,' Aaron smiled, 'does that make us so very different from the adult community?'

He again folded his hands. At this moment there was no significant difference between Aaron and other boys his age. Except for the way he looked at me. It was the first time I'd seen the look, on Aaron or any other child – on any other human being.

I considered resigning the game, because it was obvious he had lost interest in continuing the competition. Or, more likely, that he had never intended to compete in the first place, calling, as the look urged, that I abandon my accustomed stance and meet with him on an equal and neutral ground.

'Don't you see it, Mister Packer? I'm just like you. There is no young and old, good and evil, man and woman. Those are just wedges from the same orange, words from the same language, seasons of the same year. I am old, you are young. You've been twelve; I've been twelve. Will you tell me I haven't been forty? Would I tell you you've never been my twelve? Should we use the same yardstick to measure years and awareness? And why is it that mankind finds it so very necessary to measure at all? Simply because without some method of measuring, a man would have to accept that he is a fraction of three billion, rather than a one of one. He finds this intolerable. Somehow he must be just a little better than everyone else: older, stronger, brighter, bigger, more attractive, more talented.

'Oh, we have great equalisers: speed limit fifty-five, no parking between five an seven a.m.; five tons of grain-per-acre limitations; set your clocks ahead, set your clocks back; tobacco legal, marijuana illegal; no nude bathing in public places, otherwise people will come from miles around to gawk, and then complain to the police about indecent exposure.

'Then we have the inequalities: vote at twenty-one, drink at eighteen; retire at sixty-five, drive at sixteen; kill abroad, but don't kill at home.

'A year ago in Des Moines, Iowa, a municipal committee endorsed the city's removal of two home-made headstones that a young mother and father on welfare had placed on the graves of their two infant children. It was the committee's considered opinion that the headstones detracted from the appearance of the city's "show place" cemetery. They removed the eyesores and passed an ordinance that permitted only granite or bronze headstones, certainly within the buying power of the young couple's more affluent neighbours.

'Two years ago in California, a Doctor David Rosenhan and seven of his colleagues from Stanford University posed as patients concerned about their mental health. They were admitted to mental hospitals, diagnosed as insane, treated for two months, and released – not as cured, mind you – but merely as improved or "in remission", as their doctors reported. During the time they were treated, the only people who suspected they weren't really crazy were their fellow patients. Thirty-five of the hundred-and-eighteen authentic inmates challenged them. "You're *not* crazy!' they insisted. "You're a journalist or a professor. You're checking up on the hospital." But the staff never fell for it. One nurse, observing that one of the pseudo-patients was taking regular notes, saw it as a symptom of a crazy compulsion. "Patient engages in writing behaviour", she wrote in her report.

'How about the two guys back in nineteen-seventy-three, who rescued a pig swimming fifteen miles off shore from Miami? The pig squealed its delight, but it was killed the same day by the united States Department of Agriculture, because it was feared the pig might be carrying a dangerous disease. No verification tests were performed, before or after.

'How about the naked girl who was washed ashore outside of Melbourne, Australia last year. Her left arm had been severed. Later, the police found a clay figure hanging in a tree. The left arm was missing. They deducted the girl had been a victim of a sacrificial witchcraft killing.

'True, Mister Packer, all true. I have a file a foot thick of such items. Sane or insane, Mister Packer, good or evil? Are you presumptuous enough to judge? Justified or unjustified, Mister Packer, life or death? Will you define? Do you possess such omnipotence?

'Let me ask you a question. Please accept that it is asked

with sincerity, not condescension. Can you get your mind around this? First you have to take it for granted that your mother and father are going to be dead; and then you must accept that your children are going to take it for granted that you are going to be dead. It is an example of thinking in jump-time. A form of psychic teleportation. It is to develop the ability to see yourself at the age of six feeding a swan, and at seventy-two feeding the pigeons on a park bench, no matter what age you are when you see.

'When you are able to see in this way, when you grasp that your life is in the raindrop falling into a puddle creating momentary ripples, you are prepared to take the next step. You *must* take the next step; there is no choice, because you perceive the step beyond*that* as lucidly as you see and hear me at this moment in this room and once seen, it cannot be denied. It is axiomatic.

'The intermediary step is in the protection of a right, and that is the one and only right we must all have: I am allowed, you are allowed, to come and go and do as our inclinations direct, as long as it isn't injurious to others. The only justification of injury is in the preservation of that right. Those who would inhibit or threaten that right either can't see or won't see. Their reasons come in various phrases and volumes, but the motivation is essentially the same: Their yardstick has been violated. Deemed impotent. They are no longer older, stronger, brighter, because somehow, for a reason ostensibly incoherent to them, the dissenters have walked away, peacefully, without rancour. Yet the tyrants are insulted. So they must pursue. They must have their pound of flesh. Because to renounce one man's way, particularly without a clear vision of another, is heretical.

'The step beyond is some distance away in terms of years, but not far at all considering the relative youth of our planet. It is a place where man will accept himself as a species first and as unique within that species second. Ego will occupy a subordinate position, the nurturing and care of mankind, regardless of boundaries, will be primary. It is only at this point that we will be able to prepare ourselves for the next evolutionary phase, because the prerequisite for that stage is the same as having attained it: the linkage of consciousness. As of now, we are but particles. Can you imagine the beauty of that whole?'

'Do you honestly believe that, Aaron?'

'How can you honestly consider the otherwise, Mister Packer? To do so would be to deny the lessons of anthropology. It's inevitable. How long it will take is up to us.'

'How do you define "the otherwise"?'

'As spiritual stasis.'

'I'm sorry, Aaron. It's either beyond me or something inside me refuses to accept it.'

'Because there are too few words, Mister Packer. Or, perhaps, too many. Certainly the right words are not available.'

'Possibly.'

'Listen with your hands, Mister Packer not to the sounds, but to the pictures. Hear with all of you, but also listen and hear with me. It is the only way. I . . . I want you to understand, Mister Packer, I want you to believe. I don't know why it's important, but right now, in this room, it's very important. Five minutes from now, later tonight, it may not be important at all.

'I'm afraid of death – we are afraid of death. You are afraid of living too full; we have lived too full. You feel cold, I feel cold; we both know what warmth is. It goes by different names, but we both sense the same warmth.

'I see feathers falling, standing still on the air, bursting from a pillow. You see a roll of dust tumbling along the floor and think broom.

'I see a moth trapped on a day window, trying to reach the sun. I let him out. You see a fly and think swatter.

'Ahh, listen, though! *I* see a girl with white smiles and orange fragrance. I think beautiful. *You* see a woman with lovely breasts and a ballet walk. You think beautiful. We are seeing from the same place. Do you hear?

'All is now. I went to a small town once. It is with me now. I sit on a stone wall. I am alone. I pick an apple from the tree above. As I feel the wall, taste the apple, listen to the locusts, I see a couple lying in a green, swaying field, having a picnic. Then I hear a clumsy bell, and a black goat comes nodding out from behind a red shed. From the other direction, I hear many bells, and when I turn to look, I see a shepherd with hundreds of sheep funnelling from a shallow canyon. I take a bite of my apple. Then I hear another bell, a deeper and slower bell. I look down, and there below me is a church; people in black are coming through the front door in slow twos and threes. In the narrow street is a hearse drawn by a horse with a man in black holding the bridle. His hair is white.

'A second bell joins the first and they play back and forth with each other, one trying to get ahead of the other, then laughing and falling back to let the other have the fun of ringing first. A coffin is carried from inside and placed in the hearse by twenty-four white hands. They gently lift, gently push, gently close the back door.

'A third bell joins the first two, and you should see them play; separate, together, all the thousands of ways three bells can play together – fast-slow, soft-loud, happy-sad.

'The man in the white hair climbs into a seat above the horse, puts on his black top hat, and jiggles the reins. The people watch.

'Now a fourth and fifth bell, higher in tone, join the game. A sixth, seventh and eighth, and the sky bursts with bells flying north and east, valley floor to mountain top, climbing up and tumbling down. And the couple and the black goat with his clumsy bell and the shepherd and the hundreds of sheep with their carillon playing and the people crying black, people feeling goodbye, people holding people – all was happy, all was beautiful. And in that one moment in a single day of my life, I saw *all* of life happening at once, with its own orchestra booming for everyone to hear, for all to see.

'I'd finished my apple, so I just sat there shaking my head, laughing and crying, laughing and crying. I would have sung, but I can't sing worth a damn.

'Mister Packer, I could have died that day without having to learn anything else for the rest of my life. I understood. Everyone was doing the same thing! Everyone, at some time in their life, would be doing what everyone else was doing. Everyone as one. And if ever, ever, we all do *one* thing together, *all* at the same time, can you imagine how beautiful that would be?'

'Yes,' I said, 'it would be.'

'Prodigies die young, Mister Packer. I know what I am. A little freaky in your language. I don't know how to measure young any more. Perhaps now . . . perhaps now you might have some difficulty?

'I don't want you to come to the preview tonight, Mister Packer. It's not that it's you. It's what I'm hoping you'll become. Right now is just not the right time. Do you understand what I'm saying when I say, "not the right time"?'

'I'm not sure. I'm sorry, Aaron.'

'I mean there are things I must do, and there are things you must do before it's time for certain things to happen. When the time is right, you will know. And you will know that I will know.'

'How will that happen?'

'Don't waste time watching the ugliness. Don't measure it's closeness. Because as long as you watch and measure, you can't see.' He smiled. 'It happens, Mister Packer.'

'I'll . . . I'll have to think about it.'

'It'd be simpler if you didn't.'

'I can't do that, Aaron.'

'You won't do that, Mister Packer?'

'I guess you could put it that way.'

'Please don't say you won't try.'

'All right.'

He went to the door and turned around, as if there were more he wanted to say, as if more needed being said. 'I enjoyed this. I don't want you to think that because you didn't say much you didn't talk to me . You did. You said a great deal. I want you to know I appreciate that. It's not often I have the opportunity. I wish there were time to know you better. But I feel I know you well. And there will be a time when you know me well.'

He smiled openly. 'I'm acting childish again, right? Good night, Mister Packer.'

FIVE

1

'Good night, Aaron.'

The door closed behind him. The car noises were gone. The light was darker. And Aaron would have said, 'The dark is lighter.' The radiators had stopped. Somewhere in the heart of the school someone had cut off the circulation.

I sat back, exhausted. I hadn't said more than ten words, yet I was as drained as if I'd just hosted a live, twenty-four-hour telethon. My head ached. I chuckled to myself with a giddiness of relief. It must've been the strain. I hadn't worked so hard trying to understand someone since I'd called it quits with my wife. I also felt lighter. Perhaps I hadn't understood all of it, but I'd scored high enough to see a glimpse and follow a drift.

I respected him. Here I'd prepared for a father-son, prosecutor-defendant talk. The father-son intention had materialised, but I felt decidedly type-cast in the role of the son. Yet unlike many of my childhood (to use the word in our language) experiences with my own father, I felt I had learned something. I assumed the understanding would be forthcoming, probably in uneven doses. I understood enough at this moment to realise that further understanding wasn't in the far, too distant future.

I noticed my copy of Wilder's *Bridge of San Luis Rey* on the corner of my desk. I'd taken it from the library earlier. Did I understand enough *not* to read it? Did I understand enough to justify or at least rationalise Rod Angstrom, the Witts and the Kaskos? I decided I'd decide later, after my habitual, much needed scotch.

The smell of lamb greeted me as I entered the apartment. Margie'd outdone herself. The candles were lit on the table, a bottle of vintage Bordeaux was 'breathing' on the centrepiece.

'It's not my birthday, is it?'

Margie appeared from the kitchen, all smiles. 'I don't know. You tell me.'

'Oh, please! No double-entendres or innuendoes. It's been an exhausting afternoon.'

'Your talk with Aaron?'

'How'd you know about . . . never mind.'

'That's what I meant by birthday.'

'Come on, Margie, I realise that! I'm not all that thick, you know. Let's just say "I'm in labour", to use your language.'

The smile left. 'Didn't go well, huh?'

'It went very well. *Too* well. I'm confused all over again. He's . . . he's a very thoughtful boy.'

'Boy?'

'All right! Person, human being, whatever fits in with your vocabulary.'

'What'd he say?'

I poured my drink. Fast. Sipped. 'I don't know if I could even begin to tell you. He's very convincing . . . he's very convincing. Particularly since I don't even know what I'm convinced about.'

'Hmmm,' she smiled again. 'Couldn't have been all that bad, after all.'

'Bad is not good, good is not bad, bad is not bad, good is not good. Jesus! How do you guys plan to get through life always thinking that way?'

'By thinking that way.'

I sat down and cracked the book to the first page, the title page. I'd never liked Wilder, except for *Our Town.*

'No time for that,' Margie shouted from the kitchen. 'It's time to eat.'

It was a dinner I'd remember for my old age (by our language). Though the food was brilliant, it couldn't compare to the conversation. It was as if a veil had been lifted. I'd been to the same shrink she had. We talked about things like swimming and Mozart, hot peanuts and Hemingway, the youthfulness of Monet's last canvases. The occasion, for whatever reason, was special enough for Margie to enjoy the wine. I suddenly felt like a parent-chauvinist pig; she should have wine every night if she felt like it. No, goddammit, she shouldn't!

By the time we'd finished with the chocolate eclairs and coffee, it was eight-thirty, half an hour later than the preview had been scheduled to begin. In arriving late, could I convince Aaron I'd wrestled with my mind? And his reasoning had lost out? Or whatever? I pretended I hadn't looked at my watch as I sat down to read Wilder's first page.

I read the first line and slammed the book shut. Whatever Aaron's definition of 'it happens' was, I couldn't be sure. I was only sure of my own. Similar or not, I knew I had to get over to that preview as fast as I could. I suddenly knew what Aaron had planned for this night, and it would be beyond the understanding and comprehension of everyone I knew. At that moment it was still quite beyond my own.

The snow had stopped falling as I raced and skidded down Colby Road. No one had chains. The scene was out of Charlie Chaplin – dozens of cars swerving drunkenly in all directions.

Sirens in the distance came from all directions, telling me I was too late; I drove faster, refusing to believe it. Too late is not too late. Is that how Aaron would think it? Or would it be 'Nothing is ever too late or too soon?'

Parked, snow-covered cars like hippopotamus ghosts. Rainbowed street lamps. The sirens come closer. I turn left on to Bellevue Boulevard, street of mansions. My windshield filled with bloodshot eyes. The fire engines, police cars and ambulances huddle together in the distance. 'It can't happen,' I think. But then, 'It must happen.'

The street had been cordoned off, two blocks from the house. I parked and raced the remaining distance. A crowd of nearly a hundred had already gathered. I took one look. I knew I was too late. It had already happened.

Flames poured from every window of the house. The bronze plaque pulsed in the orange glow as if titling the episode, 'The Bridge'. Fire hoses snaked across the glazed snow towards the house. The sycamores shimmered and dripped in the heat, the manicured privet smoked and burst into pockets of flame. Arcs of water from the hoses steamed in the cold air and surrounded the house in garlands. A snowman near the front door appeared shellacked. The nose was gone. An eye dropped to the ground as I watched. The black bars criss-crossing the basement windows stencilled themselves like cattle brands into the orange body of the house. The viewing was to have taken place behind those bars.

Squinting from the heat, the firemen stood at least fifteen yards back from the blaze, their faces appearing to melt as they reflected the advances and retreats of the flames.

I took a few steps forward to cross the street and was stopped by a policeman. Ambulance attendants leaned against their vehicles smoking cigarettes, watching.

'But, I've got to get over there.'

'Who're you kidding, Mister? You'd be fried in five minutes.'

I saw a fireman next to an engine, keeping an eye on the pump gauges. I ran up to him. 'Jesus, get your men inside. There's people in there.'

'Not any more.'

'Did anyone get out?'

'Not that I know of.'

'Who would know?'

He shrugged, bored. 'Ask around.'

'How did it start?'

'Never got close enough to find out. Started in that

bottom room with the bars. That's all we know for sure. Went up like a Christmas tree.'

I frantically wedged my way through the crowd; shadowed bodies, orange faces, the smell of wet wool. Frightened whispers.

'Good way to keep warm,' says a nervous lady.

A familiar face, where's a familiar face? A dog lifted his leg at a mound of snow and trotted off down the street.

Coming to the end of the crowd, I was able to get across the street just opposite the house next door. Looking back I could see the spectators, frozen together, eyes locked forward, breaths held. A person in over-sized ear muffs suddenly pointed at the blaze. I followed the direction of the arm, looked back. A boy stood in the front yard, alone, hands in pockets, staring through the line of firefighters. He turned slightly and looked up into the trees. Was it Aaron? Looked like Aaron.

'Aaron!' I shouted into the noise. Then I recognised the profile, the smaller stature. 'Robbie!' I yelled. 'Robbie! Over here.'

Either he didn't hear me or his concentration was directed elsewhere. I followed his gaze into the trees as he began to motion with his right arm. What I saw drained all the remaining warmth from my body, as if Camilla had slipped a new, untried drug into the wine, and the entire orange, black and white Hallowe'en tableau was a hallucination.

Ski masks, melting snowmen , steaming faces, and there, there, wedged into the crook of a tree, was Chris Kasko, eye pressed into the socket of the sixteen-millimetre Arriflex camera, panning the windows of the bottom floor, stopping, setting new position, zooming into flame. I looked at the windows, each in turn, forcing my eyes to penetrate the heat. A face? An outline? A blackened hand gripping a metal bar? A human cry above the roar? Or imagination. I couldn't be sure.

I followed Robbie's gaze, watched his arm again give a signal. From the bushes on the other side of the driveway jumped Peter Robinson, a Super-eight camera in hand. He dropped to one knee at a position twenty feet closer to the house, and flipped the on-switch, his new camera position set. Then, from the foot of the driveway, Amy Witt, carrying a new magazine of film, running to Peter; followed by Camilla Saddleford, the Nagra sound equipment slung from her shoulder, microphone in hand, picking up the sound effects, the orders shouted from one red helmet to the other, the murmurs of the bewildered crowd.

Nausea waved through me. Dizziness and weakness. I reached for the trunk of a tree for support. Closed eyes, open again, the children still there. 'Oh, God,' I whispered, 'Oh, my God.'

I watched as Robbie backpedalled away from the house to a location closer to me. 'Robbie!' I screamed, my voice breaking. He turned, saw me. Looked down, didn't move. Then slowly, deliberately, walked towards me cutting black holes into the new snow. He stopped a few feet in front of me and looked up. He didn't speak, just stood there waiting for me to say something. The nausea swept by, my throat remaining tight. I watched for something to read on his face. It was illegible.

'Who was in there, Robbie?' Staccato words.

'People,' he answered simply.

'*Names*, Robbie!' The anger rushed out. 'Names! Not your goddamned philosophy.'

'Aaron said you'd . . . '

'Some other time, Robbie! Who was in there?'

'The Saddlefords.'

He stopped, as if that should be enough to say it all.

'Who else?'

'The Kaskos.'

I looked beyond Robbie to Camilla Saddleford, close to a hose recording the rush of water; to Chris Kasko, still slotted in his tree. I was dreaming. They had concocted a potion to rid the body of souls.

'Who else?' I asked, staring into the darkening window.

'My father. My mother.'

Sylvia, my God, Sylvia. Perhaps a kinder place, a place where thirty-eight and seventy-two and twelve are only numerals and not years. What she had said at the Kaskos' party kept repeating: 'I keep hoping it'll be different somewhere else.'

I remembered the clipping from the New York paper, the two-alarm blaze, the man called William Penn Robinson. I looked back to the house. The windows transformed into caves as the fire abated under the constant streams of a dozen hoses. Worship of the phoenix? It would fit.

'That's what happened to Peter Robinson's father, isn't it, Robbie? Same thing.'

I felt moisture under my collar; the waste, the waste, I would never understand all of it. I couldn't take any more.

'I want to talk to Aaron, Robbie. Right now. I want to see Aaron.' I looked around the front yard. 'You tell Aaron I want to see him. Here. Where is he?'

'With them, Mister Packer,' he stared at me.

'With who?'

'Them in the house.' He didn't take his eyes from me.

I shook my head. 'He's not in that house, Robbie!'

'No,' he looked at his shoes, crunched some snow, 'No, I suppose he isn't any more.'

I crouched in front of him, took his shoulders. 'Robbie, *why*? For God's sake, why?'

'He said he was pretty sure you'd know.'

'Well, I don't!' I shouted, shaking him. A glimpse of the note I'd found with the news clipping: 'Now he's got to go with the rest. As might *I*, as might *I*.'

'I'm very sorry you don't, Mister Packer. I do. It's the way it is.'

'It *isn't* the way it is!' I could feel his arms begin to tense, his eyes wavering as if I'd begun to shake him out of some hypnotic trance he'd been in. A look of panic, the beginning terror, of 'What if I'm wrong?' Then it was gone as quickly as it had appeared. The brown eyes were clear. His body relaxed. That same look I'd seen on Aaron earlier in the afternoon.

'I try not to be afraid of you, Mister Packer. Aaron said not to be afraid of you. Not to be afraid of anything. He said you would come around in time.'

'I won't be around to come around, Robbie.'

'It doesn't matter where you'll be. It'll happen anyway.'

'Oh, Christ, you sound like Aaron.'

'I hope so.' The first smile.

I looked down, took a deep breath, hoping a return to sanity wasn't too far off. Goddamn you, Aaron, goddamn you. It didn't have to be like this. Not like this.

As I looked again to the house, still disbelieving, Agatha Wickware and Margie were walking hurriedly towards us. Miss Wickware appeared a shambles; Margie looked plain frightened. The humanness of her response was my return to sense. The snow began to feel cold again.

'Margie called, Mister Packer. I would have come sooner but I go to bed at nine. I . . . I just couldn't get here any faster, the roads are iced, you know, and accidents every . . . Oh, my God, Mister Packer, what are we going to do? This is just . . . this is just impossible.'

I felt a tug on my sleeve. It was Robbie. I was struck by what a natural, childlike thing it was to do. He was much shorter than Aaron, had to look much higher.

'What is it, Robbie?'

'Aaron left a note for you, Mister Packer. Do you want it now? He asked me to give it to you.' He held it up to me.

I took the note. Looked at the handwriting on the envelope. The perfect printing. Aaron's trademark. My breath caught. I gritted my teeth. I'd lost someone. Someone I'd just learned to care for. Glanced at Margie.

Tears were streaming down her cheeks. She had known. She would also know of the one word on the envelope: 'Matt.'

I opened the flap and closed it. 'Where will you stay tonight, Robbie?'

He pointed at the envelope. 'It's in the note, Mister Packer.'

'And the others?'

'They have their homes, Daddy.' Margie blinking, holding together as best she could.

'They need rides. Miss Wickware?'

'Of . . . of course, Mister Packer. But . . . what about all this? What do we have to do?'

'Nothing, Miss Wickware. I think it's all been done. Nothing tonight. I'll call you tomorrow. We'll work something out then.'

The flames were gone. A few remaining flickers from deep inside. The new sound of steam. The now colour of black. The light was gone. The remaining faces glowed in headlamps and spinning red smears.

Miss Wickware's voice was quiet, as if somehow implying a secret from the children: 'Mister Packer, we just can't *leave* it this way. Something's got to be done. You know how kids are . . . '

'Yes, Miss Wickware, I' beginning to know how kids are. Which is why I think we should go home and get some sleep.'

What would Aaron have said? 'Today is yesterday, so there's no rush for tomorrow.'

'Tomorrow, Miss Wickware. We'll work it out then.'

'Very well.' Her voice was clipped as she started to walk away.

'Miss Wickware?'

'Yes,' she stopped and turned around.

'This . . . this has been a difficult night for everyone. There are feelings that are shown, and those that are hidden. I don't understand all of it. Neither do you. Let's take it slowly and patiently, shall we? Be as gentle as you can.'

She watched me a moment, then nodded. 'All right. I'll do the best I can. Should I take Robbie with me?'

'Not tonight, no.'

'I'll gather the others. Should I talk to the police?'

'No. I'll handle that before I leave.'

'If . . . there's anything else I can do, please call.'

'I will. Thank you.'

She walked off. The stride was purposeful. She called out, and from hollows of darkness the children appeared and followed, Camilla and Amy falling in beneath her arms, Chris and Peter trudging ahead of her, camera gear over their shoulders.

I opened the envelope and read in the half-light.

> DEAR MATT,
>
> Try not to be angry. Try not to be sad. As I mentioned, it is a way of seeing, and as it is with all seeing, the beholder is either rich or poor, warm or cold, here or, hopefully, some day there. Robbie is fine. I would like it if he would be with you, and you would be with him for the week-end. He will tell you of a house where we shall live. You understand my 'we'. Robbie will finish the film. I am not beyond hoping you will like it. See it through many eyes.
>
> Take care of Margie . . .

I looked down. She was watching me, the tears still fresh. She knew the words.

> Take care of Margie, as I know you shall. She is often sad when she should be happy. She soesn't know yet that being together never ends. Perhaps that's just girls though. I still haven't figured that one out.

Hope you enjoyed the dinner Margie and I planned. It was meant as a thank you for all your help. I chose the wine.

I'd like you to help us by helping others to understand. You are so close. We need your perspective, your reason. And so do they. You understand my 'they'.

If you choose 'the otherwise', I can accept that it's not time. You have your way to go, and you have given Margie the best part of you. As have I. We live together within her. Can you think of better friends?

LOVE, AARON

P.S. That damn moviola broke again.

When I looked up, the ambulance attendants had started their engines. It was time to go home. They would leave empty.

THE BRIDGE OF ERIEVIEW LAKE

Nicholas [illegible]
intimidated by [illegible]
The accusations [illegible]
that it was [illegible]
he would have [illegible]

I recounted [illegible]
resolve my feelings [illegible]
stood, and I didn't [illegible]
him. Considering [illegible]
lines were a [illegible]
of the film would [illegible]
so outraged [illegible]
appalled. Although [illegible]
particular scene [illegible]
controversial [illegible]

Inevitably [illegible]
The better [illegible]
actors, we [illegible]
literally explode [illegible]

Robin [illegible]
Heights HOD [illegible]
other chapters [illegible]
one would replace [illegible]

In [illegible]
the viewing [illegible]
brilliant [illegible]
beauty and [illegible]
continued the [illegible]
him. Well. [illegible]

Wednesday [illegible]
brunch [illegible]

1

Numbness settled in over the community. The adults functioned by rote. The children talked in hushed corners. The members of HOD worked feverishly to complete the film. It was as if Aaron had never left. Had he been around, he would have told us he never had.

I reconciled one internal war: I would never be able to resolve my feelings towards Aaron and HOD. I understood, and I didn't understand. I damned him and I loved him. Considering the attitudes of my contemporaries, I felt this was no mean accomplishment. I also knew that viewing the film would not bring me any closer to a personal resolution. I would be sympathetic, and I would be appalled. Aaron had taught me much, but one thing in particular stood out; I would never again be able to utilise conventional yardsticks.

The school board met and appointed a new principal. The police and fire departments had found no trace of arson, yet were hard pressed to explain why the house had literally exploded into flames. Relatives were notified.

Robbie was elected the new president of the Erieview Heights HOD, and his name immediately submitted to the other chapters to replace Aaron as national chairman. No one would replace Aaron as founder.

In Tuesday's mail was a note from Sylvia, written before the viewing. One paragraph stood out: 'The twist of the brilliant mind is in the flick of an eye; the distance between beauty and ugliness can be measured between the leap of a deer and the crack of a gun. That is why I cannot condemn him, Matt. The loss belongs to all of us. Yours, Gilda.'

Wednesday morning, following the necessary twenty-four-hour waiting period required by law, Robbie and

Peter insisted on returning to 'The Bridge' to examine what was left. I hadn't wanted them to go, but the registering of my disapproval was as far as I got.

That afternoon all of them took me to a musty, old house on Avonshire Road. Planted on the weed-strewn front lawn was a hand-stencilled sign: Erieview Heights Young People's Liberation House – Mother Chapter, Home of David. The sling was centred below the words. Once inside, I was introduced to two teenagers who had recently succeeded in getting their Emancipated Minor documents. They were busy cleaning up, moving in second-hand furniture.

'This is our new home,' Robbie explained. 'Chris, Amy and Camilla move in tomorrow.'

'How about you?'

'Is it all right?'

'I'd like to know how far I'd get if I said it wasn't.'

Margie squeezed my hand.

'Who's setting all this up?' I asked.

'Ozzie. He's also handling all that "Ward of the State" crap.'

'Lucky to have him.'

'He's talking about moving in. That would make him our oldest member.'

'You have no age limit?'

Robbie shook his head and looked exasperated. 'Mister Packer, is that all the further you've come?'

The following Wednesday, Martin Birdly, the new principal, rejected a request by the libbers that their film be shown a week later in the school auditorium. It was hastily decided that the premiere would be held in the living room of the Avonshire Road house.

The afternoon before the viewing, Margie told me I'd be the only adult in attendance. I wasn't apprehensive so much about what I would see, as I was about what I'd do after seeing.

Margie and I arrived five minutes late. The others had all been early or on time. The living room was festooned with children; the familiar chapter members and, I assumed, prospective inductees. To one side there was a refreshment table with cookies, cake, punch and beer. I was given a chair at the rear of the room. Margie joined the others. Before the lights went out I sensed a few sidelong glances, some outwardly friendly, some candidly hostile. They were seventy-five. I was one. I thought about Aaron. 'Seventy-six,' he would have corrected.

The room, dark, the whirr of the projector fan, the clockwise fan of count-downing numbers. Focus. 5 – 4 – 3 – 2 Black.

The room remains black, as does the screen. For at least half a minute. Subtly, far in the background, the sound begins a slow fade-in. First indistinguishable, it begins to define itself. It is laboured breathing, a woman in pain. The first title flashes on the screen:

THE END

The screen returns to black, but as the breathing becomes heavier and faster, a white pinpoint of light begins to iris-open at centre frame. The sound increases with the widening of the hole, the woman choking, on the verge of screams. As the black disappears off the edges of the frame, the screen fills with a pair of hands, rubber gloved, blood streaked. They reach on top of the lens, blotting out, momentarily. Then the room spins, floor, ceiling, walls nurses, hospital equipment. There is a slap as the room flips upside down; the first sensation and view of the world of a newborn baby. His first reaction: crying.

The helpless bleating continues during a dissolve to a long, unbroken surface of skin being panned in profile. The camera is so tight that, moving along the body, its clefts and contours give the impression of sand dunes, the body hair appearing as thin strands of pampas grass. The sound of the baby's cries is joined by wind, as the camera take us along this landscape – barren, unforgiving. We reach a hill and slowly I climb until, at the peak, we stop. The camera pushes tighter, tighter, fills the screen with nipple. As we again fade to black, the baby's crying stops, and we now hear the soft, yet ravenous sounds of nursing.

The sound diminishes and we begin a pull back, starting as tight on the breast as before, but now shot from an overhead angle. The woman's chest appears, then her face, but it is no longer the same breast, the same woman. It is a girl who smiles lasciviously into camera.

> *GIRL*: Did you like that?
> *MALE VOICE*: (OFF CAMERA) I liked that.

I didn't recognise the girl or the voice.

Quick cut to a close-up shot of a plate with one bite of chocolate cake remaining. A fork removes the piece. The plate is empty.

> *WOMAN'S VOICE*: (OFF CAMERA) Did you enjoy that?
> *MAN'S VOICE*: (OFF CAMERA) Yes, but I always want more.

Cut to wide shot of the man and woman, in their eighties, sitting in a Victorian parlour. She slices him another piece of cake.

The sequence continued; the words were variations on the original theme, the participants changing, reality to allegory and returning. A policeman, having just shot a suspect.

> *SUSPECT*: (DYING) You enjoyed that.
> *POLICEMAN*: (SHRUGS) It's a job.

A butcher stamping carcasses hanging in a refrigerated room; a little girl blowing dandelion seeds to the wind; and finally, a vignette where I recognised the talent.

Michael Farrow, somewhere in downtown Cleveland, hustling a teenage boy in front of an adult movie house. Money passes hands. The boy goes home with Michael. My stomach grabbed as a new horror was revealed. The next shot had been taken from the secret wall compartment where I'd found the Nikon. I hadn't realised there had been enough room to house a super-8 hooked to a portable tape recorder. As usual, I had looked but not far enough. The vault had been intended for much more than stills for blackmail.

Involuntary revulsion. Michael and the boy, the boy staring ceilingwards, Michael crouching over him, a close shot on moving buttocks, the lines off-camera, obviously recorded at some other time.

> *MICHAEL*: Did you like that?
> *BOY*: Getting paid doesn't mean I have to like it.
> *MICHAEL*: I didn't say you had to.
> *BOY*: Good. Then you shouldn't feel cheated.

Slow dissolve to a garden party, shot at some time before my arrival. Pastel colours, a soft and pastoral setting. All the clan. The camera pushes in on a conversation between Gabe and Michael, jovial, sipping martinis.

> *GABE*: You'd be willing to sponsor the boys' camp then?
> *MICHAEL*: Why, Gabe, of course. I'm a boys' best friend. You know that. I'll even volunteer my services as a counsellor.

Two other sequences followed, equally as chilling. People I didn't know; didn't want to know. The room was silent.

A simple and charming Mozart melody faded in behind a group of stills: wedding and honeymoon snapshots of the Saddlefords, the Kaskos and the Farrows. Sound effects of laughter and merrymaking joined the music. But then, cutting into the advertised happiness, the voice of a newscaster.

> *NEWSCASTER*: In Lancaster, Wyoming, last night, Mister and Mrs Harold Vreeland were arrested for child abuse. Their fifteen-month-old boy was found dead, a cord knotted around his penis resulting in fatal uremic poisoning.

Two similar incidents, by different newscasters, ostensibly from different sections of the country, followed the flat and documentary reading of the first.

Each holiday-spirited still then gave way to scenes at the dinner party I'd attended at the Kaskos. The laughter was gone, the expressions were worn, weddings to whining, honeymoons to hassels.

The sound track that had been recorded at the time of the party was dipped far below recognition, unintelligible. Now, as the phony smiles and cocktail gestures continued, as people began to waver and drinks began to spill, as Saddleford sniped at Sylvia and Peggy Kasko berated Chris, the Mozart melody diminished and gave way to the first, threatening indications of *The Rite of Spring*, that subtle prefacing, where the violins are plucked, promising the explosion to come.

The shot is now of Gabe talking to Michael, Sylvia in the background, her hand on Michael's shoulder. There are flash cuts of the wedding picture in perfect synchronisation with the building music. But the words have become silent; the mouths move and smile, yet we hear the woodwinds joining the strings, crescendoing. Sound effects join the music, to the same rhythm, building to the same intensity: heavy breathing, panting, groaning, caught breaths, moans and single words such as 'yes' and 'more' and 'there' and 'harder' and again, 'there', all the animal sounds of passion juxtaposed to a picture of a supposedly innocent cocktail party.

The music explodes and the footage of Gabe and Marty Kyle thrashing in bed takes the screen. And now – replacing the sound of the last scene – is the dialogue, the innocuous patter of Gabe talking to Michael on the couch, breezy, Sunday-afternoon amenities over hard-core pornography.

GABE: Marty was a . . . fine boy, Michael.
MICHAEL: If you got him in the right mood.
GABE: Fine co-operative attitude.
MICHAEL: I assume you mean that the way I think you mean it . . .
(LAUGHTER FROM BOTH)

The music drops back to strings, as in the beginning, starts to build again. The scene is Bill and Sylvia talking formally from one Louis XIV chair to the other. Their voices are unheard as the sounds and breathing of passion again rise to ear-splitting level, *The Rite of Spring* thundering forwards, as if it were the bed itself.

I quickly glance around the room. Attentions are unbroken. The impulse to leave is sudden and resolute. I have no stomach for seeing myself in this film. It is more than I can put myself through. I quietly stand up as the next bedroom scene comes to the screen, now Bill and Sylvia. Next . . . I start for the door and then stop as the nonsense dialogue begins over grotesque close-ups of genitalia. The voice is mine.

MATT: It's a pleasure to be here, Mrs Farrow.
SYLVIA: I'd be interested in hearing about your first impressions of the community.
MATT: Well, Mrs Farrow, thus far I find myself most impressed with the relaxed atmosphere and quick friendliness.
SYLVIA: Tell me . . . do you find it easier or more difficult to make friends here?

The camera zooms in for a close-up: Bill Kasko, mouth open, eyes closed, oblivious.

> *MATT*: Oddly enough, Mrs Farrow, people here seem to be more accessible.

Close-up shot of Sylvia biting flesh, music driving to finale.

> *MATT*: I am delighted to find that people here are more concerned with *real* values, *real* relationships, an emphasis on intellectual development.

I sit back down, trying to control the bursting inside. My cheeks become sore with the strain. Finally, I can control it no longer, the laughter erupts. It is impossible to contain. Heads snap around and stare. *That's* why Aaron had laughed so uproariously at the party. He *knew*. He saw how it was to be heard. As suddenly as it started, it stopped. I was gagged with embarrassment.

One person stood at the front of the room, clapping. Through the darkness. It was Robbie, smiling, clapping for me. He knew where I'd been and why.

As if by telepathy, I also knew something else. Regardless of what Aaron's intentions had originally been, he had deleted all on-camera footage of me. He had also removed all references to 'Mister Packer' in the sound track. That's why my name had been scratched out in the script. All this, in addition to keeping me away from the deadly preview. Whatever I had seen, whatever I was to see, one thing became clear: Aaron had at one point given in to feelings. He had cared. Ill is not all ill. Healthy is not all healthy. A very complex human being.

Seconds only had passed. Sylvia was on the screen. A freeze frame: her eyes closed, her face relaxed, the faintest tinge of a smile. Strands of her hair lay across her cheek, the slight glistening of moisture on her forehead. Her open hand relaxed on the pillow. Satisfaction. Fulfillment. In the momentary places she'd been able to find it. The Mozart theme returns, unhurried, from nowhere. Sylvia's soft reading begins.

> *SYLVIA*: . . . a red-hot poker will burn you if you hold it too long; and that if you cut your finger *very* deeply with a knife, it usually bleeds; and she had never forgotten that if you drink much from a bottle marked 'poison', it is almost certain to disagree with you, sooner or later. Alice ventured to taste it, and finding it very nice (it had, in fact, a sort of mixed flavour of cherry-tart, custard, pineapple, roast turkey, toffee and hot buttered toast), she very soon finished it off.

The freeze frame faded to black. The sound diminished to silence. Some under-breath mumblings from the audience: shock waves, nervousness, shifting bodies.

A small squeak and our attention is again drawn to the screen. A small door has been partially opened. An eye peers at the lens. The door opens full, and Aaron stared in at us, as if we are jammed-up occupants of the camera vault.

> *AARON*: Welcome. 'On Friday noon, July twentieth, seventeen-fourteen, the finest bridge in all Peru broke and precipitated five travellers into the gulf below.

As he stepped out of frame and let the opening of *The Bridge of San Luis Rey* take its effect, the camera re-focused on the background tableau. It was a scene of contemporary revelry: the Kaskos, the Saddlefords and Michael Farrow, drinking, laughing, exaggerating their enjoyment to compensate for being trapped into watching Aaron's 'student' film. All but Sylvia, who carefully followed Aaron's every move. A cut to black.

Another opening of a small door, this time on another side of the room, facing the back of the group, a small movie screen for their viewing just beyond.

AARON: Welcome. On Monday night, September twenty-sixth, nineteen-seventy-seven, the finest 'Bridge' in all Erieview Heights burned and precipitated seven travellers into a gulf further below than that first.

Again I felt the demanding impulse to leave the room. We would now see on-the-spot news footage of the conflagration. From within. That was why Robbie and Peter had wanted to go through the rubble. To retrieve the exposed stock from the wall camera.

The revellry of the adults continued as Aaron went to the recreation-room door, pulled a pin from the doorknob. A slight click. Sylvia watches him, starts to get up, changes her mind. Aaron moves to the barred window closest to the door, opens it, and throws the pin beyond the window well. He shuts the window, turns, and addresses the group.

AARON: It is time for your preview.
SADDLEFORD: (RAISING HIS GLASS IN A TOAST) Hail to the chief.
MICHAEL: That's my boy.
PEGGY: You can have him.

Aaron returns to a position just below the rear camera position and flicks the projector switch, dims the lights.

The same footage we have just seen, in uncut form, as shot in Sylvia's bedroom, appears on the screen within the screen.

The raucous laughter stops abruptly as Michael and the boy appear.

A wisecrack from Bill Kasko is interrupted as he next sees himself with Sylvia. The ice in cocktail glasses stops tinkling.

Gabe's vulgar laughter is cut off as he sees himself with Marty Kyle.

The three sequences now intercut with one another,

progressing together, each becoming more frenzied, the movements accelerating.

A silhouette jumps up from the couch and smashes the screen to the floor, turns to Aaron and is revealed by the light from the projector.

SADDLEFORD: You little, fucking bastard!

The writhing forms of the film now melt and curve grotesquely as they are projected on his face, shirt and pants. A close-up of Sylvia, mouth open, moves up his chest as he comes towards Aaron. The others stand up, pieces of the projected film now dappling their faces and bodies.

Bill Kasko leaps up and rushes for the projector, lifts it high, the scenes briefly sweeping the entire room, crashes it to the floor.

The dimmed lights come up full, just as Saddleford reaches Aaron, grabs him by the collar and begins slapping him, open-handed, back and forth, back and forth.

SADDLEFORD: Bastard! Bastard! Bastard!

Sylvia remains in her chair, hands limp at her sides, a long cigarette ash about to fall. There are tears in her eyes, moisture on her cheeks. She doesn't move. She watches.

Kasko now stomping on the projector pieces, then grabbing Aaron from Saddleford and hurling him across the room into a wall, where he slumps to the floor. He is dazed. Blood comes from his nose. There is the slight smile, the cheshire look in his eyes. Kasko rushes for him again. Michael gets in his way, holds him off.

MICHAEL: No! Mine!

Michael lifts him by his shirt, presses him into the wall, face inches from Aaron's, blood red, mouth wet.

MICHAEL: Consider this, my little monster. Sick, yes; we may be . . . but, *none* as sick as you!

He slams Aaron's head against the wall with every other word, the blond hair matting, a crimson spot, the black eyes dazed.

MICHAEL: You're not of me! You never were. Someone else. Someone dirty. Your mother's kind. A man I never saw.
AARON: (SCREAMS) Mother!
(Sylvia slowly stands.)
SYLVIA: (HARD) Michael!
AARON: (BARELY AUDIBLE) You promised, Mother.
SYLVIA: He knew, Michael. He's always known. About everything. About you and Gabe and Marty Kyle.

Peggy Kasko sits frozen, fingers of both hands pressed to her lips.

SYLVIA: About Amy Witt's father making sure Marty never got out of the detention home alive.

Mrs Saddleford stares at Gabe, unmoving, except a slow, bewildered shaking of her head.

SYLVIA: About Gabe inducting kids by threats and blackmail. He knows you well.

Bill, Michael and Gabe freeze in their positions over Aaron, wet with perspiration, out of breath, shirt tails messed, hair stringy.

SYLVIA: (WORDS NOW CATCHING IN HER THROAT) But not well enough, Michael, not well enough to know that you'd stand by and watch him being molested. By a stranger. For a film *you* made.

Aaron looks at her, an elbow propped under him, keeping him from the floor, his shirt spattered red.

> *AARON*: (SHAKING HEAD) Please, Mother. You promised. You can see. Now you can see.

Sylvia comes towards him, stops at the back of the couch, looks down at it, flicks the ash from her cigarette. Her face still moist.

> *SYLVIA*: Yes, Aaron, I promised. You're right. You're right about all of us.

She looks once at the red tip of her cigarette, touches it to the fabric on the back of the couch just above the hidden reservoir. It bursts into flame.

Aaron closes his eyes, rests his head on the floor.

> *PEGGY*: (SCREAMS) Oh, my God, you're crazy!

She rushes to the door as Michael and Bill pull the rug from beneath the chairs. The door is locked. The rug is thrown over the couch. It, too, ignites; white, magnesium flames now leaping to the ceiling.

Gabe stumbles to the door.

Sylvia slowly, methodically walks to the curtains, touches them; to the stuffed chair, touches the arm.

It is too late. Too far to climb. The room fills with orange and white. Gabe swings a chair at the door. It splinters. Bill throws open a window, pressing himself into the cage formed by the iron bars, now his back against the window side, pressing with his feet, now his back on the ground, pressing up. The cage holding fast.

Mrs Saddleford screams as her dress catches.

Sylvia walks slowly to where Aaron lies on the floor. Peggy stands in a far corner, arms pressed into her chest, sliding to her knees.

Sylvia sits on the floor next to Aaron and lightly, with

her fingertips, brushes the wisps of fine, blond hair from his forehead.

Michael grabs the poker from the fireplace and rushes to the locked door. He pries, there is splintering, but the door remains tight to the jamb.

Gabe yanks the poker away from him, tries, fails.

Michael pulls Gabe out of the way.

Bill tears the poker from Michael.

Sylvia quietly strokes Aaron's head, takes a handkerchief from her skirt pocket and gently dabs the blood away from beneath his nose.

The rhythms of *The Rite of Spring* continue relentlessly in the background.

Cutaways to the exterior camera positions.

Tight on a face pressed into the bars, contorted.

Pan to the next window. A tangle of six hands. One pair loosens, falls away. Another face, between arms, hair afire, falls away.

Pull back, slow, to reveal the entire house engulfed in flames.

Cut to interior, bathed in orange, the outline of a female figure bent over a boy figure, covering it.

The small door of the vault housing the camera begins to close, triggered, I assumed, by a thermostat built into the inside wall. With one, final, crashing chord, the screen returned to black. And remained so, silent, for what seemed to be agonising minutes.

Silence in our living room theatre. Not a movement. Only the distant squeak of a projector drive wheel needing a drop of oil.

Then, without warning, the vault door began to re-open, slowly, precisely, revealing the recreation room – untouched.

The same room, exactly as it had been in the beginning, only now, in place of the adults, in exactly the same seated positions, were the children: Margie and Amy, Peter and

Chris, Camilla and Robbie. Aaron walked about, just as he had with the adults, a knowing look in his eye, a look insisting he was here as well as there. The ashtrays were empty. The cocktail glasses contained soft drinks. Sun came in the two windows, not night. The kids were laughing, teasing one another. Aaron stopped just behind Margie's chair.

> *AARON*: It's agreed then? That's how we'll end the film?
> *GROUP*: Yes!

All their hands shot into the air as the affirmative splintered into individual voices.

Aaron looked directly into the lens of the wall camera and smiled. The camera moved in on Aaron's face until it filled the frame. A freeze on the smile, that open, all-knowing smile. Then, slowly, bleeding through the freeze, the beginnings of a dissolve.

Gradually, Aaron's features were replaced by others, the head of someone else being born, it appeared, out of Aaron's face, out of Aaron's mind. A superimposure.

It was the face of a baby, five, perhaps six months old, also smiling, also in freeze frame. When the metamorphosis was complete and the last tracings of Aaron's face had disappeared, the baby moved.

A spoon touched his lips. He took a mouthful and forced it back out. The spoon caught the remains and forced them back in. The camera pulled back slightly to include the mother, in a state of obvious irritation packing the food into the baby's mouth as best she could. The dish rested on the tray of the high chair. The baby became impatient, darting his head back and forth, waving his arms, anything to avoid the spoon. He knew what he wanted. He knew what he didn't want.

With a quick thrash of an arm, he sent the baby plate crashing to the floor. At first he looked startled. But then, as the despairing mother stooped to clean up the food, the baby grinned broadly, gleefully, and pounded his little fist on his empty tray.

A slow fade to black. The final words appeared on the screen:

THE BEGINNING

A few seconds later, in small lettering, there appeared the credits:

Written, Directed and Produced
by The Home of David
for The Home of David

There were no names.

As the lights came on I quickly scanned the room for reactions. There was no applause. There were no shouts. There was nothing.

Amy and Camilla stood behind the refreshment table. Most of the kids in the audience looked at each other without expression. Occasionally there was some mumbling, some stretching. A mention of a hamburger at Bob's Big Boy. Another two or three groups left. Saying nothing.

Robbie, standing quiet and small in front of the screen, glanced around, disappointed, but steady. 'We have food . . . if you're hungry.'

Margie got up and stood next to him. 'If you have any questions, please speak up.'

As if in silent understanding, the remainder of the room slowly emptied towards the front door. Silently. All but three, scattered in different places about the room, three not knowing each other, possibly not knowing exactly what they'd seen. But they stayed. Sitting very still, a boy and two girls. The boy looked around, watched the last of the others leave. Then he, too, stood up, but went to the refreshment table.

The two girls joined him, poured themselves some

punch. Those that had departed looked to be in their mid or late teens. The remaining three appeared to be younger.

They asked Camilla if she had been in Ethel Newby's geography class. They asked Amy if she were planning to go out for tennis again that spring. Robbie listened.

I got up and walked over to him. Peter and Chris joined the others at the table. As I stood in front of him, he kept listening.

'Robbie . . . ?'

He didn't look up.

'Robbie, it wasn't an enjoyable film.'

'It wasn't meant to be.'

'I . . . I could be wrong, but I think kids your age – the majority of them anyway – just want to be entertained.'

He looked up at me. 'Nineteen-thirteen, Mister Packer.'

'What about it?'

'In nineteen-thirteen, *The Rite of Spring* had its premiere performance. In Paris. The auditorium was packed. But before the music ended, more than three-quarters of that audience had walked out.' He gave me that same, open smile I had assumed was Aaron's individual trademark.

'Nineteen-thirteens happen every year,' he said. 'You know that. Aaron knew that. He said it would be this way. And Stravinsky went right on composing music.' He glanced over at the table and listened again. All eight of them, the five old-timers and the three newcomers, were now talking about the film.

'You see, Mister Packer, it's still just the beginning. That's all we ever hoped for during our childhoods. Another way to begin.'

'I think I'd like some ice cream, too, Robbie.'

'All right.'

When he returned I decided it most politic to discuss technicalities rather than subject matter. 'Robbie, I realise the casements in which you housed those wall cameras were fire proof, but what I don't understand is why the film within the magazines didn't disintegrate from the intensity of that heat.'

'They were refrigerated, Mister Packer.'

'But the electricity would have been cut off by the fire.'

'The casements were insulated with a two-inch layer of dry ice.'

'But, the camera engines . . . '

'Battery driven.' Then he'd smiled. 'Aaron's fairly bright, you know.' He never used the past tense in speaking of Aaron. None of them did.

'The couch? The curtains? The . . .'

'Camilla.'

Of course. I thought, of course. I wondered where it would end. I wanted to go home. I finished the ice cream and picked up my coat. Robbie followed me to the door.

'Mister Packer?'

'Yes, Robbie?'

'The film isn't enjoyable to see. It also wasn't enjoyable to make. For the most part. I wanted you to know that. I couldn't assume you already did.'

I didn't know what to say. The same intense eyes, the same assured expression. Aaron remained.

I pushed my hands deep into my pockets at the doorway. The snow had begun again.

'I'm feeling old, Robbie. I like my scotch and evening paper. Coffee and a warm bed. I can't join you.'

'You won't join us,' he corrected.

'Very well. And I won't judge you. I'm afraid I'm just going to go off . . . and do what pleases me.'

'Without demanding that it please someone else?'

'That's right. And without you demanding that what you've done must please me.'

'Of course. That's not where we are.'

'Thus far.'

'Like I said, Mister Packer, it's a beginning.'

I got in the car and put the key in the ignition. I hesitated before turning it. It would have been nice not to feel the hesitation. My whole outlook might have been different had I turned the key without a second thought. I wondered what Aaron would have said.

I

Forty thousand brothers
Could not, with all their quantity of love,
Make up my sum.
Hamlet – Act V, Scene 1, Line 291
– William Shakespeare

I: On a Saturday Morning in November

Robbie Farrow went to Cammie Saddleford's room. She'd asked him to stop by the evening before so she could give him an update.

He knocked twice.

'Come on in, Robbie.'

He opened the door, stood in the entryway, always a bit awed by the quantity and intricacy of the equipment and instruments. The room was wall-to-wall with floor-to-ceiling shelves. Hundreds of bottles of varying shapes and sizes filled the spaces, all marked with exotic names, such as anhydride, benzoate, fulminate and sal ammoniac. On a long rectangular table stretching from one end of the room to the other were Buchner funnels, Bunsen burners, desiccators, stills, etnas and aspirators.

He gazed at the winding, twisting, contorted, distended glass assemblage pulsing with bubbles and steam in the middle of the table.

'Looks like a transparent roller coaster.'

'You finish your amplifer?' Cammie looked up and smiled.

'Yeah, but I'm getting some kind of feedback hum: I blew it somewhere along the way.' He walked to the small cubic freezer in one corner, opened the door.

'Don't leave it open too long,' Cammie warned.

'I won't.' He pushed aside a greenish bottle, found what he was looking for, touched it: a small, metal container the size of a children's block. The label on top was in Cammie's handwriting. There were two words: Aaron Farrow. He closed the door. turned around.

'Any luck?'

Cammie stopped what she was doing over a rack of test tubes and smiled. 'I don't know, Robbie, I honest-to-God don't know. It looks good on paper,' she walked to the largest beaker of the table assemblage. 'And so far it's looking good in application. I'm also getting positive reports from the East Chester unit.'

'Then what?'

'It's just too soon to tell.'

'How come?'

'Because there's no precedent. There's very little available data. And beyond that, it's a hush-hush subject, loaded with controversy.' She shrugged. 'It's virgin ground.' Then smiled. 'We'll get there. Amy got her first period last week. She'll be what's called the "host".' She laughed. 'Or hostess.'

'What's it called again?'

She turned to face him. 'Cloning.'

EPILOGUE

It is very harsh to say this and I know I am going to shock a lot of people, but in my mind these youngsters will be less damaged if left out on the street than if exposed to the downward spiral of our juvenile justice system. The answer is not to jail these kids, but to provide more and better counselling agencies to which they can turn if they wish.

I have great faith in the amazing capacity of young people to resolve their own problems and take care of themselves. Much of the time they're running away from a really crummy situation anyway – beatings, sexual abuse, the works. So why in God's name should the state step in and complicate their lives even more?

Bob Smith – Deputy Director, California Youth Authority

You're going to see the law changing more and more towards allowing children to determine their own lives in a number of areas. In particular, adolescents will be increasingly treated as young adults with the full complement of legal and civil rights to back them up.

Stephen Wizner – Lecturer, Yale Law School

I'd say that within five years, most states will adopt laws that exclude status offenders from the purview of the juvenile court. What this means is that the court will be allowed to concentrate entirely on criminal offenders and communities will be developing more and better programmes to deal with ungovernable and disturbed kids.

Milton Rector – President, National Council on Crime and Delinquency

Washington Post, Monday, January 5, 1976

From the living hell of her watery grave she rises again . . .

THE NIGHT BOAT

By Robert R. McCammon

Deep under the calm water of a Caribbean lagoon, salvage diver David Moore discovers a sunken Nazi U-boat entombed in the sand. A mysterious relic from the last war. Slowly the U-boat rises from the depths laden with a long-dead crew, cancerous with rot, mummified for eternity.
Or so Moore thought.

UNTIL HE HEARD THE DEEP, HOLLOW BOOM OF SOMETHING HAMMERING WITH FEVERISH INTENSITY . . . SOMETHING DESPERATELY TRYING TO GET OUT!

If you've read either of Robert McCammon's other horror masterpieces, you won't be disappointed with **THE NIGHT BOAT**, but if this is your first McCammon encounter, be prepared for a bit of a shock!

HORROR 0 7221 5871 8 £1.25

Robert R. McCammon's
BAAL
and
BETHANY'S SIN
are also available in Sphere Books

keeper of the children

BY WILLIAM H. HALLAHAN

NOTHING CAN PREPARE YOU FOR
THE NERVE-WRENCHING FRENZY OF . . .
KEEPER OF THE CHILDREN

Alone in a child's bedroom in a suburban Philadelphia home,
Eddie Benson listens for footsteps on the stairs.

The footfall Eddie is waiting for will not be human.
It could be someone's pet cat, or a stuffed teddy bear,
or even a smiling marionette doll.

But whatever it is that comes creeping up the stairs it will
have two horrifying qualities: it will be propelled by a
diabolic force and it will have only one intention – murder.

If Eddie Benson wants his daughter back, he will have to
fight a battle no human has ever fought before. And he
must win. For only the victor can return with his life –
and soul – from the realms of such dark, unnatural evil.

**'Eerie, scary . . . utterly fascinating . . .
this is not going to be what you think'**
Publishers Weekly

HORROR 0 7221 4246 3 £1.00

BETHANY'S SIN

BY ROBERT R. McCAMMON

When Evan Reid brought his wife and small daughter to Bethany's Sin it seemed the perfect setting. A small village, far from the noise and pollution of the city, it was quaint and very peaceful.

Too peaceful. There were no sounds at all . . . almost as if the night had been frightened into silence.

Then Evan noticed there were very few men in the village, and that those he knew of were crippled. And sometimes he thought he heard the sound of horses galloping in the dead of night.

Soon he would know the superhuman secret that kept the village alive. And he would watch in horror as Kay and Laurie underwent a hideous transformation right before his eyes. He would know the terror that happened at night – and only to men . . . in *Bethany's Sin.*

HORROR 0 7221 5869 6 £1.40